Confidence

Confidence
Henry James

WILDSIDE PRESS
Doylestown, Pennsylvania

1879

Confidence
A publication of
WILDSIDE PRESS
P.O. Box 301
Holicong, PA 18928-0301

www.wildsidepress.com

Chapter I

*I*t was in the early days of April; Bernard Longueville had been spending the winter in Rome. He had traveled northward with the consciousness of several social duties that appealed to him from the further side of the Alps, but he was under the charm of the Italian spring, and he made a pretext for lingering. He had spent five days at Siena, where he had intended to spend but two, and still it was impossible to continue his journey. He was a young man of a contemplative and speculative turn, and this was his first visit to Italy, so that if he dallied by the way he should not be harshly judged. He had a fancy for sketching, and it was on his conscience to take a few pictorial notes. There were two old inns at Siena, both of them very shabby and very dirty. The one at which Longueville had taken up his abode was entered by a dark, pestiferous archway, surmounted by a sign which at a distance might have been read by the travelers as the Dantean injunction to renounce all hope. The other was not far off, and the day after his arrival, as he passed it, he saw two ladies going in who evidently belonged to the large fraternity of Anglo-Saxon tourists, and one of whom

was young and carried herself very well. Longueville
had his share – or more than his share – of gallantry,
and this incident awakened a regret. If he had gone to
the other inn he might have had charming company:
at his own establishment there was no one but an
aesthetic German who smoked bad tobacco in the
dining room. He remarked to himself that this was
always his luck, and the remark was characteristic of
the man; it was charged with the feeling of the moment,
but it was not absolutely just; it was the result of an
acute impression made by the particular occasion; but
it failed in appreciation of a providence which had
sprinkled Longueville's career with happy accidents –
accidents, especially, in which his characteristic gallantry was not allowed to rust for want of exercise. He
lounged, however, contentedly enough through these
bright, still days of a Tuscan April, drawing much
entertainment from the high picturesqueness of the
things about him. Siena, a few years since, was a flawless
gift of the Middle Ages to the modern imagination.
No other Italian city could have been more interesting
to an observer fond of reconstructing obsolete manners. This was a taste of Bernard Longueville's, who
had a relish for serious literature, and at one time had
made several lively excursions into mediaeval history.
His friends thought him very clever, and at the same
time had an easy feeling about him which was a tribute
to his freedom from pedantry. He was clever indeed,
and an excellent companion; but the real measure of
his brilliancy was in the success with which he entertained himself. He was much addicted to conversing
with his own wit, and he greatly enjoyed his own
society. Clever as he often was in talking with his
friends, I am not sure that his best things, as the phrase
is, were not for his own ears. And this was not on
account of any cynical contempt for the under-

standing of his fellow-creatures: it was simply because what I have called his own society was more of a stimulus than that of most other people. And yet he was not for this reason fond of solitude; he was, on the contrary, a very sociable animal. It must be admitted at the outset that he had a nature which seemed at several points to contradict itself, as will probably be perceived in the course of this narration.

He entertained himself greatly with his reflections and meditations upon Sienese architecture and early Tuscan art, upon Italian street-life and the geological idiosyncrasies of the Apennines. If he had only gone to the other inn, that nice-looking girl whom he had seen passing under the dusky portal with her face turned away from him might have broken bread with him at this intellectual banquet. Then came a day, however, when it seemed for a moment that if she were disposed she might gather up the crumbs of the feast. Longueville, every morning after breakfast, took a turn in the great square of Siena — the vast *piazza*, shaped like a horse-shoe, where the market is held beneath the windows of that crenellated palace from whose over-hanging cornice a tall, straight tower springs up with a movement as light as that of a single plume in the bonnet of a captain. Here he strolled about, watching a brown *contadino* disembarrass his donkey, noting the progress of half an hour's chaffer over a bundle of carrots, wishing a young girl with eyes like animated agates would let him sketch her, and gazing up at intervals at the beautiful, slim tower, as it played at contrasts with the large blue air. After he had spent the greater part of a week in these grave considerations, he made up his mind to leave Siena. But he was not content with what he had done for his portfolio. Siena was eminently sketchable, but he had not been indus-trious. On the last morning of his visit, as he stood staring about him in the crowded piazza, and feeling that, in spite of its picturesqueness, this was an awkward place for setting up an easel, he bethought himself, by contrast, of a quiet corner in another part of the town, which he had chanced upon in one of his first walks — an angle of a lonely terrace that abutted upon the city-wall, where three or four superannuated objects seemed to slumber in the sunshine — the open door of an empty church, with a faded fresco exposed to the air in the arch above it, and an ancient beggar-woman sitting beside it on a three-legged stool. The little terrace had an old polished parapet, about as high as a man's breast, above which was a view of strange, sad-colored hills. Outside, to the left, the wall of the town made an outward bend, and exposed its rugged and rusty complexion. There was a smooth stone bench set into the wall of the church, on which Longueville had rested for an hour, observing the composition of the little picture of which I have indicated the elements, and of which the parapet of the terrace would form the foreground. The thing was what painters call a subject, and he had promised himself to come back with his utensils. This morning he returned to the inn and took possession of them, and then he made his way through a labyrinth of empty streets, lying on the edge of the town, within the wall, like the superfluous folds of a garment whose wearer has shrunken with old age. He reached his little grass-grown terrace, and found it as sunny and as private as before. The old mendicant was mumbling petitions, sacred and profane, at the church door; but save for this the stillness was unbroken. The yellow sunshine warmed the brown surface of the city-wall, and lighted the hollows of the Etruscan hills. Longueville settled himself on the empty bench, and, arranging his little portable apparatus, began to ply his brushes. He worked for some time smoothly and rapidly, with an agreeable sense of the absence of obstacles. It seemed almost an interruption when, in the silent air, he heard a distant bell in the town strike noon. Shortly after this, there was another interruption. The sound of a soft footstep caused him to look up; whereupon he saw a young woman standing there and bending her eyes upon the graceful artist. A second glance assured him that she was that nice girl whom he had seen going into the other inn with her mother, and suggested that she had just emerged from the little church. He suspected, however — I hardly know why — that she had been looking at him for some moments before he perceived her. It would perhaps be impertinent to inquire what she thought of him; but Longueville, in the space of an instant, made two or three reflections upon the young lady. One of them was to the effect that she was a handsome creature, but that she looked rather bold; the burden of the other was that — yes, decidedly — she was a compatriot. She turned away almost as soon as she met his eyes; he had hardly time to raise his hat, as, after a moment's hesitation, he proceeded to do. She herself appeared to feel a certain hesitation; she glanced back at the church door, as if under the impulse to retrace her steps. She stood there a moment longer — long enough to let him see that she was a person of easy attitudes — and then she walked away slowly to the parapet of the terrace. Here she stationed herself, leaning her arms upon the high stone ledge, presenting her back to Longueville, and gazing at rural Italy. Longueville went on with his sketch, but less attentively than before. He wondered what this young lady was doing there alone, and then it occurred to him that her companion — her mother, presumably — was in the church. The two ladies had been in the church when he arrived; women liked to sit in churches; they had been there more than half an hour, and the mother had not enough of it even yet. The young lady, however, at present preferred the view that Longueville was painting; he became aware that she had placed herself in the very center of his foreground. His first feeling was that she would spoil it; his second was that she would improve it. Little by little she turned more into profile, leaning only one arm upon the parapet, while the other hand, holding her folded parasol, hung down at her side. She was motionless; it was almost as if she were standing there on purpose to be drawn. Yes, certainly she improved the picture. Her profile, delicate and thin, defined itself against the sky, in the clear shadow of a coquettish hat; her figure was light; she bent and leaned easily; she wore a gray dress, fastened up as was then the fashion, and displaying the broad edge of a crimson petticoat. She kept her position; she seemed absorbed in the view. "Is she *posing* — is she attitudinizing for my benefit?" Longueville asked of himself. And then it seemed to him that this was a needless assumption, for the prospect was quite beautiful enough to be looked at for itself, and there was nothing impossible in a pretty girl having a love of fine landscape. "But posing or not," he went on, "I will put her into my sketch. She has simply put herself in. It will give it a human interest. There is nothing like having a human interest." So, with the ready skill that he possessed, he introduced the young girl's figure into his foreground, and at the end of ten minutes he had almost made something that had the form of a likeness. "If she will only be quiet for another ten minutes," he said, "the thing will really be a picture." Unfortunately, the young lady was not quiet; she had apparently had enough of her attitude and her view. She turned away, facing Longueville again, and slowly came back, as if to reenter the church. To do so she had to pass near him, and as she approached he instinctively got up, holding his drawing in one hand. She looked at him again, with that expression that he had mentally characterized as "bold," a few minutes before — with dark, intelligent eyes. Her hair was dark and dense; she was a strikingly handsome girl.

"I am so sorry you moved," he said, confidently, in English. "You were so — so beautiful."

She stopped, looking at him more directly than ever; and she looked at his sketch, which he held out toward her. At the sketch, however, she only glanced, whereas there was observation in the eye that she bent upon Longueville. He never knew whether she had blushed; he afterward thought she might have been frightened. Nevertheless, it was not exactly terror that appeared to dictate her answer to Longueville's speech.

"I am much obliged to you. Don't you think you have looked at me enough?"

"By no means. I should like so much to finish my drawing."

"I am not a professional model," said the young lady.

"No. That's my difficulty," Longueville answered, laughing. "I can't propose to remunerate you."

The young lady seemed to think this joke in indifferent taste. She turned away in silence; but something in her expression, in his feeling at the time, in the situation, incited Longueville to higher play. He felt a lively need of carrying his point.

"You see it will be pure kindness," he went on, — "a simple act of charity. Five minutes will be enough. Treat me as an Italian beggar."

She had laid down his sketch and had stepped forward. He stood there, obsequious, clasping his hands and smiling.

His interruptress stopped and looked at him again, as if she thought him a very odd person; but she seemed amused. Now, at any rate, she was not frightened. She seemed even disposed to provoke him a little.

"I wish to go to my mother," she said.

"Where is your mother?" the young man asked.

"In the church, of course. I didn't come here alone!"

"Of course not; but you may be sure that your mother is very contented. I have been in that little church. It is charming. She is just resting there; she is probably tired. If you will kindly give me five minutes more, she will come out to you."

"Five minutes?" the young girl asked.

"Five minutes will do. I shall be eternally grateful." Longueville was amused at himself as he said this. He cared infinitely less for his sketch than the words appeared to imply; but, somehow, he cared greatly that this graceful stranger should do what he had proposed.

The graceful stranger dropped an eye on the sketch again.

"Is your picture so good as that?" she asked.

"I have a great deal of talent," he answered, laughing. "You shall see for yourself, when it is finished."

She turned slowly toward the terrace again.

"You certainly have a great deal of talent, to induce me to do what you ask." And she walked to where she had stood before. Longueville made a movement to go with her, as if to show her the attitude he meant; but, pointing with decision to his easel, she said —

"You have only five minutes." He immediately went back to his work, and she made a vague attempt to take up her position. "You must tell me if this will do," she added, in a moment.

"It will do beautifully," Longueville answered, in a happy tone, looking at her and plying his brush. "It is immensely good of you to take so much trouble."

For a moment she made no rejoinder, but presently she said —

"Of course if I pose at all I wish to pose well."

"You pose admirably," said Longueville.

After this she said nothing, and for several minutes he painted rapidly and in silence. He felt a certain excitement, and the movement of his thoughts kept pace with that of his brush. It was very true that she posed admirably; she was a fine creature to paint. Her prettiness inspired him, and also her audacity, as he was content to regard it for the moment. He wondered about her — who she was, and what she was — perceiving that the so-called audacity was not vulgar boldness, but the play of an original and probably interesting character. It was obvious that she was a perfect lady, but it was equally obvious that she was irregularly clever. Longueville's little figure was a success — a charming success, he thought, as he put on the last touches. While he was doing this, his model's companion came into view. She came out of the church, pausing a moment as she looked from her daughter to the young man in the corner of the terrace; then she walked straight over to the young girl. She was a delicate little gentlewoman, with a light, quick step.

Longueville's five minutes were up; so, leaving his place, he approached the two ladies, sketch in hand. The elder one, who had passed her hand into her daughter's arm, looked up at him with clear, surprised eyes; she was a charming old woman. Her eyes were very pretty, and on either side of them, above a pair of fine dark brows, was a band of silvery hair, rather coquettishly arranged.

"It is my portrait," said her daughter, as Longueville drew near. "This gentleman has been sketching me."

"Sketching you, dearest?" murmured her mother. "Wasn't it rather sudden?"

"Very sudden — very abrupt!" exclaimed the young girl with a laugh.

"Considering all that, it's very good," said Longueville, offering his picture to the elder lady, who took it and began to examine it. "I can't tell you how much I thank you," he said to his model.

"It's very well for you to thank me now," she replied. "You really had no right to begin."

"The temptation was so great."

"We should resist temptation. And you should have asked my leave."

"I was afraid you would refuse it; and you stood there, just in my line of vision."

"You should have asked me to get out of it."

"I should have been very sorry. Besides, it would have been extremely rude."

The young girl looked at him a moment.

"Yes, I think it would. But what you have done is ruder."

"It is a hard case!" said Longueville. "What could I have done, then, decently?"

"It's a beautiful drawing," murmured the elder lady, handing the thing back to Longueville. Her daughter, meanwhile, had not even glanced at it.

"You might have waited till I should go away," this argumentative young person continued.

Longueville shook his head.

"I never lose opportunities!"

"You might have sketched me afterwards, from memory."

Longueville looked at her, smiling.

"Judge how much better my memory will be now!"

She also smiled a little, but instantly became serious.

"For myself, it's an episode I shall try to forget. I don't like the part I have played in it."

"May you never play a less becoming one!" cried Longueville. "I hope that your mother, at least, will accept a memento of the occasion." And he turned again with his sketch to her companion, who had been listening to the girl's conversation with this enterprising stranger, and looking from one to the other with an air of earnest confusion. "Won't you do me the honor of keeping my sketch?" he said. "I think it really looks like your daughter."

"Oh, thank you, thank you; I hardly dare," murmured the lady, with a deprecating gesture.

"It will serve as a kind of amends for the liberty I have taken," Longueville added; and he began to remove the drawing from its paper block.

"It makes it worse for you to give it to us," said the young girl.

"Oh, my dear, I am sure it's lovely!" exclaimed her mother. "It's wonderfully like you."

"I think that also makes it worse!"

Longueville was at last nettled. The young lady's perversity was perhaps not exactly malignant; but it was certainly ungracious. She seemed to desire to present herself as a beautiful tormentress.

"How does it make it worse?" he asked, with a frown.

He believed she was clever, and she was certainly ready. Now, however, she reflected a moment before answering.

"That you should give us your sketch," she said at last.

"It was to your mother I offered it," Longueville observed.

But this observation, the fruit of his irritation, appeared to have no effect upon the young girl.

"Isn't it what painters call a study?" she went on. "A study is of use to the painter himself. Your justification would be that you should keep your sketch, and that it might be of use to you."

"My daughter is a study, sir, you will say," said the elder lady in a little, light, conciliating voice, and graciously accepting the drawing again.

"I will admit," said Longueville, "that I am very inconsistent. Set it down to my esteem, madam," he added, looking at the mother.

"That's for you, mamma," said his model, disengaging her arm from her mother's hand and turning away.

The mamma stood looking at the sketch with a smile which seemed to express a tender desire to reconcile all accidents.

"It's extremely beautiful," she murmured, "and if you insist on my taking it —"

"I shall regard it as a great honor."

"Very well, then; with many thanks, I will keep it." She looked at the young man a moment, while her daughter walked away. Longueville thought her a delightful little person; she struck him as a sort of transfigured Quakeress — a mystic with a practical side. "I am sure you think she's a strange girl," she said.

"She is extremely pretty."

"She is very clever," said the mother.

"She is wonderfully graceful."

"Ah, but she's good!" cried the old lady.

"I am sure she comes honestly by that," said Longueville, expressively, while his companion, returning his salutation with a certain scrupulous grace of her own, hurried after her daughter.

Longueville remained there staring at the view but not especially seeing it. He felt as if he had at once enjoyed and lost an opportunity. After a while he tried to make a sketch of the old beggar-woman who sat there in a sort of palsied immobility, like a rickety statue at a church-door. But his attempt to reproduce her features was not gratifying, and he suddenly laid down his brush. She was not pretty enough — she had a bad profile.

Chapter II

*T*wo months later Bernard Longueville was at Venice, still under the impression that he was leaving Italy. He was not a man who made plans and held to them. He made them, indeed — few men made more — but he made them as a basis for variation. He had gone to Venice to spend a fortnight, and his fortnight had taken the form of eight enchanting weeks. He had still a sort of conviction that he was carrying out his plans; for it must be confessed that where his pleasure was concerned he had considerable skill in accommodating his theory to his practice. His enjoyment of Venice was extreme, but he was roused from it by a summons he was indisposed to resist. This consisted of a letter from an intimate friend who was living in Germany — a friend whose name was Gordon Wright. He had been spending the winter in Dresden, but his letter bore the date of Baden-Baden. As it was not long, I may give it entire.

"I wish very much that you would come to this place. I think you have been here before, so that you know how pretty it is, and how amusing. I shall probably be here the rest of the summer. There are some people I know and whom I want you to know. Be so good as to arrive. Then I will thank you properly for your various Italian rhapsodies. I can't reply on the same scale — I haven't the time. Do you know what I am doing? I am making love. I find it a most absorbing occupation. That is literally why I have not written to you before. I have been making love ever since the last of May. It takes an immense amount of time, and everything else has got terribly behindhand. I don't mean to say that the experiment itself has gone on very fast; but I am trying to push it forward. I haven't yet had time to test its success; but in this I want your help. You know we great physicists never make an experiment without an 'assistant' — a humble individual who burns his fingers and stains his clothes in the cause of science, but whose interest in the problem is only indirect. I want you to be my assistant, and I will guarantee that your burns and stains shall not be dangerous. She is an extremely interesting girl, and I really want you to see her — I want to know what you think of her. She wants to know you, too, for I have talked a good deal about you. There you have it, if gratified vanity will help you on the way. Seriously, this is a real request. I want your opinion, your impression. I want to see how she will affect you. I don't say I ask for your advice; that, of course, you will not undertake to give. But I desire a definition, a characterization; you know you toss off those things. I don't see why I shouldn't tell you all this — I have always told you everything. I have never pretended to know anything about women, but I have always supposed that you knew everything. You certainly have always had the tone of that sort of omniscience. So come here as soon as possible and let me see that you are not a humbug. She's a very handsome girl."

Longueville was so much amused with this appeal that he very soon started for Germany. In the reader, Gordon Wright's letter will, perhaps, excite surprise rather than hilarity; but Longueville thought it highly characteristic of his friend. What it especially pointed to was Gordon's want of imagination — a deficiency which was a matter of common jocular allusion between the two young men, each of whom kept a collection of acknowledged oddities as a playground for the other's wit. Bernard had often spoken of his comrade's want of imagination as a bottomless pit, into which Gordon was perpetually inviting him to lower himself. "My dear fellow," Bernard said, "you must really excuse me; I cannot take these subterranean excursions. I should lose my breath down there; I should never come up alive. You know I have dropped things down — little jokes and metaphors, little fantasies and paradoxes — and I have never heard them touch bottom!" This was an epigram on the part of a young man who had a lively play of fancy; but it was nonetheless true that Gordon Wright had a firmly-treading, rather than a winged, intellect. Every phrase in his letter seemed, to Bernard, to march in stout-soled walking-boots, and nothing could better express his attachment to the process of reasoning things out than this proposal that his friend should come and make a chemical analysis — a geometrical survey — of the lady of his love. "That I shall have any difficulty in forming an opinion, and any difficulty in expressing it when formed — of this he has as little idea as that he shall have any difficulty in accepting it when expressed." So Bernard reflected, as he rolled in the train to Munich. "Gordon's mind," he went on, "has no atmosphere; his intellectual process goes on in the void. There are no currents and eddies to affect it, no high winds nor hot suns, no changes of season and temperature. His premises are neatly arranged, and his conclusions are perfectly calculable."

Yet for the man on whose character he so freely exercised his wit Bernard Longueville had a strong affection. It is nothing against the validity of a friendship that the parties to it have not a mutual resemblance. There must be a basis of agreement, but the structure reared upon it may contain a thousand disparities. These two young men had formed an alliance of old, in college days, and the bond between them had been strengthened by the simple fact of its having survived the sentimental revolutions of early life. Its strongest link was a sort of mutual respect. Their tastes, their pursuits were different; but each of them had a high esteem for the other's character. It may be said that they were easily pleased; for it is certain that neither of them had performed any very conspicuous action. They were highly civilized young Americans, born to an easy fortune and a tranquil destiny, and unfamiliar with the glitter of golden opportunities. If I did not shrink from disparaging the constitution of their native land for their own credit, I should say that it had never been very definitely proposed to these young gentlemen to distinguish themselves. On reaching manhood, they had each come into property sufficient to make violent exertion superfluous. Gordon Wright, indeed, had inherited a large estate. Their wants being tolerably modest, they had not been tempted to strive for the glory of building up commercial fortunes — the most obvious career open to young Americans. They had, indeed, embraced no career at all, and if summoned to give an account of themselves would, perhaps, have found it hard to tell any very impressive story. Gordon Wright was much interested in physical science, and had ideas of his own on what is called the endowment of research. His ideas had taken a practical shape, and he had distributed money very freely among the investigating classes, after which he had gone to spend a couple of years in Germany, supposing it to be the land of laboratories. Here we find him at present, cultivating relations with several learned bodies and promoting the study of various tough branches of human knowledge, by paying the expenses of difficult experiments. The experiments, it must be added, were often of his own making, and he must have the honor of whatever brilliancy attaches, in the estimation of the world, to such pursuits. It was not, indeed, a brilliancy that dazzled Bernard Longueville, who, however, was not easily dazzled by anything. It was because he regarded him in so plain and direct a fashion, that Bernard had an affection for his friend — an affection to which it would perhaps be difficult to assign a definite cause. Personal sympathies are doubtless caused by something; but the causes are remote, mysterious to our daily vision, like those of the particular state of the weather. We content ourselves with remarking that it is fine or that it rains, and the enjoyment of our likes and dislikes is by no means apt to borrow its edge from the keenness of our analysis. Longueville had a relish for fine quality — superior savor; and he was sensible of this merit in the simple, candid, manly, affectionate nature of his comrade, which seemed to him an excellent thing of its kind. Gordon Wright had a tender heart and a strong will — a combination which, when the understanding is not too limited, is often the motive of admirable actions. There might sometimes be a question whether Gordon's understanding were sufficiently unlimited, but the impulses of a generous temper often play a useful part in filling up the gaps of an incomplete imagination, and the general impression that Wright produced was certainly that of intelligent good nature. The reasons for appreciating Bernard Longueville were much more manifest. He pleased superficially, as well as fundamentally. Nature had sent him into the world with an armful of good gifts. He was very good-looking — tall, dark, agile, perfectly finished, so good-looking that he might have been a fool and yet be forgiven. As has already been intimated, however, he was far from being a fool. He had a number of talents, which, during three or four years that followed his leaving college, had received the discipline of the study of the law. He had not made much of the law; but he had made something of his talents. He was almost always spoken of as "accomplished;" people asked why he didn't do something. This question was never satisfactorily answered, the feeling being that Longueville did more than many people in causing it to be asked. Moreover, there was one thing he did constantly — he enjoyed himself. This is manifestly not a career, and it has been said at the outset that he was not attached to any of the recognized professions. But without going into details, he was a charming fellow — clever, urbane, free-handed, and with that fortunate quality in his appearance which is known as distinction.

Chapter III

*H*e had not specified, in writing to Gordon Wright, the day on which he should arrive at Baden-Baden; it must be confessed that he was not addicted to specifying days. He came to his journey's end in the evening, and, on presenting himself at the hotel from which his friend had dated his letter, he learned that Gordon Wright had betaken himself after dinner, according to the custom of Baden-Baden, to the grounds of the Conversation-house. It was eight o'clock, and Longueville, after removing the stains of travel, sat down to dine. His first impulse had been to send for Gordon to come and keep him company at his repast; but on second thought he determined to make it as brief as possible. Having brought it to a close, he took his way to the Kursaal. The great German watering-place is one of the prettiest nooks in Europe, and of a summer evening in the gaming days, five-and-twenty years ago, it was one of the most brilliant scenes. The lighted windows of the great temple of hazard (of as chaste an architecture as if it had been devoted to a much purer divinity) opened wide upon the gardens and groves;

the little river that issues from the bosky mountains of the Black Forest flowed, with an air of brooklike innocence, past the expensive hotels and lodging-houses; the orchestra, in a high pavilion on the terrace of the Kursaal, played a discreet accompaniment to the conversation of the ladies and gentlemen who, scattered over the large expanse on a thousand little chairs, preferred for the time the beauties of nature to the shuffle of coin and the calculation of chance; while the faint summer stars, twinkling above the vague black hills and woods, looked down at the indifferent groups without venturing to drop their light upon them.

Longueville, noting all this, went straight into the gaming-rooms; he was curious to see whether his friend, being fond of experiments, was trying combinations at roulette. But he was not to be found in any of the gilded chambers, among the crowd that pressed in silence about the tables; so that Bernard presently came and began to wander about the lamp-lit terrace, where innumerable groups, seated and strolling, made the place a gigantic *conversazione.* It seemed to him very agreeable and amusing, and he remarked to himself that, for a man who was supposed not to take especially the Epicurean view of life, Gordon Wright, in coming to Baden, had certainly made himself comfortable. Longueville went his way, glancing from one cluster of talkers to another; and at last he saw a face which brought him to a stop. He stood a moment looking at it; he knew he had seen it before. He had an excellent memory for faces; but it was some time before he was able to attach an identity to this one. Where had he seen a little elderly lady with an expression of timorous vigilance, and a band of hair as softly white as a dove's wing? The answer to the question presently came — Where but in a grass-grown corner of an old Italian town? The lady was the mother of his inconsequent model, so that this mysterious personage was probably herself not far off. Before Longueville had time to verify this induction, he found his eyes resting upon the broad back of a gentleman seated close to the old lady, and who, turning away from her, was talking to a young girl. It was nothing but the back of this gentleman that he saw, but nevertheless, with the instinct of true friendship, he recognized in this feature-less expanse the robust personality of Gordon Wright. In a moment he had stepped forward and laid his hand upon Wright's shoulder.

His friend looked round, and then sprang up with a joyous exclamation and grasp of the hand.

"My dear fellow — my dear Bernard! What on earth — when did you arrive?"

While Bernard answered and explained a little, he glanced from his friend's good, gratified face at the young girl with whom Wright had been talking, and then at the lady on the other side, who was giving him a bright little stare. He raised his hat to her and to the young girl, and he became conscious, as regards the latter, of a certain disappointment. She was very pretty; she was looking at him; but she was not the heroine of the little incident of the terrace at Siena.

"It's just like Longueville, you know," Gordon Wright went on; "he always comes at you from behind; he's so awfully fond of surprises." He was laughing; he was greatly pleased; he introduced Bernard to the two ladies. "You must know Mrs. Vivian; you must know Miss Blanche Evers."

Bernard took his place in the little circle; he wondered whether he ought to venture upon a special recognition of Mrs. Vivian. Then it seemed to him that he should leave the option of this step with the lady, especially as he had detected recognition in her eye. But Mrs. Vivian ventured upon nothing special; she contented herself with soft generalities — with remarking that she always liked to know when people would arrive; that, for herself, she never enjoyed surprises.

"And yet I imagine you have had your share," said Longueville, with a smile. He thought this might remind her of the moment when she came out of the little church at Siena and found her daughter posturing to an unknown painter.

But Mrs. Vivian, turning her benignant head about, gave but a superficial reply.

"Oh, I have had my share of everything, good and bad. I don't complain of anything." And she gave a little deprecating laugh.

Gordon Wright shook hands with Bernard again; he seemed really very glad to see him. Longueville, remembering that Gordon had written to him that he had been "making love," began to seek in his countenance for the ravages of passion. For the moment, however, they were not apparent; the excellent, honest fellow looked placid and contented. Gordon Wright had a clear gray eye, short, straight, flaxen hair, and a healthy diffusion of color. His features were thick and rather irregular; but his countenance — in addition to the merit of its expression — derived a certain grace from a powerful yellow moustache, to which its wearer occasionally gave a martial twist. Gordon Wright was not tall, but he was strong, and in his whole person there was something well-planted and sturdy. He almost always dressed in light-colored garments, and he wore round his neck an eternal blue cravat. When he was agitated he grew very red. While he questioned Longueville about his journey and his health, his whereabouts and his intentions, the latter, among his own replies, endeavored to read in Wright's eyes some account of his present situation. Was that pretty girl at his side the ambiguous object of his adoration, and, in that case, what was the function of the elder lady, and what had become of her argumentative daughter? Perhaps this was another, a younger daughter, though, indeed, she bore no resemblance to either of Longueville's friends. Gordon Wright, in spite of Bernard's interrogative glances, indulged in no optical confidences. He had too much to tell. He would keep his story till they should be alone together. It was impossible that they should adjourn just yet to social solitude; the two ladies were under Gordon's protection. Mrs. Vivian — Bernard felt a satisfaction in learning her name; it was as if a curtain, half pulled up and stopped by a hitch, had suddenly been raised altogether — Mrs. Vivian sat looking up and down the terrace at the crowd of loungers and talkers with an air of tender expectation. She was probably looking for her elder daughter, and Longueville could not help wishing also that this young lady would arrive. Meanwhile, he saw that the young girl to whom Gordon had been devoting himself was extremely pretty, and appeared eminently approachable. Longueville had some talk with her, reflecting that if she were the person concerning whom Gordon had written him, it behooved him to appear to take an interest in her. This view of the case was confirmed by Gordon Wright's presently turning away to talk with Mrs. Vivian, so that his friend might be at liberty to make acquaintance with their companion.

Though she had not been with the others at Siena, it seemed to Longueville, with regard to her, too, that this was not the first time he had seen her. She was simply the American pretty girl, whom he had seen a thousand times. It was a numerous sisterhood, pervaded by a strong family likeness. This young lady had charming eyes (of the color of Gordon's cravats), which looked everywhere at once and yet found time to linger

in some places, where Longueville's own eyes fre-
quently met them. She had soft brown hair, with a
silky-golden thread in it, beautifully arranged and
crowned by a smart little hat that savored of Paris. She
had also a slender little figure, neatly rounded, and
delicate, narrow hands, prettily gloved. She moved
about a great deal in her place, twisted her little flexible
body and tossed her head, fingered her hair and examined the ornaments of her dress. She had a great deal
of conversation, Longueville speedily learned, and she
expressed herself with extreme frankness and decision.
He asked her, to begin with, if she had been long at
Baden, but the impetus of this question was all she
required. Turning her charming, conscious, coquettish
little face upon him, she instantly began to chatter.

"I have been here about four weeks. I don't know
whether you call that long. It doesn't seem long to me;
I have had such a lovely time. I have met ever so many
people here I know — every day some one turns up.
Now you have turned up today."

"Ah, but you don't know me," said Longueville,
laughing.

"Well, I have heard a great deal about you!" cried the
young girl, with a pretty little stare of contradiction.
"I think you know a great friend of mine, Miss Ella
Maclane, of Baltimore. She's traveling in Europe now."
Longueville's memory did not instantly respond to
this signal, but he expressed that rapturous assent
which the occasion demanded, and even risked the
observation that the young lady from Baltimore was
very pretty. "She's far too lovely," his companion went
on. "I have often heard her speak of you. I think you
know her sister rather better than you know her. She
has not been out very long. She is just as interesting as
she can be. Her hair comes down to her feet. She's
traveling in Norway. She has been everywhere you can

think of, and she's going to finish off with Finland.
You can't go any further than that, can you? That's one
comfort; she will have to turn round and come back.
I want her dreadfully to come to Baden-Baden."

"I wish she would," said Longueville. "Is she traveling alone?"

"Oh, no. They've got some Englishman. They say
he's devoted to Ella. Everyone seems to have an Englishman, now. We've got one here, Captain Lovelock,
the Honorable Augustus Lovelock. Well, they're awfully handsome. Ella Maclane is dying to come to
Baden-Baden. I wish you'd write to her. Her father and
mother have got some idea in their heads; they think
it's improper — what do you call it? — immoral. I wish
you would write to her and tell her it isn't. I wonder
if they think that Mrs. Vivian would come to a place
that's immoral. Mrs. Vivian says she would take her in
a moment; she doesn't seem to care how many she has.
I declare, she's only too kind. You know I'm in Mrs.
Vivian's care. My mother's gone to Marienbad. She
would let me go with Mrs. Vivian anywhere, on account of the influence — she thinks so much of Mrs.
Vivian's influence. I have always heard a great deal
about it, haven't you? I must say it's lovely; it's had a
wonderful effect upon me. I don't want to praise
myself, but it has. You ask Mrs. Vivian if I haven't been
good. I have been just as good as I can be. I have been
so peaceful, I have just sat here this way. Do you call
this immoral? You're not obliged to gamble if you
don't want to. Ella Maclane's father seems to think you
get drawn in. I'm sure I haven't been drawn in. I know
what you're going to say — you're going to say I have
been drawn out. Well, I have, tonight. We just sit here
so quietly — there's nothing to do but to talk. We make
a little party by ourselves — are you going to belong to
our party? Two of us are missing — Miss Vivian and

Captain Lovelock. Captain Lovelock has gone with her into the rooms to explain the gambling — Miss Vivian always wants everything explained. I am sure I understood it the first time I looked at the tables. Have you ever seen Miss Vivian? She's very much admired, she's so very unusual. Black hair's so uncommon — I see you have got it too — but I mean for young ladies. I am sure one sees everything here. There's a woman that comes to the tables — a Portuguese countess — who has hair that is positively blue. I can't say I admire it when it comes to that shade. Blue's my favorite color, but I prefer it in the eyes," continued Longueville's companion, resting upon him her own two brilliant little specimens of the tint.

He listened with that expression of clear amusement which is not always an indication of high esteem, but which even pretty chatterers, who are not the reverse of estimable, often prefer to masculine inattention; and while he listened Bernard, according to his wont, made his reflections. He said to himself that there were two kinds of pretty girls — the acutely conscious and the finely unconscious. Mrs. Vivian's *protégée* was a member of the former category; she belonged to the genus coquette. We all have our conception of the indispensable, and the indispensable, to this young lady, was a spectator; almost any male biped would serve the purpose. To her spectator she addressed, for the moment, the whole volume of her being — addressed it in her glances, her attitudes, her exclamations, in a hundred little experiments of tone and gesture and position. And these rustling artifices were so innocent and obvious that the directness of her desire to be well with her observer became in itself a grace; it led Bernard afterward to say to himself that the natural vocation and *métier* of little girls for whom existence was but a shimmering surface, was to prattle and ruffle their plumage; their view of life and its duties was as simple and superficial as that of an Oriental *bayadere*. It surely could not be with regard to this transparent little flirt that Gordon Wright desired advice; you could literally see the daylight — or rather the Baden gaslight — on the other side of her. She sat there for a minute, turning her little empty head to and fro, and catching Bernard's eye every time she moved; she had for the instant the air of having exhausted all topics. Just then a young lady, with a gentleman at her side, drew near to the little group, and Longueville, perceiving her, instantly got up from his chair.

"There's a beauty of the unconscious class!" he said to himself. He knew her face very well; he had spent half an hour in copying it.

"Here comes Miss Vivian!" said Gordon Wright, also getting up, as if to make room for the daughter near the mother.

She stopped in front of them, smiling slightly, and then she rested her eyes upon Longueville. Their gaze at first was full and direct, but it expressed nothing more than civil curiosity. This was immediately followed, however, by the light of recognition — recognition embarrassed, and signaling itself by a blush.

Miss Vivian's companion was a powerful, handsome fellow, with a remarkable auburn beard, who struck the observer immediately as being uncommonly well dressed. He carried his hands in the pockets of a little jacket, the buttonhole of which was adorned with a blooming rose. He approached Blanche Evers, smiling and dandling his body a little, and making her two or three jocular bows.

"Well, I hope you have lost every penny you put on the table!" said the young girl, by way of response to his obeisances.

He began to laugh and repeat them.

"I don't care what I lose, so long — so long —"

"So long as what, pray?"

"So long as you let me sit down by you!" And he dropped, very gallantly, into a chair on the other side of her.

"I wish you would lose all your property!" she replied, glancing at Bernard.

"It would be a very small stake," said Captain Lovelock. "Would you really like to see me reduced to misery?"

While this graceful dialogue rapidly established itself, Miss Vivian removed her eyes from Longueville's face and turned toward her mother. But Gordon Wright checked this movement by laying his hand on Longueville's shoulder and proceeding to introduce his friend.

"This is the accomplished creature, Mr. Bernard Longueville, of whom you have heard me speak. One of his accomplishments, as you see, is to drop down from the moon."

"No, I don't drop from the moon," said Bernard, laughing. "I drop from — Siena!" He offered his hand to Miss Vivian, who for an appreciable instant hesitated to extend her own. Then she returned his salutation, without any response to his allusion to Siena.

She declined to take a seat, and said she was tired and preferred to go home. With this suggestion her mother immediately complied, and the two ladies appealed to the indulgence of little Miss Evers, who was obliged to renounce the society of Captain Lovelock. She enjoyed this luxury, however, on the way to Mrs. Vivian's lodgings, toward which they all slowly strolled, in the sociable Baden fashion. Longueville might naturally have found himself next Miss Vivian, but he received an impression that she avoided him. She walked in front, and Gordon Wright strolled beside her, though Longueville noticed that they appeared to exchange but few words. He himself offered his arm to Mrs. Vivian, who paced along with a little lightly-wavering step, making observations upon the beauties of Baden and the respective merits of the hotels.

Chapter IV

"Which of them is it?" asked Longueville of his friend, after they had bidden good-night to the three ladies and to Captain Lovelock, who went off to begin, as he said, the evening. They stood, when they had turned away from the door of Mrs. Vivian's lodgings, in the little, rough-paved German street.

"Which of them is what?" Gordon asked, staring at his companion.

"Oh, come," said Longueville, "you are not going to begin to play at modesty at this hour! Didn't you write to me that you had been making violent love?"

"Violent? No."

"The more shame to you! Has your love-making been feeble?"

His friend looked at him a moment rather soberly.

"I suppose you thought it a queer document — that letter I wrote you."

"I thought it characteristic," said Longueville smiling.

"Isn't that the same thing?"

"Not in the least. I have never thought you a man of oddities." Gordon stood there looking at him with a serious eye, half appealing, half questioning; but at these last words he glanced away. Even a very modest man may wince a little at hearing himself denied the distinction of a few variations from the common type. Longueville made this reflection, and it struck him, also, that his companion was in a graver mood than he had expected; though why, after all, should he have been in a state of exhilaration? "Your letter was a very natural, interesting one," Bernard added.

"Well, you see," said Gordon, facing his companion again, "I have been a good deal preoccupied."

"Obviously, my dear fellow!"

"I want very much to marry."

"It's a capital idea," said Longueville.

"I think almost as well of it," his friend declared, "as if I had invented it. It has struck me for the first time."

These words were uttered with a mild simplicity which provoked Longueville to violent laughter.

"My dear fellow," he exclaimed, "you have, after all, your little oddities."

Singularly enough, however, Gordon Wright failed to appear flattered by this concession.

"I didn't send for you to laugh at me," he said.

"Ah, but I haven't traveled three hundred miles to cry! Seriously, solemnly, then, it is one of these young ladies that has put marriage into your head?"

"Not at all. I had it in my head."

"Having a desire to marry, you proceeded to fall in love."

"I am not in love!" said Gordon Wright, with some energy.

"Ah, then, my dear fellow, why did you send for me?"

Wright looked at him an instant in silence.

"Because I thought you were a good fellow, as well as a clever one."

"A good fellow!" repeated Longueville. "I don't understand your confounded scientific nomenclature. But excuse me; I won't laugh. I am not a clever fellow; but I *am* a good one." He paused a moment, and then laid his hand on his companion's shoulder. "My dear Gordon, it's no use; you *are* in love."

"Well, I don't want to be," said Wright.

"Heavens, what a horrible sentiment!"

"I want to marry with my eyes open. I want to *know* my wife. You don't know people when you are in love with them. Your impressions are colored."

"They are supposed to be, slightly. And you object to color?"

"Well, as I say, I want to know the woman I marry, as I should know anyone else. I want to see her as clearly."

"Depend upon it, you have too great an appetite for knowledge; you set too high an esteem upon the dry light of science."

"Ah!" said Gordon promptly; "of course I want to be fond of her."

Bernard, in spite of his protest, began to laugh again.

"My dear Gordon, you are better than your theories. Your passionate heart contradicts your frigid intellect. I repeat it — you *are* in love."

"Please don't repeat it again," said Wright.

Bernard took his arm, and they walked along.

"What shall I call it, then? You are engaged in making studies for matrimony."

"I don't in the least object to your calling it that. My studies are of extreme interest."

"And one of those young ladies is the fair volume that contains the precious lesson," said Longueville. "Or perhaps your text-book is in two volumes?"

"No; there is one of them I am not studying at all. I never could do two things at once."

"That proves you are in love. One can't be in love with two women at once, but one may perfectly have two of them — or as many as you please — up for a competitive examination. However, as I asked you before, which of these young ladies is it that you have selected?"

Gordon Wright stopped abruptly, eying his friend.

"Which should you say?"

"Ah, that's not a fair question," Bernard urged. "It would be invidious for me to name one rather than the other, and if I were to mention the wrong one, I should feel as if I had been guilty of a rudeness towards the other. Don't you see?"

Gordon saw, perhaps, but he held to his idea of making his companion commit himself.

"Never mind the rudeness. I will do the same by you some day, to make it up. Which of them should you think me likely to have taken a fancy to? On general grounds, now, from what you know of me?" He proposed this problem with an animated eye.

"You forget," his friend said, "that though I know, thank heaven, a good deal of you, I know very little of either of those girls. I have had too little evidence."

"Yes, but you are a man who notices. That's why I wanted you to come."

"I spoke only to Miss Evers."

"Yes, I know you have never spoken to Miss Vivian." Gordon Wright stood looking at Bernard and urging his point as he pronounced these words. Bernard felt peculiarly conscious of his gaze. The words represented an illusion, and Longueville asked himself quickly whether it were not his duty to dispel it. The answer came more slowly than the question, but still it came, in the shape of a negative. The illusion was but a trifling one, and it was not for him, after all, to let his friend know that he had already met Miss Vivian. It was for the young girl herself, and since she had not done so — although she had the opportunity — Longueville said to himself that he was bound in honor not to speak. These reflections were very soon made, but in the midst of them our young man, thanks to a great agility of mind, found time to observe, tacitly, that it was odd, just there, to see his "honor" thrusting in its nose. Miss Vivian, in her own good time, would doubtless mention to Gordon the little incident of Siena. It was Bernard's fancy, for a moment, that he already knew it, and that the remark he had just uttered had an ironical accent; but this impression was completely dissipated by the tone in which he added — "All the same, you noticed her."

"Oh, yes; she is very noticeable."

"Well, then," said Gordon, "you will see. I should like you to make it out. Of course, if I am really giving my attention to one to the exclusion of the other, it will be easy to discover."

Longueville was half amused, half irritated by his friend's own relish of his little puzzle. "'The exclusion of the other' has an awkward sound," he answered, as they walked on. "Am I to notice that you are very rude to one of the young ladies?"

"Oh dear, no. Do you think there is a danger of that?"

"Well," said Longueville, "I have already guessed."

Gordon Wright remonstrated. "Don't guess yet — wait a few days. I won't tell you now."

"Let us see if he doesn't tell me," said Bernard, privately. And he meditated a moment. "When I presented myself, you were sitting very close to Miss Evers and talking very earnestly. Your head was bent toward her — it was very loverlike. Decidedly, Miss Evers is the object!"

For a single instant Gordon Wright hesitated, and then — "I hope I haven't seemed rude to Miss Vivian!" he exclaimed.

Bernard broke into a light laugh. "My dear Gordon, you are very much in love!" he remarked, as they arrived at their hotel.

Chapter V

*L*ife at Baden-Baden proved a very sociable affair, and Bernard Longueville perceived that he should not lack opportunity for the exercise of those gifts of intelligence to which Gordon Wright had appealed. The two friends took long walks through the woods and over the mountains, and they mingled with human life in the crowded precincts of the Conversation-house. They engaged in a ramble on the morning after Bernard's arrival, and wandered far away, over hill and dale. The

Baden forests are superb, and the composition of the landscape is most effective. There is always a bosky dell in the foreground, and a purple crag embellished with a ruined tower at a proper angle. A little timber-and-plaster village peeps out from a tangle of plum trees, and a way-side tavern, in comfortable recurrence, solicits concessions to the national custom of frequent refreshment. Gordon Wright, who was a dogged pedestrian, always enjoyed doing his ten miles, and Longueville, who was an incorrigible stroller, felt a keen relish for the picturesqueness of the country. But it was not, on this occasion, of the charms of the landscape or the pleasures of locomotion that they chiefly discoursed. Their talk took a more closely personal turn. It was a year since they had met, and there were many questions to ask and answer, many arrears of gossip to make up. As they stretched themselves on the grass on a sun-warmed hillside, beneath a great German oak whose arms were quiet in the blue summer air, there was a lively exchange of impressions, opinions, speculations, anecdotes. Gordon Wright was surely an excellent friend. He took an interest in you. He asked no idle questions and made no vague professions; but he entered into your situation, he examined it in detail, and what he learned he never forgot. Months afterwards, he asked you about things which you yourself had forgotten. He was not a man of whom it would be generally said that he had the gift of sympathy; but he gave his attention to a friend's circumstances with a conscientious fixedness which was at least very far removed from indifference. Bernard had the gift of sympathy — or at least he was supposed to have it; but even he, familiar as he must therefore have been with the practice of this charming virtue, was at times so struck with his friend's fine faculty of taking other people's affairs seriously that he constantly exclaimed to himself, "The excellent fellow — the admirable nature!"

Bernard had two or three questions to ask about the three persons who appeared to have formed for some time his companion's principal society, but he was indisposed to press them. He felt that he should see for himself, and at a prospect of entertainment of this kind, his fancy always kindled. Gordon was, moreover, at first rather shy of confidences, though after they had lain on the grass ten minutes there was a good deal said.

"Now what do you think of her face?" Gordon asked, after staring a while at the sky through the oak-boughs.

"Of course, in future," said Longueville, "whenever you make use of the personal pronoun feminine, I am to understand that Miss Vivian is indicated."

"Her name is Angela," said Gordon; "but of course I can scarcely call her that."

"It's a beautiful name," Longueville rejoined; "but I may say, in answer to your question, that I am not struck with the fact that her face corresponds to it."

"You don't think her face beautiful, then?"

"I don't think it angelic. But how can I tell? I have only had a glimpse of her."

"Wait till she looks at you and speaks — wait till she smiles," said Gordon.

"I don't think I saw her smile — at least, not at me, directly. I hope she will!" Longueville went on. "But who is she — this beautiful girl with the beautiful name?"

"She is her mother's daughter," said Gordon Wright. "I don't really know a great deal more about her than that."

"And who is her mother?"

"A delightful little woman, devoted to Miss Vivian. She is a widow, and Angela is her only child. They have lived a great deal in Europe; they have but a modest income. Over here, Mrs. Vivian says, they can get a lot of things for their money that they can't get at home. So they stay, you see. When they are at home they live in New York. They know some of my people there. When they are in Europe they live about in different places. They are fond of Italy. They are extremely nice; it's impossible to be nicer. They are very fond of books, fond of music, and art, and all that. They always read in the morning. They only come out rather late in the day."

"I see they are very superior people," said Bernard. "And little Miss Evers — what does she do in the morning? I know what she does in the evening!"

"I don't know what her regular habits are. I haven't paid much attention to her. She is very pretty."

"*Wunderschön!*" said Bernard. "But you were certainly talking to her last evening."

"Of course I talk to her sometimes. She is totally different from Angela Vivian — not nearly so culti-vated; but she seems very charming."

"A little silly, eh?" Bernard suggested.

"She certainly is not so wise as Miss Vivian."

"That would be too much to ask, eh? But the Vivians, as kind as they are wise, have taken her under their protection."

"Yes," said Gordon, "they are to keep her another month or two. Her mother has gone to Marienbad, which I believe is thought a dull place for a young girl; so that, as they were coming here, they offered to bring her with them. Mrs. Evers is an old friend of Mrs. Vivian, who, on leaving Italy, had come up to Dresden to be with her. They spent a month there together; Mrs. Evers had been there since the winter. I think Mrs. Vivian really came to Baden-Baden — she would have preferred a less expensive place — to bring Blanche

Evers. Her mother wanted her so much to come."

"And was it for her sake that Captain Lovelock came, too?" Bernard asked.

Gordon Wright stared a moment.

"I'm sure I don't know!"

"Of course you can't be interested in that," said Bernard smiling. "Who is Captain Lovelock?"

"He is an Englishman. I believe he is what's called aristocratically connected — the younger brother of a lord, or something of that sort."

"Is he a clever man?"

"I haven't talked with him much, but I doubt it. He is rather rakish; he plays a great deal."

"But is that considered here a proof of rakishness?" asked Bernard. "Haven't you played a little yourself?"

Gordon hesitated a moment.

"Yes, I have played a little. I wanted to try some experiments. I had made some arithmetical calculations of probabilities, which I wished to test."

Bernard gave a long laugh.

"I am delighted with the reasons you give for amusing yourself! Arithmetical calculations!"

"I assure you they are the real reasons!" said Gordon, blushing a little.

"That's just the beauty of it. You were not afraid of being 'drawn in,' as little Miss Evers says?"

"I am never drawn in, whatever the thing may be. I go in, or I stay out; but I am not drawn," said Gordon Wright.

"You were not drawn into coming with Mrs. Vivian and her daughter from Dresden to this place?"

"I didn't come with them; I came a week later."

"My dear fellow," said Bernard, "that distinction is unworthy of your habitual candor."

"Well, I was not fascinated; I was not overmastered. I wanted to come to Baden."

"I have no doubt you did. Had you become very intimate with your friends in Dresden?"

"I had only seen them three times."

"After which you followed them to this place? Ah, don't say you were not fascinated!" cried Bernard, laughing and springing to his feet.

Chapter VI

*T*hat evening, in the gardens of the Kursaal, he renewed acquaintance with Angela Vivian. Her mother came, as usual, to sit and listen to the music, accompanied by Blanche Evers, who was in turn attended by Captain Lovelock. This little party found privacy in the crowd; they seated themselves in a quiet corner in an angle of one of the barriers of the terrace, while the movement of the brilliant Baden world went on around them. Gordon Wright engaged in conversation with Mrs. Vivian, while Bernard enjoyed an interview with her daughter. This young lady continued to ignore the fact of their previous meeting, and our hero said to himself that all he wished was to know what she preferred — he would rigidly conform to it. He conformed to her present program; he had ventured to pronounce the word Siena the evening before, but he was careful not to pronounce it again. She had her reasons for her own reserve; he wondered what they were, and it gave him a certain pleasure to wonder. He enjoyed the consciousness of their having a secret together, and it became a kind of entertaining suspense to see how long she would continue to keep it. For himself, he was in no hurry to let the daylight in; the little incident at Siena had been, in itself, a charming affair; but Miss Vivian's present attitude gave it a sort of mystic consecration. He thought she carried it off very well — the theory that she had not seen him before; last evening she had been slightly confused, but now she was as self-possessed as if the line she had taken were a matter of conscience. Why should it be a matter of conscience? Was she in love with Gordon Wright, and did she wish, in consequence, to forget — and wish him not to suspect — that she had ever received an expression of admiration from another man? This was not likely; it was not likely, at least, that Miss Vivian wished to pass for a prodigy of innocence; for if to be admired is to pay a tribute to corruption, it was perfectly obvious that so handsome a girl must have tasted of the tree of knowledge. As for her being in love with Gordon Wright, that of course was another affair, and Bernard did not pretend, as yet, to have an opinion on this point, beyond hoping very much that she might be.

He was not wrong in the impression of her good looks that he had carried away from the short interview at Siena. She had a charmingly chiseled face, with a free, pure outline, a clear, fair complexion, and the eyes and hair of a dusky beauty. Her features had a firmness which suggested tranquility, and yet her expression was light and quick, a combination — or a contradiction — which gave an original stamp to her beauty. Bernard remembered that he had thought it a trifle "bold"; but he now perceived that this had been but a vulgar misreading of her dark, direct, observant eye. The eye was a charming one; Bernard discovered in it, little by little, all sorts of things; and Miss Vivian was, for the present, simply a handsome, intelligent, smiling girl. He gave her an opportunity to make an allusion to Siena; he said to her that his friend told him that she and her mother had been spending the winter in Italy.

"Oh yes," said Angela Vivian; "we were in the far south; we were five months at Sorrento."

"And nowhere else?"

"We spent a few days in Rome. We usually prefer the quiet places; that is my mother's taste."

"It was not your mother's taste, then," said Bernard, "that brought you to Baden?"

She looked at him a moment.

"You mean that Baden is not quiet?"

Longueville glanced about at the moving, murmuring crowd, at the lighted windows of the Conversation-house, at the great orchestra perched up in its pagoda.

"This is not my idea of absolute tranquility."

"Nor mine, either," said Miss Vivian. "I am not fond of absolute tranquility."

"How do you arrange it, then, with your mother?"

Again she looked at him a moment, with her clever, slightly mocking smile.

"As you see. By making her come where I wish."

"You have a strong will," said Bernard. "I see that."

"No. I have simply a weak mother. But I make sacrifices too, sometimes."

"What do you call sacrifices?"

"Well, spending the winter at Sorrento."

Bernard began to laugh, and then he told her she must have had a very happy life — "to call a winter at Sorrento a sacrifice."

"It depends upon what one gives up," said Miss Vivian.

"What did you give up?"

She touched him with her mocking smile again.

"That is not a very civil question, asked in that way."

"You mean that I seem to doubt your abnegation?"

"You seem to insinuate that I had nothing to renounce. I gave up — I gave up —" and she looked about her, considering a little — "I gave up society."

"I am glad you remember what it was," said Bernard. "If I have seemed uncivil, let me make it up. When a woman speaks of giving up society, what she means is giving up admiration. You can never have given up that — you can never have escaped from it. You must have found it even at Sorrento."

"It may have been there, but I never found it. It was very respectful — it never expressed itself."

"That is the deepest kind," said Bernard.

"I prefer the shallower varieties," the young girl answered.

"Well," said Bernard, "you must remember that although shallow admiration expresses itself, all the admiration that expresses itself is not shallow."

Miss Vivian hesitated a moment.

"Some of it is impertinent," she said, looking straight at him, rather gravely.

Bernard hesitated about as long.

"When it is impertinent it is shallow. That comes to the same thing."

The young girl frowned a little.

"I am not sure that I understand — I am rather stupid. But you see how right I am in my taste for such places as this. I have to come here to hear such ingenious remarks."

"You should add that my coming, as well, has something to do with it."

"Everything!" said Miss Vivian.

"Everything? Does no one else make ingenious remarks? Doesn't my friend Wright?"

"Mr. Wright says excellent things, but I should not exactly call them ingenious remarks."

"It is not what Wright says; it's what he does. That's the charm!" said Bernard.

His companion was silent for a moment. "That's not usually a charm; good conduct is not thought pleasing."

"It surely is not thought the reverse!" Bernard exclaimed.

"It doesn't rank — in the opinion of most people — among the things that make men agreeable."

"It depends upon what you call agreeable."

"Exactly so," said Miss Vivian. "It all depends on that."

"But the agreeable," Bernard went on — "it isn't after all, fortunately, such a subtle idea! The world certainly is agreed to think that virtue is a beautiful thing."

Miss Vivian dropped her eyes a moment, and then, looking up,

"Is it a charm?" she asked.

"For me there is no charm without it," Bernard declared.

"I am afraid that for me there is," said the young girl.

Bernard was puzzled — he who was not often puzzled. His companion struck him as altogether too clever to be likely to indulge in a silly affectation of cynicism. And yet, without this, how could one account for her sneering at virtue?

"You talk as if you had sounded the depths of vice!" he said, laughing. "What do you know about other than virtuous charms?"

"I know, of course, nothing about vice; but I have

known virtue when it was very tiresome."

"Ah, then it was a poor affair. It was poor virtue. The best virtue is never tiresome."

Miss Vivian looked at him a little, with her fine discriminating eye.

"What a dreadful thing to have to think any virtue poor!"

This was a touching reflection, and it might have gone further had not the conversation been interrupted by Mrs. Vivian's appealing to her daughter to aid a defective recollection of a story about a Spanish family they had met at Biarritz, with which she had undertaken to entertain Gordon Wright. After this, the little circle was joined by a party of American friends who were spending a week at Baden, and the conversation became general.

Chapter VII

*B*ut on the following evening, Bernard again found himself seated in friendly colloquy with this interesting girl, while Gordon Wright discoursed with her mother on one side, and little Blanche Evers chattered to the admiring eyes of Captain Lovelock on the other.

"You and your mother are very kind to that little girl," our hero said; "you must be a great advantage to her."

Angela Vivian directed her eyes to her neighbors, and let them rest a while on the young girl's little fidgeting figure and her fresh, coquettish face. For some moments she said nothing, and to Longueville, turning over several things in his mind, and watching her, it seemed that her glance was one of disfavor. He divined, he scarcely knew how, that her esteem for her pretty companion was small.

"I don't know that I am very kind," said Miss Vivian. "I have done nothing in particular for her."

"Mr. Wright tells me you came to this place mainly on her account."

"I came for myself," said Miss Vivian. "The consideration you speak of perhaps had weight with my mother."

"You are not an easy person to say appreciative things to," Bernard rejoined. "One is tempted to say them; but you don't take them."

The young girl colored as she listened to this observation.

"I don't think you know," she murmured, looking away. Then, "Set it down to modesty," she added.

"That, of course, is what I have done. To what else could one possibly attribute an indifference to compliments?"

"There is something else. One might be proud."

"There you are again!" Bernard exclaimed. "You won't even let me praise your modesty."

"I would rather you should rebuke my pride."

"That is so humble a speech that it leaves no room for rebuke."

For a moment Miss Vivian said nothing.

"Men are singularly base," she declared presently, with a little smile. "They don't care in the least to say things that might help a person. They only care to say things that may seem effective and agreeable."

"I see: you think that to say agreeable things is a great misdemeanor."

"It comes from their vanity," Miss Vivian went on, as if she had not heard him. "They wish to appear agreeable and get credit for cleverness and *tendresse*, no matter how silly it would be for another person to believe them."

Bernard was a good deal amused, and a little nettled.

"Women, then," he said, "have rather a fondness for producing a bad impression — they like to appear disagreeable?"

His companion bent her eyes upon her fan for a moment as she opened and closed it.

"They are capable of resigning themselves to it — for a purpose."

Bernard was moved to extreme merriment.

"For what purpose?"

"I don't know that I mean for a purpose," said Miss Vivian; "but for a necessity."

"Ah, what an odious necessity!"

"Necessities usually are odious. But women meet them. Men evade them and shirk them."

"I contest your proposition. Women are themselves necessities; but they are not odious ones!" And Bernard added, in a moment, "One couldn't evade them, if they were!"

"I object to being called a necessity," said Angela Vivian. "It diminishes one's merit."

"Ah, but it enhances the charm of life!"

"For men, doubtless!"

"The charm of life is very great," Bernard went on, looking up at the dusky hills and the summer stars, seen through a sort of mist of music and talk, and of powdery light projected from the softly lurid windows of the gaming-rooms. "The charm of life is extreme. I am unacquainted with odious necessities. I object to nothing!"

Angela Vivian looked about her as he had done — looked perhaps a moment longer at the summer stars; and if she had not already proved herself a young lady of a contradictory turn, it might have been supposed she was just then tacitly admitting the charm of life to be considerable.

"Do you suppose Miss Evers often resigns herself to being disagreeable — for a purpose?" asked Longueville, who had glanced at Captain Lovelock's companion again.

"She can't be disagreeable; she is too gentle, too soft."

"Do you mean too silly?"

"I don't know that I call her silly. She is not very wise; but she has no pretensions — absolutely none — so that one is not struck with anything incongruous."

"What a terrible description! I suppose one ought to have a few pretensions."

"You see one comes off more easily without them," said Miss Vivian.

"Do you call that coming off easily?"

She looked at him a moment gravely.

"I am very fond of Blanche," she said.

"Captain Lovelock is rather fond of her," Bernard went on.

The girl assented.

"He is completely fascinated — he is very much in love with her."

"And do they mean to make an international match?"

"I hope not; my mother and I are greatly troubled."

"Isn't he a good fellow?"

"He is a good fellow; but he is a mere trifler. He hasn't a penny, I believe, and he has very expensive habits. He gambles a great deal. We don't know what to do."

"You should send for the young lady's mother."

"We have written to her pressingly. She answers that Blanche can take care of herself, and that she must stay at Marienbad to finish her cure. She has just begun a new one."

"Ah well," said Bernard, "doubtless Blanche can take care of herself."

For a moment his companion said nothing; then she exclaimed —

"It's what a girl ought to be able to do!"

"I am sure you are!" said Bernard.

She met his eyes, and she was going to make some rejoinder; but before she had time to speak, her mother's little, clear, conciliatory voice interposed. Mrs. Vivian appealed to her daughter, as she had done the night before.

"Dear Angela, what was the name of the gentleman who delivered that delightful course of lectures that we heard in Geneva, on — what was the title? — 'The Redeeming Features of the Pagan Morality.'"

Angela flushed a little.

"I have quite forgotten his name, mamma," she said, without looking round.

"Come and sit by me, my dear, and we will talk them over. I wish Mr. Wright to hear about them," Mrs. Vivian went on.

"Do you wish to convert him to paganism?" Bernard asked.

"The lectures were very dull; they had no redeeming features," said Angela, getting up, but turning away from her mother. She stood looking at Bernard Longueville; he saw she was annoyed at her mother's interference. "Every now and then," she said, "I take a turn through the gaming-rooms. The last time, Captain Lovelock went with me. Will you come tonight?"

Bernard assented with expressive alacrity; he was charmed with her not wishing to break off her conversation with him.

"Ah, we'll all go!" said Mrs. Vivian, who had been listening, and she invited the others to accompany her to the Kursaal.

They left their places, but Angela went first, with Bernard Longueville by her side; and the idea of her having publicly braved her mother, as it were, for the sake of his society, lent for the moment an almost ecstatic energy to his tread. If he had been tempted to presume upon his triumph, however, he would have found a check in the fact that the young girl herself tasted very soberly of the sweets of defiance. She was silent and grave; she had a manner which took the edge from the wantonness of filial independence. Yet, for all this, Bernard was pleased with his position; and, as he walked with her through the lighted and crowded rooms, where they soon detached themselves from their companions, he felt that peculiar satisfaction which best expresses itself in silence. Angela looked a while at the rows of still, attentive faces, fixed upon the luminous green circle, across which little heaps of louis d'or were being pushed to and fro, and she continued to say nothing. Then at last she exclaimed simply, "Come away!" They turned away and passed into another chamber, in which there was no gambling. It was an immense apartment, apparently a ballroom; but at present it was quite unoccupied. There were green velvet benches all around it, and a great polished floor stretched away, shining in the light of chandeliers adorned with innumerable glass drops. Miss Vivian stood a moment on the threshold; then she passed in, and they stopped in the middle of the place, facing each other, and with their figures reflected as if they had been standing on a sheet of ice. There was no one in the room; they were entirely alone.

"Why don't you recognize me?" Bernard murmured quickly.

"Recognize you?"

"Why do you seem to forget our meeting at Siena?"

She might have answered if she had answered immediately; but she hesitated, and while she did so something happened at the other end of the room which caused her to shift her glance. A green velvet *portière* suspended in one of the door-ways — not that through which our friends had passed — was lifted, and Gordon Wright stood there, holding it up, and looking at them. His companions were behind him.

"Ah, here they are!" cried Gordon, in his loud, clear voice.

This appeared to strike Angela Vivian as an interruption, and Bernard saw it very much in the same light.

Chapter VIII

*H*e forbore to ask her his question again — she might tell him at her convenience. But the days passed by, and she never told him — she had her own reasons. Bernard talked with her very often; conversation formed indeed the chief entertainment of the quiet little circle of which he was a member. They sat on the terrace and talked in the mingled starlight and lamp-light, and they strolled in the deep green forests and wound along the side of the gentle Baden hills, under the influence of colloquial tendencies. The Black Forest is a country of almost unbroken shade, and in the still days of midsummer the whole place was covered with a motionless canopy of verdure. Our friends were not extravagant or audacious people, and they looked at Baden life very much from the outside — they sat aloof from the brightly lighted drama of professional revelry. Among themselves as well, however, a little drama went forward in which each member of the company had a part to play. Bernard Longueville had been surprised at first at what he would have called Miss Vivian's approachableness — at the frequency with which he encountered opportunities for sitting near her and entering into conversation. He had expected that Gordon Wright would deem himself to have established an anticipatory claim upon the young lady's attention, and that, in pursuance of this claim, he would occupy a recognized place at her side. Gordon was, after all, wooing her; it was very natural he should seek her society. In fact, he was never very far off; but Bernard, for three or four days, had the anomalous consciousness of being still nearer. Presently, however, he perceived that he owed this privilege simply to his friend's desire that he should become acquainted with Miss Vivian — should receive a vivid impression of a person in whom Gordon was so deeply interested. After this result might have been supposed to be attained, Gordon Wright stepped back into his usual place and showed her those small civilities which were the only homage that the quiet conditions of their life rendered possible — walked with her, talked with her, brought her a book to read, a chair to sit upon, a couple of flowers to place in the bosom of her gown, treated her, in a word, with a sober but by no means inexpressive gallantry. He had not been making violent love, as he told Longueville, and these demonstrations were certainly not violent. Bernard said to himself that if he were not in the secret, a spectator would scarcely make the discovery that Gordon cherished an even very safely tended flame. Angela Vivian, on her side, was not strikingly responsive. There was nothing in her deportment to indicate that she was in love with her systematic suitor. She was perfectly gracious and civil. She smiled in his face when he shook hands with her; she looked at him and listened when he talked; she let him stroll beside her in the Lichtenthal Alley; she read, or appeared to read, the books he lent her, and she decorated herself with the flowers he offered. She seemed neither bored nor embarrassed, neither irritated nor oppressed. But it was Bernard's belief that she took no more pleasure in his attentions than a pretty girl must always take in any recognition of her charms. "If she's not indifferent," he said to himself, "she is, at any rate, impartial — profoundly impartial."

It was not till the end of a week that Gordon Wright told him exactly how his business stood with Miss Vivian and what he had reason to expect and hope — a week during which their relations had been of the happiest and most comfortable cast, and during which Bernard, rejoicing in their long walks and talks, in the charming weather, in the beauty and entertainment of the place, and in other things besides, had not ceased to congratulate himself on coming to Baden. Bernard, after the first day, had asked his friend no questions. He had a great respect for opportunity, coming either to others or to himself, and he left Gordon to turn his lantern as fitfully as might be upon the subject which was tacitly open between them, but of which as yet only the mere edges had emerged into light. Gordon, on his side, seemed content for the moment with having his clever friend under his hand; he reserved him for final appeal or for some other mysterious use.

"You can't tell me you don't know her now," he said, one evening as the two young men strolled along the Lichtenthal Alley — "now that you have had a whole week's observation of her."

"What is a week's observation of a singularly clever and complicated woman?" Bernard asked.

"Ah, your week has been of some use. You have found out she is complicated!" Gordon rejoined.

"My dear Gordon," Longueville exclaimed, "I don't see what it signifies to you that I should find Miss Vivian out! When a man's in love, what need he care what other people think of the loved object?"

"It would certainly be a pity to care too much. But there is some excuse for him in the loved object being, as you say, complicated."

"Nonsense! That's no excuse. The loved object is always complicated."

Gordon walked on in silence a moment.

"Well, then, I don't care a button what you think!"

"Bravo! That's the way a man should talk," cried Longueville.

Gordon indulged in another fit of meditation, and then he said —

"Now that leaves you at liberty to say what you please."

"Ah, my dear fellow, you are ridiculous!" said Bernard.

"That's precisely what I want you to say. You always think me too reasonable."

"Well, I go back to my first assertion. I don't know Miss Vivian — I mean I don't know her to have opinions about her. I don't suppose you wish me to string you off a dozen mere *banalités* — 'she's a charming girl — evidently a superior person — has a great deal of style.'"

"Oh no," said Gordon; "I know all that. But, at any rate," he added, "you like her, eh?"

"I do more," said Longueville. "I admire her."

"Is that doing more?" asked Gordon, reflectively.

"Well, the greater, whichever it is, includes the less."

"You won't commit yourself," said Gordon. "My dear Bernard," he added, "I thought you knew such an immense deal about women!"

Gordon Wright was of so kindly and candid a nature that it is hardly conceivable that this remark should have been framed to make Bernard commit himself by putting him on his mettle. Such a view would imply indeed on Gordon's part a greater familiarity with the uses of irony than he had ever possessed, as well as a livelier conviction of the irritable nature of his friend's vanity. In fact, however, it may be confided to the reader that Bernard was pricked in a tender place, though the resentment of vanity was not visible in his answer.

"You were quite wrong," he simply said. "I am as ignorant of women as a monk in his cloister."

"You try to prove too much. You don't think her sympathetic!" And as regards this last remark, Gordon Wright must be credited with a certain ironical impulse.

Bernard stopped impatiently.

"I ask you again, what does it matter to you what I think of her?"

"It matters in this sense — that she has refused me."

"Refused you? Then it is all over, and nothing matters."

"No, it isn't over," said Gordon, with a positive head-shake. "Don't you see it isn't over?"

Bernard smiled, laid his hand on his friend's shoulder and patted it a little.

"Your attitude might almost pass for that of resignation."

"I'm not resigned!" said Gordon Wright.

"Of course not. But when were you refused?"

Gordon stood a minute with his eyes fixed on the ground. Then, at last looking up,

"Three weeks ago — a fortnight before you came. But let us walk along," he said, "and I will tell you all about it."

"I proposed to her three weeks ago," said Gordon, as they walked along. "My heart was very much set upon it. I was very hard hit — I was deeply smitten. She had been very kind to me — she had been charming — I thought she liked me. Then I thought her mother was pleased, and would have liked it. Mrs. Vivian, in fact, told me as much; for of course I spoke to her first. Well, Angela does like me — or at least she did — and I see no reason to suppose she has changed. Only she didn't like me enough. She said the friendliest and pleasantest things to me, but she thought that she knew me too little, and that I knew her even less. She made a great point of that — that I had no right, as yet, to trust her. I told her that if she would trust me, I was perfectly willing to trust her; but she answered that this was poor reasoning. She said that I was trustworthy and that she was not, and — in short, all sorts of nonsense. She abused herself roundly — accused herself of no end of defects."

"What defects, for instance?"

"Oh, I haven't remembered them. She said she had a bad temper — that she led her mother a dreadful life. Now, poor Mrs. Vivian says she is an angel."

"Ah yes," Bernard observed; "Mrs. Vivian says that, very freely."

"Angela declared that she was jealous, ungenerous, unforgiving — all sorts of things. I remember she said 'I am very false,' and I think she remarked that she was cruel."

"But this didn't put you off," said Bernard.

"Not at all. She was making up."

"She makes up very well!" Bernard exclaimed, laughing.

"Do you call that well?"

"I mean it was very clever."

"It was not clever from the point of view of wishing to discourage me."

"Possibly. But I am sure," said Bernard, "that if I had been present at your interview — excuse the impudence of the hypothesis — I should have been struck with the young lady's —" and he paused a moment.

"With her what?"

"With her ability."

"Well, her ability was not sufficient to induce me to give up my idea. She told me that after I had known her six months I should detest her."

"I have no doubt she could make you do it if she should try. That's what I mean by her ability."

"She calls herself cruel," said Gordon, "but she has not had the cruelty to try. She has been very reasonable — she has been perfect. I agreed with her that I would drop the subject for a while, and that meanwhile we should be good friends. We should take time to know each other better and act in accordance with further knowledge. There was no hurry, since we trusted each other — wrong as my trust might be. She had no wish that I should go away. I was not in the least disagreeable to her; she liked me extremely, and I was perfectly free to try and please her. Only I should drop my proposal, and be free to take it up again or leave it alone, later, as I should choose. If she felt differently then, I should have the benefit of it, and if I myself felt differently, I should also have the benefit of it."

"That's a very comfortable arrangement. And that's your present situation?" asked Bernard.

Gordon hesitated a moment.

"More or less, but not exactly."

"Miss Vivian feels differently?" said Bernard.

"Not that I know of."

Gordon's companion, with a laugh, clapped him on the shoulder again.

"Admirable youth, you are a capital match!"

"Are you alluding to my money?"

"To your money and to your modesty. There is as much of one as of the other — which is saying a great deal."

"Well," said Gordon, "in spite of that enviable combination, I am not happy."

"I thought you seemed pensive!" Bernard exclaimed. "It's you, then, who feel differently."

Gordon gave a sigh.

"To say that is to say too much."

"What shall we say, then?" his companion asked, kindly.

Gordon stopped again; he stood there looking up at a certain particularly lustrous star which twinkled — the night was cloudy — in an open patch of sky, and the vague brightness shone down on his honest and serious visage.

"I don't understand her," he said.

"Oh, I'll say that with you any day!" cried Bernard. "I can't help you there."

"You *must* help me;" and Gordon Wright deserted his star. "You must keep me in good humor."

"Please to walk on, then. I don't in the least pity you; she is very charming with you."

"True enough; but insisting on that is not the way to keep me in good humor — when I feel as I do."

"How is it you feel?"

"Puzzled to death — bewildered — depressed!"

This was but the beginning of Gordon Wright's list; he went on to say that though he "thought as highly" of Miss Vivian as he had ever done, he felt less at his ease with her than in the first weeks of their acquaintance, and this condition made him uncomfortable and unhappy.

"I don't know what's the matter," said poor Gordon. "I don't know what has come between us. It isn't her fault — I don't make her responsible for it. I began to notice it about a fortnight ago — before you came; shortly after that talk I had with her that I have just described to you. Her manner hasn't changed and I have no reason to suppose that she likes me any the less; but she makes a strange impression on me — she makes me uneasy. It's only her nature coming out, I suppose — what you might call her originality. She's thoroughly original — she's a kind of mysterious creature. I suppose that what I feel is a sort of fascination; but that is just what I don't like. Hang it, I don't want to be fascinated — I object to being fascinated!"

This little story had taken some time in the telling, so that the two young men had now reached their hotel.

"Ah, my dear Gordon," said Bernard, "we speak a different language. If you don't want to be fascinated, what is one to say to you? 'Object to being fascinated!' There's a man easy to satisfy! *Raffiné, va!*"

"Well, see here now," said Gordon, stopping in the door-way of the inn; "when it comes to the point, do you like it yourself?"

"When it comes to the point?" Bernard exclaimed. "I assure you I don't wait till then. I like the beginning — I delight in the approach of it — I revel in the prospect."

"That's just what I did. But now that the thing has come — I don't revel. To be fascinated is to be mystified. Damn it, I like my liberty — I like my judgment!"

"So do I — like yours," said Bernard, laughing, as they took their bedroom candles.

Chapter IX

*B*ernard talked of this matter rather theoretically, inasmuch as to his own sense, he was in a state neither of incipient nor of absorbed fascination. He got on very easily, however, with Angela Vivian, and felt none of the mysterious discomfort alluded to by his friend. The element of mystery attached itself rather to the young lady's mother, who gave him the impression that for undiscoverable reasons she avoided his society. He regretted her evasive deportment, for he found something agreeable in this shy and scrupulous little woman, who struck him as a curious specimen of a society of which he had once been very fond. He learned that she was of old New England stock, but he had not needed this information to perceive that Mrs. Vivian was animated by the genius of Boston. "She has the Boston temperament," he said, using a phrase with which he had become familiar and which evoked a train of associations. But then he immediately added that if Mrs. Vivian was a daughter of the Puritans, the Puritan strain in her disposition had been mingled with another element. "It is the Boston temperament sophisticated," he said; "perverted a little — perhaps even corrupted. It is the local east-wind with an infusion from climates less tonic." It seemed to him that Mrs. Vivian was a Puritan grown worldly — a Bostonian relaxed; and this impression, oddly enough, contributed to his wish to know more of her. He felt like going up to her very politely and saying, "Dear lady and most honored compatriot, what in the world have I done to displease you? You don't approve of me, and I am dying to know the reason why. I should be so happy to exert myself to be agreeable to you. It's no use; you give me the cold shoulder. When I speak to you, you look the other way; it is only when I speak to your daughter that you look at me. It is true that at those times you look at me very hard, and if I am not greatly mistaken, you are not gratified by what you see. You count the words I address to your beautiful Angela — you time our harmless little interviews. You interrupt them indeed whenever you can; you call her away — you appeal to her; you cut across the conversation. You are always laying plots to keep us apart. Why can't you leave me alone? I assure you I am the most innocent of men. Your beautiful Angela can't possibly be injured by my conversation, and I have no designs whatever upon her peace of mind. What on earth have I done to offend you?"

These observations Bernard Longueville was disposed to make, and one afternoon, the opportunity offering, they rose to his lips and came very near passing them. In fact, however, at the last moment, his eloquence took another turn. It was the custom of the orchestra at the Kursaal to play in the afternoon, and as the music was often good, a great many people assembled under the trees, at three o'clock, to listen to it. This was not, as a regular thing, an hour of re-union for the little group in which we are especially interested;

Miss Vivian, in particular, unless an excursion of some sort had been agreed upon the day before, was usually not to be seen in the precincts of the Conversation-house until the evening. Bernard, one afternoon, at three o'clock, directed his steps to this small world-center of Baden, and, passing along the terrace, soon encountered little Blanche Evers strolling there under a pink parasol and accompanied by Captain Lovelock. This young lady was always extremely sociable; it was quite in accordance with her habitual geniality that she should stop and say how d' ye do to our hero.

"Mr. Longueville is growing very frivolous," she said, "coming to the Kursaal at all sorts of hours."

"There is nothing frivolous in coming here with the hope of finding you," the young man answered. "That is very serious."

"It would be more serious to lose Miss Evers than to find her," remarked Captain Lovelock, with gallant jocosity.

"I wish you would lose me!" cried the young girl. "I think I should like to be lost. I might have all kinds of adventures."

"I 'guess' so!" said Captain Lovelock, hilariously.

"Oh, I should find my way. I can take care of myself!" Blanche went on.

"Mrs. Vivian doesn't think so," said Bernard, who had just perceived this lady, seated under a tree with a book, over the top of which she was observing her pretty *protégée*. Blanche looked toward her and gave her a little nod and a smile. Then chattering on to the young men —

"She's awfully careful. I never saw anyone so careful. But I suppose she is right. She promised my mother she would be tremendously particular; but I don't know what she thinks I would do."

"That isn't flattering to me," said Captain Lovelock.

"Mrs. Vivian doesn't approve of me — she wishes me in Jamaica. What does she think me capable of?"

"And me, now?" Bernard asked. "She likes me least of all, and I, on my side, think she's so nice."

"Can't say I'm very sweet on her," said the Captain. "She strikes me as feline."

Blanche Evers gave a little cry of horror.

"Stop, sir, this instant! I won't have you talk that way about a lady who has been so kind to me."

"She isn't so kind to you. She would like to lock you up where I can never see you."

"I'm sure I shouldn't mind that!" cried the young girl, with a little laugh and a toss of her head. "Mrs. Vivian has the most perfect character — that's why my mother wanted me to come with her. And if she promised my mother she would be careful, isn't she right to keep her promise? She's a great deal more careful than mamma ever was, and that's just what mamma wanted. She would never take the trouble herself. And then she was always scolding me. Mrs. Vivian never scolds me. She only watches me, but I don't mind that."

"I wish she would watch you a little less and scold you a little more," said Captain Lovelock.

"I have no doubt you wish a great many horrid things," his companion rejoined, with delightful asperity.

"Ah, unfortunately I never have anything I wish!" sighed Lovelock.

"Your wishes must be comprehensive," said Bernard. "It seems to me you have a good deal."

The Englishman gave a shrug.

"It's less than you might think. She is watching us more furiously than ever," he added, in a moment, looking at Mrs. Vivian. "Mr. Gordon Wright is the only man she likes. She is awfully fond of Mr. Gordon Wright."

"Ah, Mrs. Vivian shows her wisdom!" said Bernard.

"He is certainly very handsome," murmured Blanche Evers, glancing several times, with a very pretty aggressiveness, at Captain Lovelock. "I must say I like Mr. Gordon Wright. Why in the world did you come here without him?" she went on, addressing herself to Bernard. "You two are so awfully inseparable. I don't think I ever saw you alone before."

"Oh, I have often seen Mr. Gordon Wright alone," said Captain Lovelock — "that is, alone with Miss Vivian. That's what the old lady likes; she can't have too much of that."

The young girl, poised for an instant in one of her pretty attitudes, looked at him from head to foot.

"Well, I call that scandalous! Do you mean that she wants to make a match?"

"I mean that the young man has six thousand a year."

"It's no matter what he has — six thousand a year isn't much! And we don't do things in that way in our country. We haven't those horrid matchmaking arrangements that you have in your dreadful country. American mothers are not like English mothers."

"Oh, anyone can see, of course," said Captain Lovelock, "that Mr. Gordon Wright is dying of love for Miss Vivian."

"I can't see it!" cried Blanche.

"He dies easier than I, eh?"

"I wish you would die!" said Blanche. "At any rate, Angela is not dying of love for Mr. Wright."

"Well, she will marry him all the same," Lovelock declared.

Blanche Evers glanced at Bernard.

"Why don't you contradict that?" she asked. "Why don't you speak up for your friend?"

"I am quite ready to speak for my friend," said Bernard, "but I am not ready to speak for Miss Vivian."

"Well, I am," Blanche declared. "She won't marry him."

"If she doesn't, I'll eat my hat!" said Captain Lovelock. "What do you mean," he went on, "by saying that in America a pretty girl's mother doesn't care for a young fellow's property?"

"Well, they don't — we consider that dreadful. Why don't you say so, Mr. Longueville?" Blanche demanded. "I never saw anyone take things so quietly. Haven't you got any patriotism?"

"My patriotism is modified by an indisposition to generalize," said Bernard, laughing. "On this point permit me not to generalize. I am interested in the particular case — in ascertaining whether Mrs. Vivian thinks very often of Gordon Wright's income."

Miss Evers gave a little toss of disgust.

"If you are so awfully impartial, you had better go and ask her."

"That's a good idea — I think I will go and ask her," said Bernard.

Captain Lovelock returned to his argument.

"Do you mean to say that your mother would be indifferent to the fact that I haven't a shilling in the world?"

"Indifferent?" Blanche demanded. "Oh no, she would be sorry for you. She is very charitable — she would give you a shilling!"

"She wouldn't let you marry me," said Lovelock.

"She wouldn't have much trouble to prevent it!" cried the young girl.

Bernard had had enough of this intellectual fencing.

"Yes, I will go and ask Mrs. Vivian," he repeated. And he left his companions to resume their walk.

Chapter X

*I*t had seemed to him a good idea to interrogate Mrs. Vivian; but there are a great many good ideas that are never put into execution. As he approached her with a smile and a salutation, and, with the air of asking leave to take a liberty, seated himself in the empty chair beside her, he felt a humorous relish of her own probable dismay which relaxed the investigating impulse. His impulse was now simply to prove to her that he was the most unobjectionable fellow in the world – a proposition which resolved itself into several ingenious observations upon the weather, the music, the charms and the drawbacks of Baden, the merits of the volume that she held in her lap. If Mrs. Vivian should be annoyed, should be fluttered, Bernard would feel very sorry for her; there was nothing in the world that he respected more than the moral consciousness of a little Boston woman whose view of life was serious and whose imagination was subject to alarms. He held it to be a temple of delicacy, where one should walk on tiptoe, and he wished to exhibit to Mrs. Vivian the possible lightness of his own step. She herself was incapable of being rude or ungracious, and now that she was fairly confronted with the plausible object of her mistrust, she composed herself to her usual attitude of refined liberality. Her book was a volume of Victor Cousin.

"You must have an extraordinary power of abstracting your mind," Bernard said to her, observing it. "Studying philosophy at the Baden Kursaal strikes me as a real intellectual feat."

"Don't you think we need a little philosophy here?"

"By all means — what we bring with us. But I shouldn't attempt the use of the text-book on the spot."

"You shouldn't speak of yourself as if you were not clever," said Mrs. Vivian. "Everyone says you are so very clever."

Longueville stared; there was an unexpectedness in the speech and an incongruity in Mrs. Vivian's beginning to flatter him. He needed to remind himself that if she was a Bostonian, she was a Bostonian perverted.

"Ah, my dear madam, everyone is no one," he said, laughing.

"It was Mr. Wright, in particular," she rejoined. "He has always told us that."

"He is blinded by friendship."

"Ah yes, we know about your friendship," said Mrs. Vivian. "He has told us about that."

"You are making him out a terrible talker!"

"We think he talks so well — we are so very fond of his conversation."

"It's usually excellent," said Bernard. "But it depends a good deal on the subject."

"Oh," rejoined Mrs. Vivian, "we always let him choose his subjects." And dropping her eyes as if in sudden reflection, she began to smooth down the crumpled corner of her volume.

It occurred to Bernard that — by some mysterious impulse — she was suddenly presenting him with a chance to ask her the question that Blanche Evers had just suggested. Two or three other things as well occurred to him. Captain Lovelock had been struck with the fact that she favored Gordon Wright's addresses to her daughter, and Captain Lovelock had a grotesque theory that she had set her heart upon seeing this young lady come into six thousand a year. Miss Evers's devoted swain had never struck Bernard as a brilliant reasoner, but our friend suddenly found himself regarding him as one of the inspired. The form of depravity into which the New England conscience had lapsed on Mrs. Vivian's part was an undue appreciation of a possible son-in-law's income! In this illuminating discovery everything else became clear. Mrs. Vivian disliked her humble servant because he had not thirty thousand dollars a year, and because at a moment when it was Angela's prime duty to concentrate her thoughts upon Gordon Wright's great advantages, a clever young man of paltry fortune was a superfluous diversion.

"When you say clever, everything is relative," he presently observed. "Now, there is Captain Lovelock; he has a certain kind of cleverness; he is very observant."

Mrs. Vivian glanced up with a preoccupied air.

"We don't like Captain Lovelock," she said.

"I have heard him say capital things," Bernard answered.

"We think him brutal," said Mrs. Vivian. "Please don't praise Captain Lovelock."

"Oh, I only want to be just."

Mrs. Vivian for a moment said nothing.

"Do you want very much to be just?" she presently asked.

"It's my most ardent desire."

"I'm glad to hear that — and I can easily believe it," said Mrs. Vivian.

Bernard gave her a grateful smile, but while he smiled, he asked himself a serious question. "Why the deuce does she go on flattering me? — You have always been very kind to me," he said aloud.

"It's on Mr. Wright's account," she answered demurely.

In speaking the words I have just quoted, Bernard Longueville had felt himself, with a certain compunction, to be skirting the edge of clever impudence; but Mrs. Vivian's quiet little reply suggested to him that her cleverness, if not her impudence, was almost equal to his own. He remarked to himself that he had not yet done her justice.

"You bring everything back to Gordon Wright," he said, continuing to smile.

Mrs. Vivian blushed a little.

"It is because he is really at the foundation of everything that is pleasant for us here. When we first came we had some very disagreeable rooms, and as soon as he arrived he found us some excellent ones — that were less expensive. And then, Mr. Longueville," she added, with a soft, sweet emphasis which should properly have contradicted the idea of audacity, but which, to Bernard's awakened sense, seemed really to impart a vivid color to it, "he was also the cause of your joining our little party."

"Oh, among his services that should never be forgotten. You should set up a tablet to commemorate it, in the wall of the Kursaal! — The wicked little woman!" Bernard mentally subjoined.

Mrs. Vivian appeared quite unruffled by his sportive sarcasm, and she continued to enumerate her obligations to Gordon Wright.

"There are so many ways in which a gentleman can

be of assistance to three poor lonely women, especially when he is at the same time so friendly and so delicate as Mr. Wright. I don't know what we should have done without him, and I feel as if everyone ought to know it. He seems like a very old friend. My daughter and I quite worship him. I will not conceal from you that when I saw you coming through the grounds a short time ago without him I was very much disappointed. I hope he is not ill."

Bernard sat listening, with his eyes on the ground.

"Oh no, he is simply at home writing letters."

Mrs. Vivian was silent a moment.

"I suppose he has a very large correspondence."

"I really don't know. Just now that I am with him he has a smaller one than usual."

"Ah yes. When you are separated I suppose you write volumes to each other. But he must have a great many business letters."

"It is very likely," said Bernard. "And if he has, you may be sure he writes them."

"Order and method!" Mrs. Vivian exclaimed. "With his immense property those virtues are necessary."

Bernard glanced at her a moment.

"My dear Lovelock," he said to himself, "you are not such a fool as you seem. — Gordon's virtues are always necessary, doubtless," he went on. "But should you say his property was immense?"

Mrs. Vivian made a delicate little movement of deprecation. "Oh, don't ask me to say! I know nothing about it; I only supposed he was rich."

"He is rich; but he is not a Croesus."

"Oh, you fashionable young men have a standard of luxury!" said Mrs. Vivian, with a little laugh. "To a poverty-stricken widow such a fortune as Mr. Wright's seems magnificent."

"Don't call me such horrible names!" exclaimed

Bernard. "Our friend has certainly money enough and to spare."

"That was all I meant. He once had occasion to allude to his property, but he was so modest, so reserved in the tone he took about it, that one hardly knew what to think."

"He is ashamed of being rich," said Bernard. "He would be sure to represent everything unfavorably."

"That's just what I thought!" This ejaculation was more eager than Mrs. Vivian might have intended, but even had it been less so, Bernard was in a mood to appreciate it. "I felt that we should make allowances for his modesty. But it was in very good taste," Mrs. Vivian added.

"He's a fortunate man," said Bernard. "He gets credit for his good taste — and he gets credit for the full figure of his income as well!"

"Ah," murmured Mrs. Vivian, rising lightly, as if to make her words appear more casual, "I don't know the full figure of his income."

She was turning away, and Bernard, as he raised his hat and separated from her, felt that it was rather cruel that he should let her go without enlightening her ignorance. But he said to himself that she knew quite enough. Indeed, he took a walk along the Lichtenthal Alley and carried out this line of reflection. Whether or no Miss Vivian were in love with Gordon Wright, her mother was enamored of Gordon's fortune, and it had suddenly occurred to her that instead of treating the friend of her daughter's suitor with civil mistrust, she would help her case better by giving him a hint of her state of mind and appealing to his sense of propriety. Nothing could be more natural than that Mrs. Vivian should suppose that Bernard desired his friend's success; for, as our thoughtful hero said to himself, what she had hitherto taken it into her head to fear was not that Bernard should fall in love with her daughter, but that her daughter should fall in love with him. Watering-place life is notoriously conducive to idleness of mind, and Bernard strolled for half an hour along the overarched avenue, glancing alternately at these two insupposable cases.

A few days afterward, late in the evening, Gordon Wright came to his room at the hotel.

"I have just received a letter from my sister," he said. "I am afraid I shall have to go away."

"Ah, I'm sorry for that," said Bernard, who was so well pleased with the actual that he desired no mutation.

"I mean only for a short time," Gordon explained. "My poor sister writes from England, telling me that my brother-in-law is suddenly obliged to go home. She has decided not to remain behind, and they are to sail a fortnight hence. She wants very much to see me before she goes, and as I don't know when I shall see her again, I feel as if I ought to join her immediately and spend the interval with her. That will take about a fortnight."

"I appreciate the sanctity of family ties and I project myself into your situation," said Bernard. "On the other hand, I don't envy you a breathless journey from Baden to Folkestone."

"It's the coming back that will be breathless," exclaimed Gordon, smiling.

"You will certainly come back, then?"

"Most certainly. Mrs. Vivian is to be here another month."

"I understand. Well, we shall miss you very much."

Gordon Wright looked for a moment at his companion.

"You will stay here, then? I am so glad of that."

"I was taking it for granted; but on reflection — what

do you recommend?"

"I recommend you to stay."

"My dear fellow, your word is law," said Bernard.

"I want you to take care of those ladies," his friend went on. "I don't like to leave them alone."

"You are joking!" cried Bernard. "When did you ever hear of my 'taking care' of anyone? It's as much as I can do to take care of myself."

"This is very easy," said Gordon. "I simply want to feel that they have a man about them."

"They will have a man at any rate — they have the devoted Lovelock."

"That's just why I want them to have another. He has only an eye to Miss Evers, who, by the way, is extremely bored with him. You look after the others. You have made yourself very agreeable to them, and they like you extremely."

"Ah," said Bernard, laughing, "if you are going to be coarse and flattering, I collapse. If you are going to titillate my vanity, I succumb."

"It won't be so disagreeable," Gordon observed, with an intention vaguely humorous.

"Oh no, it won't be disagreeable. I will go to Mrs. Vivian every morning, hat in hand, for my orders."

Gordon Wright, with his hands in his pockets and a meditative expression, took several turns about the room.

"It will be a capital chance," he said, at last, stopping in front of his companion.

"A chance for what?"

"A chance to arrive at a conclusion about my young friend."

Bernard gave a gentle groan.

"Are you coming back to that? Didn't I arrive at a conclusion long ago? Didn't I tell you she was a delightful girl?"

"Do you call that a conclusion? The first comer could tell me that at the end of an hour."

"Do you want me to invent something different?" Bernard asked. "I can't invent anything better."

"I don't want you to invent anything. I only want you to observe her — to study her in complete independence. You will have her to yourself — my absence will leave you at liberty. Hang it, sir," Gordon declared, "I should think you would like it!"

"Damn it, sir, you're delicious!" Bernard answered; and he broke into an irrepressible laugh. "I don't suppose it's for my pleasure that you suggest the arrangement."

Gordon took a turn about the room again.

"No, it's for mine. At least, it's for my benefit."

"For your benefit?"

"I have got all sorts of ideas — I told you the other day. They are all mixed up together and I want a fresh impression."

"My impressions are never fresh," Bernard replied.

"They would be if you had a little good-will — if you entered a little into my dilemma." The note of reproach was so distinct in these words that Bernard stood staring. "You never take anything seriously," his companion went on.

Bernard tried to answer as seriously as possible.

"Your dilemma seems to me of all dilemmas the strangest."

"That may be; but different people take things differently. Don't you see," Gordon went on with a sudden outbreak of passion — "don't you see that I am horribly divided in mind? I care immensely for Angela Vivian — and yet — and yet — I am afraid of her."

"Afraid of her?"

"I am afraid she's cleverer than I — that she would be a difficult wife; that she might do strange things."

"What sort of things?"

"Well, that she might flirt, for instance."

"That's not a thing for a man to fear."

"Not when he supposes his wife to be fond of him — no. But I don't suppose that — I have given that up. If I should induce Angela Vivian to accept me she would do it on grounds purely reasonable. She would think it best, simply. That would give her a chance to repent."

Bernard sat for some time looking at his friend.

"You say she is cleverer than you. It's impossible to be cleverer than you."

"Oh, come, Longueville!" said Gordon, angrily.

"I am speaking very seriously. You have done a remarkably clever thing. You have impressed me with the reality, and with — what shall I term it? — the estimable character of what you call your dilemma. Now this fresh impression of mine — what do you propose to do with it when you get it?"

"Such things are always useful. It will be a good thing to have."

"I am much obliged to you; but do you propose to let anything depend upon it? Do you propose to take or to leave Miss Vivian — that is, to return to the charge or to give up trying — in consequence of my fresh impression?"

Gordon seemed perfectly unembarrassed by this question, in spite of the ironical light which it projected upon his sentimental perplexity.

"I propose to do what I choose!" he said.

"That's a relief to me," Bernard rejoined. "This idea of yours is, after all, only the play of the scientific mind."

"I shall contradict you flat if I choose," Gordon went on.

"Ah, it's well to warn me of that," said Bernard,

laughing. "Even the most sincere judgment in the world likes to be notified a little of the danger of being contradicted."

"Is yours the most sincere judgment in the world?" Gordon demanded.

"That's a very pertinent question. Doesn't it occur to you that you may have reason to be jealous — leaving me alone, with an open field, with the woman of your choice?"

"I wish to heaven I could be jealous!" Gordon exclaimed. "That would simplify the thing — that would give me a lift."

And the next day, after some more talk, it seemed really with a hope of this contingency — though, indeed, he laughed about it — that he started for England.

Chapter XI

For the three or four days that followed Gordon Wright's departure, Bernard saw nothing of the ladies who had been committed to his charge. They chose to remain in seclusion, and he was at liberty to interpret this fact as an expression of regret at the loss of Gordon's good offices. He knew other people at Baden, and he went to see them and endeavored, by cultivating their society, to await in patience the reappearance of Mrs. Vivian and her companions. But on the fourth day he became conscious that other people were much less interesting than the trio of American ladies who had lodgings above the confectioner's, and he made bold to go and knock at their door. He had been asked to take care of them, and this function presupposed contact. He had met Captain Lovelock the day before, wandering about with a rather crest-fallen aspect, and the young Englishman had questioned him eagerly as to the whereabouts of Mrs. Vivian.

"Gad, I believe they've left the place — left the place without giving a fellow warning!" cried Lovelock.

"Oh no, I think they are here still," said Bernard. "My friend Wright has gone away for a week or two, but I suspect the ladies are simply staying at home."

"Gad, I was afraid your friend Wright had taken them away with him; he seems to keep them all in his pocket. I was afraid he had given them marching orders; they'd have been sure to go — they're so awfully fond of his pocket! I went to look them up yesterday — upon my word I did. They live at a baker's in a little back-street; people do live in rum places when they come abroad! But I assure you, when I got there, I'm damned if I could make out whether they were there or not. I don't speak a word of German, and there was no one there but the baker's wife. She was a low brute of a woman — she couldn't understand a word I said, though she gave me plenty of her own tongue. I had to give it up. They were not at home, but whether they had left Baden or not — that was beyond my finding out. If they are here, why the deuce don't they show? Fancy coming to Baden-Baden to sit moping at a pastry-cook's!"

Captain Lovelock was evidently irritated, and it was

Bernard's impression that the turn of luck over yonder where the gold pieces were chinking had something to do with the state of his temper. But more fortunate himself, he ascertained from the baker's wife that though Mrs. Vivian and her daughter had gone out, their companion, "the youngest lady — the little young lady" — was above in the sitting room.

Blanche Evers was sitting at the window with a book, but she relinquished the volume with an alacrity that showed it had not been absorbing, and began to chatter with her customary frankness.

"Well, I must say I am glad to see *someone!*" cried the young girl, passing before the mirror and giving a touch to her charming tresses.

"Even if it's only me," Bernard exclaimed, laughing.

"I didn't mean that. I am sure I am very glad to see you — I should think you would have found out that by this time. I mean I'm glad to see anyone — especially a man. I suppose it's improper for me to say that — especially to you! There — you see I do think more of you than of some gentlemen. Why especially to you? Well, because you always seem to me to want to take advantage. I didn't say a base advantage; I didn't accuse you of anything dreadful. I'm sure I want to take advantage, too — I take it whenever I can. You see I take advantage of your being here — I've got so many things to say. I haven't spoken a word in three days, and I'm sure it is a pleasant change — a gentleman's visit. All of a sudden we have gone into mourning; I'm sure I don't know who's dead. Is it Mr. Gordon Wright? It's some idea of Mrs. Vivian's — I'm sure it isn't mine. She thinks we have been often enough to the Kursaal. I don't know whether she thinks it's wicked, or what. If it's wicked the harm's already done; I can't be any worse than I am now. I have seen all the improper people and I have learnt all their names; Captain Lovelock has told me their names, plenty of times. I don't see what good it does me to be shut up here with all those names running in my ears. I must say I do prefer society. We haven't been to the Kursaal for four days — we have only gone out for a drive. We have taken the most interminable drives. I do believe we have seen every old ruin in the whole country. Mrs. Vivian and Angela are so awfully fond of scenery — they talk about it by the half-hour. They talk about the mountains and trees as if they were people they knew — as if they were gentlemen! I mean as if the mountains and trees were gentlemen. Of course scenery's lovely, but you can't walk about with a tree. At any rate, that has been all our society — foliage! Foliage and women; but I suppose women are a sort of foliage. They are always rustling about and dropping off. That's why I couldn't make up my mind to go out with them this afternoon. They've gone to see the Waterworths — the Waterworths arrived yesterday and are staying at some hotel. Five daughters — all unmarried! I don't know what kind of foliage they are; some peculiar kind — they don't drop off. I thought I had had about enough ladies' society — three women all sticking together! I don't think it's good for a young girl to have nothing but ladies' society — it's so awfully limited. I suppose I ought to stand up for my own sex and tell you that when we are alone together we want for nothing. But we want for everything, as it happens! Women's talk *is* limited — everyone knows that. That's just what mamma didn't want when she asked Mrs. Vivian to take charge of me. Now, Mr. Longueville, what are you laughing at? — you are always laughing at me. She wanted me to be unlimited — is that what you say? Well, she didn't want me to be narrowed down; she wanted me to have plenty of conversation. She wanted me to be fitted for society — that's what mamma wanted. She wanted me to have ease of manner; she thinks that if you don't acquire it when you are young you never have it at all. She was so happy to think I should come to Baden; but she wouldn't approve of the life I've been leading the last four days. That's no way to acquire ease of manner — sitting all day in a small parlor with two persons of one's own sex! Of course Mrs. Vivian's influence — that's the great thing. Mamma said it was like the odor of a flower. But you don't want to keep smelling a flower all day, even the sweetest; that's the shortest way to get a headache. Apropos of flowers, do you happen to have heard whether Captain Lovelock is alive or dead? Do I call him a flower? No; I call him a flower-pot. He always has some fine young plant in his buttonhole. He hasn't been near me these ten years — I never heard of anything so rude!"

Captain Lovelock came on the morrow, Bernard finding him in Mrs. Vivian's little sitting room on paying a second visit. On this occasion the two other ladies were at home and Bernard was not exclusively indebted to Miss Evers for entertainment. It was to this source of hospitality, however, that Lovelock mainly appealed, following the young girl out upon the little balcony that was suspended above the confectioner's window. Mrs. Vivian sat writing at one of the windows of the sitting room, and Bernard addressed his conversation to Angela.

"Wright requested me to keep an eye on you," he said; "but you seem very much inclined to keep out of my jurisdiction."

"I supposed you had gone away," she answered — "now that your friend is gone."

"By no means. Gordon is a charming fellow, but he is by no means the only attraction of Baden. Besides, I have promised him to look after you — to take care of you."

The girl looked at him a moment in silence — a little askance.

"I thought you had probably undertaken something of that sort," she presently said.

"It was of course a very natural request for Gordon to make."

Angela got up and turned away; she wandered about the room and went and stood at one of the windows. Bernard found the movement abrupt and not particularly gracious; but the young man was not easy to snub. He followed her, and they stood at the second window — the long window that opened upon the balcony. Miss Evers and Captain Lovelock were leaning on the railing, looking into the street and apparently amusing themselves highly with what they saw.

"I am not sure it was a natural request for him to make," said Angela.

"What could have been more so — devoted as he is to you?"

She hesitated a moment; then with a little laugh —

"He ought to have locked us up and said nothing about it."

"It's not so easy to lock you up," said Bernard. "I know Wright has great influence with you, but you are after all independent beings."

"I am not an independent being. If my mother and Mr. Wright were to agree together to put me out of harm's way they could easily manage it."

"You seem to have been trying something of that sort," said Bernard. "You have been so terribly invisible."

"It was because I thought you had designs upon us; that you were watching for us — to take care of us."

"You contradict yourself! You said just now that you believed I had left Baden."

"That was an artificial — a conventional speech. Isn't

a lady always supposed to say something of that sort to a visitor by way of pretending to have noticed that she has not seen him?"

"You know I would never have left Baden without coming to bid you good-bye," said Bernard.

The girl made no rejoinder; she stood looking out at the little sunny, slanting, rough-paved German street.

"Are you taking care of us now?" she asked in a moment. "Has the operation begun? Have you heard the news, mamma?" she went on. "Do you know that Mr. Wright has made us over to Mr. Longueville, to be kept till called for? Suppose Mr. Wright should never call for us!"

Mrs. Vivian left her writing-table and came toward Bernard, smiling at him and pressing her hands together.

"There is no fear of that, I think," she said. "I am sure I am very glad we have a gentleman near us. I think you will be a very good care-taker, Mr. Longueville, and I recommend my daughter to put great faith in your judgment." And Mrs. Vivian gave him an intense — a pleading, almost affecting — little smile.

"I am greatly touched by your confidence and I shall do everything I can think of to merit it," said the young man.

"Ah, mamma's confidence is wonderful!" Angela exclaimed. "There was never anything like mamma's confidence. I am very different; I have no confidence. And then I don't like being deposited, like a parcel, or being watched, like a curious animal. I am too fond of my liberty."

"That is the second time you have contradicted yourself," said Bernard. "You said just now that you were not an independent being."

Angela turned toward him quickly, smiling and

frowning at once.

"You *do* watch one, certainly! I see it has already begun." Mrs. Vivian laid her hand upon her daughter's with a little murmur of tender deprecation, and the girl bent over and kissed her. "Mamma will tell you it's the effect of agitation," she said — "that I am nervous, and don't know what I say. I am supposed to be agitated by Mr. Wright's departure; isn't that it, mamma?"

Mrs. Vivian turned away, with a certain soft severity.

"I don't know, my daughter. I don't understand you."

A charming pink flush had come into Angela's cheek and a noticeable light into her eye. She looked admirably handsome, and Bernard frankly gazed at her. She met his gaze an instant, and then she went on.

"Mr. Longueville doesn't understand me either. You must know that I *am* agitated," she continued. "Every now and then I have moments of talking nonsense. It's the air of Baden, I think; it's too exciting. It's only lately I have been so. When you go away I shall be horribly ashamed."

"If the air of Baden has such an effect upon you," said Bernard, "it is only a proof the more that you need the solicitous attention of your friends."

"That may be; but, as I told you just now, I have no confidence — none whatever, in anyone or anything. Therefore, for the present, I shall withdraw from the world — I shall seclude myself. Let us go on being quiet, mamma. Three or four days of it have been so charming. Let the parcel lie till it's called for. It is much safer it shouldn't be touched at all. I shall assume that, metaphorically speaking, Mr. Wright, who, as you have intimated, is our earthly providence, has turned the key upon us. I am locked up. I shall not go out, except upon the balcony!" And with this, Angela stepped out of the long window and went and stood beside Miss Evers.

Bernard was extremely amused, but he was also a good deal puzzled, and it came over him that it was not a wonder that poor Wright should not have found this young lady's disposition a perfectly decipherable page. He remained in the room with Mrs. Vivian — he stood there looking at her with his agreeably mystified smile. She had turned away, but on perceiving that her daughter had gone outside she came toward Bernard again, with her habitual little air of eagerness mitigated by discretion. There instantly rose before his mind the vision of that moment when he had stood face to face with this same apologetic mamma, after Angela had turned her back, on the grass-grown terrace at Siena. To make the vision complete, Mrs. Vivian took it into her head to utter the same words.

"I am sure you think she is a strange girl."

Bernard recognized them, and he gave a light laugh.

"You told me that the first time you ever saw me — in that quiet little corner of an Italian town."

Mrs. Vivian gave a little faded, elderly blush.

"Don't speak of that," she murmured, glancing at the open window. "It was a little accident of travel."

"I am dying to speak of it," said Bernard. "It was such a charming accident for me! Tell me this, at least — have you kept my sketch?"

Mrs. Vivian colored more deeply and glanced at the window again.

"No," she just whispered.

Bernard looked out of the window too. Angela was leaning against the railing of the balcony, in profile, just as she had stood while he painted her, against the polished parapet at Siena. The young man's eyes rested on her a moment, then, as he glanced back at her mother:

"Has *she* kept it?" he asked.

"I don't know," said Mrs. Vivian, with decision.

The decision was excessive — it expressed the poor lady's distress at having her veracity tested. "Dear little daughter of the Puritans — she can't tell a fib!" Bernard exclaimed to himself. And with this flattering conclusion he took leave of her.

Chapter XII

*I*t was affirmed at an early stage of this narrative that he was a young man of a contemplative and speculative turn, and he had perhaps never been more true to his character than during an hour or two that evening as he sat by himself on the terrace of the Conversation-house, surrounded by the crowd of its frequenters, but lost in his meditations. The place was full of movement and sound, but he had tilted back his chair against the great green box of an orange tree, and in this easy attitude, vaguely and agreeably conscious of the music, he directed his gaze to the star-sprinkled vault of the night. There were people coming and going whom he knew, but he said nothing to anyone — he preferred to be alone; he found his own company quite absorbing.

He felt very happy, very much amused, very curiously preoccupied. The feeling was a singular one. It partook of the nature of intellectual excitement. He had a sense of having received *carte blanche* for the expenditure of his wits. Bernard liked to feel his intelligence at play; this is, perhaps, the highest luxury of a clever man. It played at present over the whole field of Angela Vivian's oddities of conduct — for, since his visit in the afternoon, Bernard had felt that the spectacle was considerably enlarged. He had come to feel, also, that poor Gordon's predicament was by no means an unnatural one. Longueville had begun to take his friend's dilemma very seriously indeed. The girl was certainly a curious study.

The evening drew to a close and the crowd of Bernard's fellow-loungers dispersed. The lighted windows of the Kursaal still glittered in the bosky darkness, and the lamps along the terrace had not been extinguished; but the great promenade was almost deserted; here and there only a lingering couple — the red tip of a cigar and the vague radiance of a light dress — gave animation to the place. But Bernard sat there still in his tilted chair, beneath his orange tree; his imagination had wandered very far and he was awaiting its return to the fold. He was on the point of rising, however, when he saw three figures come down the empty vista of the terrace — figures which even at a distance had a familiar air. He immediately left his seat and, taking a dozen steps, recognized Angela Vivian, Blanche Evers and Captain Lovelock. In a moment he met them in the middle of the terrace.

Blanche immediately announced that they had come for a midnight walk.

"And if you think it's improper," she exclaimed, "it's not my invention — it's Miss Vivian's."

"I beg pardon — it's mine," said Captain Lovelock.

"I desire the credit of it. I started the idea; you never would have come without me."

"I think it would have been more proper to come without you than with you," Blanche declared. "You know you're a dreadful character."

"I'm much worse when I'm away from you than when I'm with you," said Lovelock. "You keep me in order."

The young girl gave a little cry.

"I don't know what you call order! You can't be worse than you have been tonight."

Angela was not listening to this; she turned away a little, looking about at the empty garden.

"This is the third time today that you have contradicted yourself," he said. Though he spoke softly he went nearer to her; but she appeared not to hear him — she looked away.

"You ought to have been there, Mr. Longueville," Blanche went on. "We have had a most lovely night; we sat all the evening on Mrs. Vivian's balcony, eating ices. To sit on a balcony, eating ices — that's my idea of heaven."

"With an angel by your side," said Captain Lovelock.

"You are not my idea of an angel," retorted Blanche.

"I'm afraid you'll never learn what the angels are really like," said the Captain. "That's why Miss Evers got Mrs. Vivian to take rooms over the baker's — so that she could have ices sent up several times a day. Well, I'm bound to say the baker's ices are not bad."

"Considering that they have been baked! But they affect the mind," Blanche went on. "They would have affected Captain Lovelock's — only he hasn't any. They certainly affected Angela's — putting it into her head, at eleven o'clock, to come out to walk."

Angela did nothing whatever to defend herself against this ingenious sally; she simply stood there in graceful abstraction. Bernard was vaguely vexed at her neither looking at him nor speaking to him; her indifference seemed a contravention of that right of criticism which Gordon had bequeathed to him.

"I supposed people went to bed at eleven o'clock," he said.

Angela glanced about her, without meeting his eye.

"They seem to have gone."

Miss Evers strolled on, and her Captain of course kept pace with her; so that Bernard and Miss Vivian were left standing together. He looked at her a moment in silence, but her eye still avoided his own.

"You are remarkably inconsistent," Bernard presently said. "You take a solemn vow of seclusion this afternoon, and no sooner have you taken it than you proceed to break it in this outrageous manner."

She looked at him now – a long time – longer than she had ever done before.

"This is part of the examination, I suppose," she said.

Bernard hesitated an instant.

"What examination?"

"The one you have undertaken – on Mr. Wright's behalf."

"What do you know about that?"

"Ah, you admit it then?" the girl exclaimed, with an eager laugh.

"I don't in the least admit it," said Bernard, conscious only for the moment of the duty of loyalty to his friend and feeling that negation here was simply a point of honor.

"I trust more to my own conviction than to your denial. You have engaged to bring your superior wisdom and your immense experience to bear upon me! That's the understanding."

"You must think us a pretty pair of wiseacres," said Bernard.

"There it is — you already begin to answer for what I think. When Mr. Wright comes back you will be able to tell him that I am 'outrageous'!" And she turned away and walked on, slowly following her companions.

"What do you care what I tell him?" Bernard asked. "You don't care a straw."

She said nothing for a moment, then, suddenly, she stopped again, dropping her eyes.

"I beg your pardon," she said, very gently; "I care a great deal. It's as well that you should know that."

Bernard stood looking at her; her eyes were still lowered.

"Do you know what I shall tell him? I shall tell him that about eleven o'clock at night you become peculiarly attractive."

She went on again a few steps; Miss Evers and Captain Lovelock had turned round and were coming toward her.

"It is very true that I am outrageous," she said; "it was extremely silly and in very bad taste to come out at this hour. Mamma was not at all pleased, and I was very unkind to her. I only wanted to take a turn, and now we will go back." On the others coming up she announced this resolution, and though Captain Lovelock and his companion made a great outcry, she carried her point. Bernard offered no opposition. He contented himself with walking back to her mother's lodging with her almost in silence. The little winding streets were still and empty; there was no sound but the chatter and laughter of Blanche and her attendant swain. Angela said nothing.

This incident presented itself at first to Bernard's mind as a sort of declaration of war. The girl had guessed that she was to be made a subject of speculative scrutiny. The idea was not agreeable to her independent spirit, and she placed herself boldly on the defensive. She took her stand upon her right to defeat his purpose by every possible means — to perplex, elude, deceive him — in plain English, to make a fool of him. This was the construction which for several days Bernard put upon her deportment, at the same time that he thought it immensely clever of her to have guessed what had been going on in his mind. She made him feel very much ashamed of his critical attitude, and he did everything he could think of to put her off her guard and persuade her that for the moment he had ceased to be an observer. His position at moments seemed to him an odious one, for he was firmly re-solved that between him and the woman to whom his friend had proposed there should be nothing in the way of a vulgar flirtation. Under the circumstances, it savored both of flirtation and of vulgarity that they should even fall out with each other — a consumma-tion which appeared to be more or less definitely impending. Bernard remarked to himself that his own only reasonable line of conduct would be instantly to leave Baden, but I am almost ashamed to mention the fact which led him to modify this decision. It was simply that he was induced to make the reflection that he had really succeeded in putting Miss Vivian off her guard. How he had done so he would have found it difficult to explain, inasmuch as in one way or another, for a week, he had spent several hours in talk with her. The most effective way of putting her off her guard would have been to leave her alone, to forswear the privilege of conversation with her, to pass the days in other society. This course would have had the draw-back of not enabling him to measure the operation of so ingenious a policy, and Bernard liked, of all the things in the world, to know when he was successful. He believed, at all events, that he was successful now, and that the virtue of his conversation itself had persuaded this keen and brilliant girl that he was thinking of anything in the world but herself. He flattered himself that the civil indifference of his manner, the abstract character of the topics he selected, the irrelevancy of his allusions and the laxity of his attention, all contributed to this result.

Such a result was certainly a remarkable one, for it is almost superfluous to intimate that Miss Vivian was, in fact, perpetually in his thoughts. He made it a point of conscience not to think of her, but he was thinking of her most when his conscience was most lively. Bernard had a conscience — a conscience which, though a little irregular in its motions, gave itself in the long run a great deal of exercise; but nothing could have been more natural than that, curious, imaginative, audacious as he was, and delighting, as I have said, in the play of his singularly nimble intelligence, he should have given himself up to a sort of unconscious experimentation. "I will leave her alone — I will be hanged if I attempt to draw her out!" he said to himself; and meanwhile he was roaming afield and plucking personal impressions in great fragrant handfuls. All this, as I say, was natural, given the man and the situation; the only oddity is that he should have fancied himself able to persuade the person most interested that he had renounced his advantage.

He remembered her telling him that she cared very much what he should say of her on Gordon Wright's return, and he felt that this declaration had a particular significance. After this, of her own movement, she never spoke of Gordon, and Bernard made up his mind that she had promised her mother to accept him if he should repeat his proposal, and that as her heart was not in the matter she preferred to drop a veil over the prospect. "She is going to marry him for his money," he said, "because her mother has brought out the advantages of the thing. Mrs. Vivian's persuasive powers have carried the day, and the girl has made herself believe that it doesn't matter that she doesn't love him. Perhaps it doesn't — to her; it's hard, in such a case, to put one's self in the woman's point of view. But I should think it would matter, some day or other, to poor Gordon. She herself can't help suspecting it may make a difference in his happiness, and she therefore doesn't wish to seem any worse to him than is necessary. She wants me to speak well of her; if she intends to deceive him she expects me to back her up. The wish is doubtless natural, but for a proud girl it is rather an odd favor to ask. Oh yes, she's a proud girl, even though she has been able to arrange it with her conscience to make a mercenary marriage. To expect me to help her is perhaps to treat me as a friend; but she ought to remember — or at least I ought to remember — that Gordon is an older friend than she. Inviting me to help her as against my oldest friend — isn't there a grain of impudence in that?"

It will be gathered that Bernard's meditations were not on the whole favorable to this young lady, and it must be affirmed that he was forcibly struck with an element of cynicism in her conduct. On the evening of her so-called midnight visit to the Kursaal she had suddenly sounded a note of sweet submissiveness which re-appeared again at frequent intervals. She was gentle, accessible, tenderly gracious, expressive, demonstrative, almost flattering. From his own personal point of view Bernard had no complaint to make of this maidenly urbanity, but he kept reminding himself that *he* was not in question and that everything must be looked at in the light of Gordon's requirements. There was all this time an absurd logical twist in his view of things. In the first place he was not to judge at all; and in the second he was to judge strictly on

Gordon's behalf. This latter clause always served as a justification when the former had failed to serve as a deterrent. When Bernard reproached himself for thinking too much of the girl, he drew comfort from the reflection that he was not thinking well. To let it gradually filter into one's mind, through a superficial complexity of more reverent preconceptions, that she was an extremely clever coquette — *this*, surely, was not to think well! Bernard had luminous glimpses of another situation, in which Angela Vivian's coquetry should meet with a different appreciation; but just now it was not an item to be entered on the credit side of Wright's account. Bernard wiped his pen, mentally speaking, as he made this reflection, and felt like a grizzled old book-keeper, of incorruptible probity. He saw her, as I have said, very often; she continued to break her vow of shutting herself up, and at the end of a fortnight she had reduced it to imperceptible particles. On four different occasions, presenting himself at Mrs. Vivian's lodgings, Bernard found Angela there alone. She made him welcome, receiving him as an American girl, in such circumstances, is free to receive the most gallant of visitors. She smiled and talked and gave herself up to charming gayety, so that there was nothing for Bernard to say but that now at least she was off her guard with a vengeance. Happily he was on his own! He flattered himself that he remained so on occasions that were even more insidiously relaxing — when, in the evening, she strolled away with him to parts of the grounds of the Conversation-house, where the music sank to sweeter softness and the murmur of the tree-tops of the Black Forest, stirred by the warm night-air, became almost audible; or when, in the long afternoons, they wandered in the woods apart from the others — from Mrs. Vivian and the amiable object of her more avowed solicitude, the object of the sportive adoration of the irrepressible, the ever-present Lovelock. They were constantly having parties in the woods at this time — driving over the hills to points of interest which Bernard had looked out in the guide-book. Bernard, in such matters, was extremely alert and considerate; he developed an unexpected talent for arranging excursions, and he had taken regularly into his service the red-waistcoated proprietor of a big Teutonic landau, which had a courier's seat behind and was always at the service of the ladies. The functionary in the red waistcoat was a capital charioteer; he was constantly proposing new drives, and he introduced our little party to treasures of romantic scenery.

Chapter XIII

More than a fortnight had elapsed, but Gordon Wright had not re-appeared, and Bernard suddenly decided that he would leave Baden. He found Mrs. Vivian and her daughter, very opportunely, in the garden of the pleasant, homely Schloss which forms the residence of the Grand Dukes of Baden during their visits to the scene of our narrative, and which, perched upon the hillside directly above the little town, is surrounded with charming old shrubberies and terraces. To this garden a portion of the public is admitted, and Bernard, who liked the place, had been there more than once. One of the terraces had a high parapet, against which Angela was leaning, looking across the valley. Mrs. Vivian was not at first in sight, but Bernard presently perceived her seated under a tree with Victor Cousin in her hand. As Bernard approached the young girl, Angela, who had not seen him, turned round.

"Don't move," he said. "You were just in the position in which I painted your portrait at Siena."

"Don't speak of that," she answered.

"I have never understood," said Bernard, "why you insist upon ignoring that charming incident."

She resumed for a moment her former position, and stood looking at the opposite hills.

"That's just how you were — in profile — with your head a little thrown back."

"It was an odious incident!" Angela exclaimed, rapidly changing her attitude.

Bernard was on the point of making a rejoinder, but he thought of Gordon Wright and held his tongue. He presently told her that he intended to leave Baden on the morrow.

They were walking toward her mother. She looked round at him quickly.

"Where are you going?"

"To Paris," he said, quite at hazard; for he had not in the least determined where to go.

"To Paris — in the month of August?" And she gave a little laugh. "What a happy inspiration!"

She gave a little laugh, but she said nothing more, and Bernard gave no further account of his plan. They went and sat down near Mrs. Vivian for ten minutes, and then they got up again and strolled to another part of the garden. They had it all to themselves, and it was filled with things that Bernard liked — inequalities of level, with mossy steps connecting them, rose trees trained upon old brick walls, horizontal trellises arranged like Italian pergolas, and here and there a towering poplar, looking as if it had survived from some more primitive stage of culture, with its stiff boughs motionless and its leaves forever trembling. They made almost the whole circuit of the garden, and then Angela mentioned very quietly that she had heard that morning from Mr. Wright, and that he would not return for another week.

"You had better stay," she presently added, as if Gordon's continued absence were an added reason.

"I don't know," said Bernard. "It is sometimes difficult to say what one had better do."

I hesitate to bring against him that most inglorious of all charges, an accusation of sentimental fatuity, of the disposition to invent obstacles to enjoyment so that he might have the pleasure of seeing a pretty girl attempt to remove them. But it must be admitted that if Bernard really thought at present that he had better leave Baden, the observation I have just quoted was not so much a sign of this conviction as of the hope that his companion would proceed to gainsay it. The hope was not disappointed, though I must add that no sooner had it been gratified than Bernard began to feel ashamed of it.

"This certainly is not one of those cases," said Angela. "The thing is surely very simple now."

"What makes it so simple?"

She hesitated a moment.

"The fact that I ask you to stay."

"You ask me?" he repeated, softly.

"Ah," she exclaimed, "one doesn't say those things twice!"

She turned away, and they went back to her mother, who gave Bernard a wonderful little look of half urgent, half remonstrant inquiry. As they left the garden he walked beside Mrs. Vivian, Angela going in front of them at a distance. The elder lady began immediately to talk to him of Gordon Wright.

"He's not coming back for another week, you know," she said. "I am sorry he stays away so long."

"Ah yes," Bernard answered, "it seems very long indeed."

And it had, in fact, seemed to him very long.

"I suppose he is always likely to have business," said Mrs. Vivian.

"You may be very sure it is not for his pleasure that he stays away."

"I know he is faithful to old friends," said Mrs. Vivian. "I am sure he has not forgotten us."

"I certainly count upon that," Bernard exclaimed – "remembering him as we do!"

Mrs. Vivian glanced at him gratefully.

"Oh yes, we remember him – we remember him daily, hourly. At least, I can speak for my daughter and myself. He has been so very kind to us." Bernard said nothing, and she went on. "And you have been so very kind to us, too, Mr. Longueville. I want so much to thank you."

"Oh no, don't!" said Bernard, frowning. "I would rather you shouldn't."

"Of course," Mrs. Vivian added, "I know it's all on his account; but that makes me wish to thank you all the more. Let me express my gratitude, in advance, for the rest of the time, till he comes back. That's more responsibility than you bargained for," she said, with a little nervous laugh.

"Yes, it's more than I bargained for. I am thinking of going away."

Mrs. Vivian almost gave a little jump, and then she paused on the Baden cobble-stones, looking up at him.

"If you *must* go, Mr. Longueville — don't sacrifice yourself!"

The exclamation fell upon Bernard's ear with a certain softly mocking cadence which was sufficient, however, to make this organ tingle.

"Oh, after all, you know," he said, as they walked on — "after all, you know, I am not like Wright — I have no business."

He walked with the ladies to the door of their lodging. Angela kept always in front. She stood there, however, at the little confectioner's window until the others came up. She let her mother pass in, and then she said to Bernard, looking at him —

"Shall I see you again?"

"Some time, I hope."

"I mean — are you going away?"

Bernard looked for a moment at a little pink sugar cherub — a species of Cupid, with a gilded bow — which figured among the pastry-cook's enticements. Then he said —

"I will come and tell you this evening."

And in the evening he went to tell her; she had mentioned during the walk in the garden of the Schloss that they should not go out. As he approached Mrs. Vivian's door he saw a figure in a light dress standing in the little balcony. He stopped and looked up, and then the person in the light dress, leaning her hands on the railing, with her shoulders a little raised, bent over and looked down at him. It was very dark, but even through the thick dusk he thought he perceived the finest brilliancy of Angela Vivian's smile.

"I shall not go away," he said, lifting his voice a little.

She made no answer; she only stood looking down at him through the warm dusk and smiling. He went into the house, and he remained at Baden-Baden till Gordon came back.

Chapter XIV

Gordon asked him no questions for twenty-four hours after his return, then suddenly he began:

"Well, haven't you something to say to me?"

It was at the hotel, in Gordon's apartment, late in the afternoon. A heavy thunderstorm had broken over the place an hour before, and Bernard had been standing at one of his friend's windows, rather idly, with his hands in his pockets, watching the rain-torrents dance upon the empty pavements. At last the deluge abated, the clouds began to break — there was a promise of a fine evening. Gordon Wright, while the storm was at its climax, sat down to write letters, and wrote half a dozen. It was after he had sealed, directed and affixed a postage-stamp to the last of the series that he addressed to his companion the question I have just quoted.

"Do you mean about Miss Vivian?" Bernard asked, without turning round from the window.

"About Miss Vivian, of course." Bernard said nothing and his companion went on. "Have you nothing to tell me about Miss Vivian?"

Bernard presently turned round looking at Gordon and smiling a little.

"She's a delightful creature!"

"That won't do — you have tried that before," said Gordon. "No," he added in a moment, "that won't do." Bernard turned back to the window, and Gordon continued, as he remained silent. "I shall have a right to consider your saying nothing a proof of an unfavorable judgment. You don't like her!"

Bernard faced quickly about again, and for an instant the two men looked at each other.

"Ah, my dear Gordon," Longueville murmured.

"*Do* you like her then?" asked Wright, getting up.

"No!" said Longueville.

"That's just what I wanted to know, and I am much obliged to you for telling me."

"I am not obliged to you for asking me. I was in hopes you wouldn't."

"You dislike her very much then?" Gordon exclaimed, gravely.

"Won't disliking her, simply, do?" said Bernard.

"It will do very well. But it will do a little better if you will tell me why. Give me a reason or two."

"Well," said Bernard, "I tried to make love to her and she boxed my ears."

"The devil!" cried Gordon.

"I mean morally, you know."

Gordon stared; he seemed a little puzzled.

"You tried to make love to her morally?"

"She boxed my ears morally," said Bernard, laughing out.

"Why did you try to make love to her?"

This inquiry was made in a tone so expressive of an

unbiased truth-seeking habit that Bernard's mirth was not immediately quenched. Nevertheless, he replied with sufficient gravity —

"To test her fidelity to you. Could you have expected anything else? You told me you were afraid she was a latent coquette. You gave me a chance, and I tried to ascertain."

"And you found she was not. Is that what you mean?"

"She's as firm as a rock. My dear Gordon, Miss Vivian is as firm as the firmest of your geological formations."

Gordon shook his head with a strange positive persistence.

"You are talking nonsense. You are not serious. You are not telling me the truth. I don't believe that you attempted to make love to her. You wouldn't have played such a game as that. It wouldn't have been honorable."

Bernard flushed a little; he was irritated.

"Oh come, don't make too much of a point of that! Didn't you tell me before that it was a great opportunity?"

"An opportunity to be wise — not to be foolish!"

"Ah, there is only one sort of opportunity," cried Bernard. "You exaggerate the reach of human wisdom."

"Suppose she had let you make love to her," said Gordon. "That would have been a beautiful result of your experiment."

"I should have seemed to you a rascal, perhaps, but I should have saved you from a latent coquette. You would owe some thanks for that."

"And now you haven't saved me," said Gordon, with a simple air of noting a fact.

"You assume — in spite of what I say — that she *is* a coquette!"

"I assume something because you evidently conceal something. I want the whole truth."

Bernard turned back to the window with increasing irritation.

"If he wants the whole truth he shall have it," he said to himself.

He stood a moment in thought and then he looked at his companion again.

"I think she would marry you — but I don't think she cares for you."

Gordon turned a little pale, but he clapped his hands together.

"Very good," he exclaimed. "That's exactly how I want you to speak."

"Her mother has taken a great fancy to your fortune and it has rubbed off on the girl, who has made up her mind that it would be a pleasant thing to have thirty thousand a year, and that her not caring for you is an unimportant detail."

"I see — I see," said Gordon, looking at his friend with an air of admiration for his frank and lucid way of putting things.

Now that he had begun to be frank and lucid, Bernard found a charm in it, and the impulse under which he had spoken urged him almost violently forward.

"The mother and daughter have agreed together to bag you, and Angela, I am sure, has made a vow to be as nice to you after marriage as possible. Mrs. Vivian has insisted upon the importance of that; Mrs. Vivian is a great moralist."

Gordon kept gazing at his friend; he seemed positively fascinated.

"Yes, I have noticed that in Mrs. Vivian," he said.

"Ah, she's a very nice woman!"

"It's not true, then," said Gordon, "that you tried to

make love to Angela?"

Bernard hesitated a single instant.

"No, it isn't true. I calumniated myself, to save her reputation. You insisted on my giving you a reason for my not liking her — I gave you that one."

"And your real reason —"

"My real reason is that I believe she would do you what I can't help regarding as an injury."

"Of course!" and Gordon, dropping his interested eyes, stared for some moments at the carpet. "But it isn't true, then, that you discovered her to be a coquette?"

"Ah, that's another matter."

"You did discover it all the same?"

"Since you want the whole truth — I did!"

"How did you discover it?" Gordon asked, clinging to his right of interrogation.

Bernard hesitated.

"You must remember that I saw a great deal of her."

"You mean that she encouraged you?"

"If I had not been a very faithful friend I might have thought so."

Gordon laid his hand appreciatively, gratefully, on Bernard's shoulder.

"And even that didn't make you like her?"

"Confound it, you make me blush!" cried Bernard, blushing a little in fact. "I have said quite enough; excuse me from drawing the portrait of too insensible a man. It was my point of view; I kept thinking of you."

Gordon, with his hand still on his friend's arm, patted it an instant in response to this declaration; then he turned away.

"I am much obliged to you. That's my notion of friendship. You have spoken out like a man."

"Like a man, yes. Remember that. Not in the least

like an oracle."

"I prefer an honest man to all the oracles," said Gordon.

"An honest man has his impressions! I have given you mine — they pretend to be nothing more. I hope they haven't offended you."

"Not in the least."

"Nor distressed, nor depressed, nor in any way discomposed you?"

"For what do you take me? I asked you a favor — a service; I imposed it on you. You have done the thing, and my part is simple gratitude."

"Thank you for nothing," said Bernard, smiling. "You have asked me a great many questions; there is one that in turn I have a right to ask you. What do you propose to do in consequence of what I have told you?"

"I propose to do nothing."

This declaration closed the colloquy, and the young men separated. Bernard saw Gordon no more that evening; he took for granted he had gone to Mrs. Vivian's. The burden of Longueville's confidences was a heavy load to carry there, but Bernard ventured to hope that he would deposit it at the door. He had given Gordon his impressions, and the latter might do with them what he chose — toss them out of the window, or let them grow stale with heedless keeping. So Bernard meditated, as he wandered about alone for the rest of the evening. It was useless to look for Mrs. Vivian's little circle, on the terrace of the Conversation-house, for the storm in the afternoon had made the place so damp that it was almost forsaken of its frequenters. Bernard spent the evening in the gaming-rooms, in the thick of the crowd that pressed about the tables, and by way of a change — he had hitherto been almost nothing of a gambler — he laid down a couple of pieces at roulette. He had played but two or three times, without winning a penny; but now he had the agreeable sensation of drawing in a small handful of gold. He continued to play, and he continued to win. His luck surprised and excited him — so much so that after it had repeated itself half a dozen times he left the place and walked about for half an hour in the outer darkness. He felt amused and exhilarated, but the feeling amounted almost to agitation. He, nevertheless, returned to the tables, where he again found success awaiting him. Again and again he put his money on a happy number, and so steady a run of luck began at last to attract attention. The rumor of it spread through the rooms, and the crowd about the roulette received a large contingent of spectators. Bernard felt that they were looking more or less eagerly for a turn of the tide; but he was in the humor for disappointing them, and he left the place, while his luck was still running high, with ten thousand francs in his pocket. It was very late when he returned to the inn — so late that he forbore to knock at Gordon's door. But though he betook himself to his own quarters, he was far from finding, or even seeking, immediate rest. He knocked about, as he would have said, for half the night — not because he was delighted at having won ten thousand francs, but rather because all of a sudden he found himself disgusted at the manner in which he had spent the evening. It was extremely characteristic of Bernard Longueville that his pleasure should suddenly transform itself into flatness. What he felt was not regret or repentance. He had it not in the least on his conscience that he had given countenance to the reprehensible practice of gaming. It was annoyance that he had passed out of his own control — that he had obeyed a force which he was unable to measure at the time. He had been drunk and he was turning sober. In spite of a great momentary appearance of frankness and a lively relish of any conjunction of agreeable circumstances exerting a pressure to which one could respond, Bernard had really little taste for giving himself up, and he never did so without very soon wishing to take himself back. He had now given himself to something that was not himself, and the fact that he had gained ten thousand francs by it was an insufficient salve to an aching sense of having ceased to be his own master. He had not been playing – he had been played with. He had been the sport of a blind, brutal chance, and he felt humiliated by having been favored by so rudely-operating a divinity. Good luck and bad luck? Bernard felt very scornful of the distinction, save that good luck seemed to him rather the more vulgar. As the night went on his disgust deepened, and at last the weariness it brought with it sent him to sleep. He slept very late, and woke up to a disagreeable consciousness. At first, before collecting his thoughts, he could not imagine what he had on his mind – was it that he had spoken ill of Angela Vivian? It brought him extraordinary relief to remember that he had gone to bed in extreme ill-humor with his exploits at roulette. After he had dressed himself and just as he was leaving his room, a servant brought him a note superscribed in Gordon's hand – a note of which the following proved to be the contents.

                                        "Seven o'clock, A.M.
    "My dear Bernard:
    "Circumstances have determined me to leave Baden immediately, and I shall take the train that starts an hour hence. I am told that you came in very late last night, so I won't disturb you for a painful parting at this unnatural hour. I came to this decision last evening, and I put up my things;

so I have nothing to do but to take myself off. I shall go to Basel, but after that I don't know where, and in so comfortless an uncertainty I don't ask you to follow me. Perhaps I shall go to America; but in any case I shall see you sooner or later. Meanwhile, my dear Bernard, be as happy as your brilliant talents should properly make you, and believe me yours ever,

"G.W.

"P.S. It is perhaps as well that I should say that I am leaving in consequence of something that happened last evening, but not — by any traceable process — in consequence of the talk we had together. I may also add that I am in very good health and spirits."

Bernard lost no time in learning that his friend had in fact departed by the eight o'clock train — the morning was now well advanced; and then, over his breakfast, he gave himself up to meditative surprise. What had happened during the evening — what had happened after their conversation in Gordon's room? He had gone to Mrs. Vivian's — what had happened there? Bernard found it difficult to believe that he had gone there simply to notify her that, having talked it over with an intimate friend, he gave up her daughter, or to mention to the young lady herself that he had ceased to desire the honor of her hand. Gordon alluded to some definite occurrence, yet it was inconceivable that he should have allowed himself to be determined by Bernard's words — his diffident and irresponsible impression. Bernard resented this idea as an injury to himself, yet it was difficult to imagine what else could have happened. There was Gordon's word for it, however, that there was no "traceable" connection between the circumstances which led to his sudden departure and the information he had succeeded in extracting from his friend. What did he mean by a "traceable" connection? Gordon never used words idly, and he meant to make of this point an intelligible distinction. It was this sense of his usual accuracy of expression that assisted Bernard in fitting a meaning to his late companion's letter. He intended to intimate that he had come back to Baden with his mind made up to relinquish his suit, and that he had questioned Bernard simply from moral curiosity — for the sake of intellectual satisfaction. Nothing was altered by the fact that Bernard had told him a sorry tale; it had not modified his behavior — that effect would have been traceable. It had simply affected his imagination, which was a consequence of the imponderable sort. This view of the case was supported by Gordon's mention of his good spirits. A man always had good spirits when he had acted in harmony with a conviction. Of course, after renouncing the attempt to make himself acceptable to Miss Vivian, the only possible thing for Gordon had been to leave Baden. Bernard, continuing to meditate, at last convinced himself that there had been no explicit rupture, that Gordon's last visit had simply been a visit of farewell, that its character had sufficiently signified his withdrawal, and that he had now gone away because, after giving the girl up, he wished very naturally not to meet her again. This was, on Bernard's part, a sufficiently coherent view of the case; but nevertheless, an hour afterward, as he strolled along the Lichtenthal Alley, he found himself stopping suddenly and exclaiming under his breath — "Have I done her an injury? Have I affected her prospects?" Later in the day he said to himself half a dozen times that he had simply warned Gordon against an incongruous union.

Chapter XV

Now that Gordon was gone, at any rate, gone for good, and not to return, he felt a sudden and singular sense of freedom. It was a feeling of unbounded expansion, quite out of proportion, as he said to himself, to any assignable cause. Everything suddenly appeared to have become very optional; but he was quite at a loss what to do with his liberty. It seemed a harmless use to make of it, in the afternoon, to go and pay another visit to the ladies who lived at the confectioner's. Here, however, he met a reception which introduced a fresh element of perplexity into the situation that Gordon had left behind him. The door was opened to him by Mrs. Vivian's maid-servant, a sturdy daughter of the Schwartzwald, who informed him that the ladies — with much regret — were unable to receive anyone.

"They are very busy — and they are ill," said the young woman, by way of explanation.

Bernard was disappointed, and he felt like arguing the case.

"Surely," he said, "they are not both ill and busy! When you make excuses, you should make them agree with each other."

The Teutonic soubrette fixed her round blue eyes a minute upon the patch of blue sky revealed to her by her open door.

"I say what I can, *lieber Herr*. It's not my fault if I'm not so clever as a French mamsell. One of the ladies is busy, the other is ill. There you have it."

"Not quite," said Bernard. "You must remember that there are three of them."

"Oh, the little one — the little one weeps."

"Miss Evers weeps!" exclaimed Bernard, to whom the vision of this young lady in tears had never presented itself.

"That happens to young ladies when they are unhappy," said the girl; and with an artless yet significant smile she carried a big red hand to the left side of a broad bosom.

"I am sorry she is unhappy; but which of the other ladies is ill?"

"The mother is very busy."

"And the daughter is ill?"

The young woman looked at him an instant, smiling again, and the light in her little blue eyes indicated confusion, but not perversity.

"No, the mamma is ill," she exclaimed, "and the daughter is very busy. They are preparing to leave Baden."

"To leave Baden? When do they go?"

"I don't quite know, *lieber Herr;* but very soon."

With this information Bernard turned away. He was rather surprised, but he reflected that Mrs. Vivian had not proposed to spend her life on the banks of the Oos, and that people were leaving Baden every day in the year. In the evening, at the Kursaal, he met Captain Lovelock, who was wandering about with an air of explosive sadness.

"Damn it, they're going — yes, they're going," said the Captain, after the two young men had exchanged a few allusions to current events. "Fancy their leaving us in that heartless manner! It's not the time to run away — it's the time to keep your rooms, if you're so lucky as to have any. The races begin next week and there'll be a tremendous crowd. All the grand-ducal people are coming. Miss Evers wanted awfully to see the Grand Duke, and I promised her an introduction. I can't make out what Mrs. Vivian is up to. I bet you a ten-pound note she's giving chase. Our friend Wright has come back and gone off again, and Mrs. Vivian means to strike camp and follow. She'll pot him yet; you see if she doesn't!"

"She is running away from you, dangerous man!" said Bernard.

"Do you mean on account of Miss Evers? Well, I admire Miss Evers — I don't mind admitting that; but I ain't dangerous," said Captain Lovelock, with a lusterless eye. "How can a fellow be dangerous when he hasn't ten shillings in his pocket? Desperation, do you call it? But Miss Evers hasn't money, so far as I have heard. I don't ask you," Lovelock continued — "I don't care a damn whether she has or not. She's a devilish charming girl, and I don't mind telling you I'm hit. I stand no chance — I know I stand no chance. Mrs. Vivian's down on me, and, by Jove, Mrs. Vivian's right. I'm not the husband to pick out for a young woman of expensive habits and no expectations. Gordon Wright's the sort of young man that's wanted, and, hang me, if Mrs. Vivian didn't want him so much for her own daughter, I believe she'd try and bag him for the little one. Gad, I believe that to keep me off she would like to cut him in two and give half to each of them! I'm afraid of that little woman. She has got a little voice like a screw-driver. But for all that, if I could get away from this cursed place, I would keep the girl in sight — hang me if I wouldn't! I'd cut the races — dash me if I wouldn't! But I'm in pawn, if you know what that means. I owe a beastly lot of money at the inn, and that impudent little beggar of a landlord won't let me out of his sight. The luck's dead against me at those filthy tables; I haven't won a farthing in three weeks. I wrote to my brother the other day, and this morning I got an answer from him — a cursed, canting letter of good advice, remarking that he had already paid my debts seven times. It doesn't happen to be seven; it's only six, or six and a half! Does he expect me to spend the rest of my life at the Hotel de Hollande? Perhaps he would like me to engage as a waiter there and pay it off by serving at the table d'hôte. It would be convenient for him the next time he comes abroad with his seven daughters and two governesses. I hate the smell of their beastly table d'hôte! You're sorry I'm hard up? I'm sure I'm much obliged to you. Can you be of any service? My dear fellow, if you are bent on throwing your money about the place I'm not the man to stop you." Bernard's winnings of the previous night were burning a hole, as the phrase is, in his pocket. Ten thousand francs had never before seemed to him so heavy a load to carry, and to lighten the weight of his good luck by lending fifty pounds to a less fortunate fellow-player was an operation that not only gratified his good nature but strongly commended itself to his conscience. His conscience, however, made its conditions. "My dear Longueville," Lovelock went on, "I have always gone in for family feeling, early associations, and all that sort of thing. That's what made me confide my difficulties to Dovedale. But, upon my honor, you remind me of the good Samaritan, or that sort of person; you are fonder of me than my own brother! I'll take fifty pounds with pleasure, thank you, and you shall have them again — at the earliest opportunity. My earliest convenience — will that do? Damn it, it *is* a convenience, isn't it? You make your conditions. My dear fellow, I accept them in advance. That I'm not to follow up Miss Evers — is that what you mean? Have you been commissioned by the family to buy me off? It's devilish cruel to take advantage of my poverty! Though I'm poor, I'm honest. But I *am* honest, my dear Longueville; that's the point. I'll give you my word, and I'll keep it. I won't go near that girl again — I won't think of her till I've got rid of your fifty pounds. It's a dreadful encouragement to extravagance, but that's your lookout. I'll stop for their beastly races and the young lady shall be sacred."

Longueville called the next morning at Mrs. Vivian's, and learned that the three ladies had left Baden by the early train, a couple of hours before. This fact produced in his mind a variety of emotions — surprise, annoyance, embarrassment. In spite of his effort to think it natural they should go, he found something precipitate and inexplicable in the manner of their going, and he declared to himself that one of the party, at least, had been unkind and ungracious in not giving him a chance to say good-bye. He took refuge by anticipation, as it were, in this reflection, whenever, for the next three or four days, he foresaw himself stopping short, as he had done before, and asking himself whether he had done an injury to Angela Vivian. This was an idle and unpractical question, inasmuch as the answer was not forthcoming; whereas it was quite simple and conclusive to say, without the note of interrogation, that she was, in spite of many attractive points, an abrupt and capricious young woman. During the three or four days in question, Bernard lingered on at Baden, uncertain what to do or where to go, feeling as if he had received a sudden check — a sort of spiritual snub — which arrested the accumulation of motive. Lovelock, also, whom Bernard saw every day, appeared to think that destiny had given him a slap in the face, for he had not enjoyed the satisfaction of a last interview with Miss Evers.

"I thought she might have written me a note," said the Captain; "but it appears she doesn't write. Some girls don't write, you know."

Bernard remarked that it was possible Lovelock would still have news of Miss Blanche; and before he left Baden he learned that she had addressed her forsaken swain a charming little note from Lausanne, where the three ladies had paused in their flight from Baden, and where Mrs. Vivian had decreed that for the present they should remain.

"I'm devilish glad she writes," said Captain Lovelock; "some girls do write, you know."

Blanche found Lausanne most horrid after Baden, for whose delights she languished. The delights of Baden, however, were not obvious just now to her correspondent, who had taken Bernard's fifty pounds into the Kursaal and left them there. Bernard, on learning his misfortune, lent him another fifty, with which he performed a second series of unsuccessful experiments; and our hero was not at his ease until he had passed over to his luckless friend the whole amount of his own winnings, every penny of which found its way through Captain Lovelock's fingers back into the bank. When this operation was completed, Bernard left Baden, the Captain gloomily accompanying him to the station.

I have said that there had come over Bernard a singular sense of freedom. One of the uses he made of his freedom was to undertake a long journey. He went to the East and remained absent from Europe for

upward of two years — a period of his life of which it
is not proposed to offer a complete history. The East
is a wonderful region, and Bernard, investigating the
mysteries of Asia, saw a great many curious and beautiful things. He had moments of keen enjoyment; he
laid up a great store of impressions and even a considerable sum of knowledge. But, nevertheless, he was not
destined to look back upon this episode with any
particular complacency. It was less delightful than it
was supposed to be; it was less successful than it might
have been. By what unnatural element the cup of
pleasure was adulterated, he would have been very
much at a loss to say; but it was an incontestable fact
that at times he sipped it as a medicine, rather than
quaffed it as a nectar. When people congratulated him
on his opportunity of seeing the world, and said they
envied him the privilege of seeing it so well, he felt
even more than the usual degree of irritation produced
by an insinuation that fortune thinks so poorly of us
as to give us easy terms. Misplaced sympathy is the least
available of superfluities, and Bernard at this time
found himself thinking that there was a good deal of
impertinence in the world. He would, however, readily
have confessed that, in so far as he failed to enjoy his
Oriental wanderings, the fault was his own; though he
would have made mentally the gratifying reflection
that never was a fault less deliberate. If, during the
period of which I speak, his natural gayety had sunk
to a minor key, a partial explanation may be found in
the fact that he was deprived of the society of his late
companion. It was an odd circumstance that the two
young men had not met since Gordon's abrupt departure from Baden. Gordon went to Berlin, and shortly
afterward to America, so that they were on opposite
sides of the globe. Before he returned to his own
country, Bernard made by letter two or three offers to

join him in Europe, anywhere that was agreeable to him. Gordon answered that his movements were very uncertain, and that he should be sorry to trouble Bernard to follow him about. He had put him to this inconvenience in making him travel from Venice to Baden, and one such favor at a time was enough to ask, even of the most obliging of men. Bernard was, of course, afraid that what he had told Gordon about Angela Vivian was really the cause of a state of things which, as between two such good friends, wore a perceptible resemblance to alienation. Gordon had given her up; but he bore Bernard a grudge for speaking ill of her, and so long as this disagreeable impression should last, he preferred not to see him. Bernard was frank enough to charge the poor fellow with a lingering rancor, of which he made, indeed, no great crime. But Gordon denied the allegation, and assured him that, to his own perception, there was no decline in their intimacy. He only requested, as a favor and as a tribute to "just susceptibilities," that Bernard would allude no more either to Miss Vivian or to what had happened at Baden. This request was easy to comply with, and Bernard, in writing, strictly conformed to it; but it seemed to him that the act of doing so was in itself a cooling-off. What would be a better proof of what is called a "tension" than an agreement to avoid a natural topic? Bernard moralized a little over Gordon's "just susceptibilities," and felt that the existence of a perverse resentment in so honest a nature was a fact gained to his acquaintance with psychological science. It cannot be said, however, that he suffered this fact to occupy at all times the foreground of his consciousness. Bernard was like some great painters; his foregrounds were very happily arranged. He heard nothing of Mrs. Vivian and her daughter, beyond a rumor that they had gone to Italy; and he learned, on apparently good authority, that Blanche Evers had returned to New York with her mother. He wondered whether Captain Lovelock was still in pawn at the Hotel de Hollande. If he did not allow himself to wonder too curiously whether he had done a harm to Gordon, it may be affirmed that he was haunted by the recurrence of that other question, of which mention has already been made. Had he done a harm to Angela Vivian, and did she know that he had done it? This inquiry by no means made him miserable, and it was far from awaiting him regularly on his pillow. But it visited him at intervals, and sometimes in the strangest places — suddenly, abruptly, in the stillness of an Indian temple, or amid the shrillness of an Oriental crowd. He became familiar with it at last; he called it his Jack-in-the-box. Some invisible touch of circumstance would press the spring, and the little image would pop up, staring him in the face and grinning an interrogation. Bernard always clapped down the lid, for he regarded this phenomenon as strikingly inane. But if it was more frequent than any pang of conscience connected with the remembrance of Gordon himself, this last sentiment was certainly lively enough to make it a great relief to hear at last a rumor that the excellent fellow was about to be married. The rumor reached him at Athens; it was vague and indirect, and it omitted the name of his betrothed. But Bernard made the most of it, and took comfort in the thought that his friend had recovered his spirits and his appetite for matrimony.

Chapter XVI

*I*t was not till our hero reached Paris, on his return from the distant East, that the rumor I have just mentioned acquired an appreciable consistency. Here, indeed, it took the shape of authentic information. Among a number of delayed letters which had been awaiting him at his banker's he found a communication from Gordon Wright. During the previous year or two his correspondence with this trusted – and trusting – friend had not been frequent, and Bernard had received little direct news of him. Three or four short letters had overtaken him in his wanderings – letters as cordial, to all appearance, if not as voluminous, as the punctual missives of an earlier time. Bernard made a point of satisfying himself that they were as cordial; he weighed them in the scales of impartial suspicion. It seemed to him on the whole that there was no relaxation of Gordon's epistolary tone. If he wrote less often than he used to do, that was a thing that very commonly happened as men grew older. The closest intimacies, moreover, had phases and seasons, intermissions and revivals, and even if his friend had, in fact, averted his countenance from him, this was simply the accomplishment of a periodical revolution which would bring them in due order face to face again. Bernard made a point, himself, of writing tolerably often and writing always in the friendliest tone. He made it a matter of conscience — he liked to feel that he was treating Gordon generously, and not demanding an eye for an eye. The letter he found in Paris was so short that I may give it entire.

"My dear Bernard (it ran), I must write to you before I write to anyone else, though unfortunately you are so far away that you can't be the first to congratulate me. Try and not be the last, however. I am going to be married — as soon as possible. You know the young lady, so you can appreciate the situation. Do you remember little Blanche Evers, whom we used to see three years ago at Baden-Baden? Of course you remember her, for I know you used often to talk with her. You will be rather surprised, perhaps, at my having selected her as the partner of a life-time; but we manage these matters according to our lights. I am very much in love with her, and I hold that an excellent reason. I have been ready anytime this year or two to fall in love with some simple, trusting, childlike nature. I find this in perfection in this charming young girl. I find her so natural and fresh. I remember telling you once that I didn't wish to be fascinated — that I wanted to estimate scientifically the woman I should marry. I have altogether got over that, and I don't know how I ever came to talk such nonsense. I am fascinated now, and I assure you I like it! The best of it is that I find it doesn't in the least prevent my estimating Blanche. I judge her very fairly — I see just what she is. She's simple — that's what I want; she's tender — that's what I long for. You will remember how pretty she is; I needn't remind you of that. She was much younger then, and she has greatly developed and improved in these two or three years. But she will always be young and innocent — I don't want her to improve too much. She came back to America with her mother the winter after we met her at Baden, but I never saw her again till three months ago. Then I saw her with new eyes, and I wondered I could have been so blind. But I wasn't ready for her till then, and what makes me so happy now is to know that I have come to my present way of feeling by experience. That gives me confidence — you see I am a reasoner still. But I am under the charm, for all my reason. We are to be married in a month — try and come back to the wedding. Blanche sends you a message, which I will give you verbatim. 'Tell him I am not such a silly little chatterbox as I used to be at Baden. I am a great deal wiser; I am almost as clever as Angela Vivian.' She has an idea you thought Miss Vivian very clever — but it is not true that she is equally so. I am very happy; come home and see."

Bernard went home, but he was not able to reach the United States in time for Gordon's wedding, which took place at midsummer. Bernard, arriving late in the autumn, found his friend a married man of some months' standing, and was able to judge, according to his invitation, whether he appeared happy. The first effect of the letter I have just quoted had been an immense surprise; the second had been a series of reflections which were quite the negative of surprise; and these operations of Bernard's mind had finally merged themselves in a simple sentiment of jollity. He was delighted that Gordon should be married; he felt jovial about it; he was almost indifferent to the question of whom he had chosen. Certainly, at first, the choice of Blanche Evers seemed highly incongruous; it was difficult to imagine a young woman less shaped to minister to Gordon's strenuous needs than the light-hearted and empty-headed little flirt whose inconsequent prattle had remained for Bernard one of the least importunate memories of a charming time. Blanche Evers was a pretty little goose — the prettiest of little geese, perhaps, and doubtless the most amiable; but she was not a companion for a peculiarly serious man, who would like his wife to share his view of human responsibilities. What a singular selection — what a queer infatuation! Bernard had no sooner committed himself to this line of criticism than he stopped short, with the sudden consciousness of error carried almost to the point of *naïveté*. He exclaimed that Blanche Evers was exactly the sort of girl that men of Gordon Wright's stamp always ended by falling in love with, and that poor Gordon knew very much better what he was about in this case than he had done in trying to solve the deep problem of a comfortable life with Angela Vivian. This was what your strong, solid, sensible fellows always came to; they paid, in this particular, a larger tribute to pure fancy than the people who were supposed habitually to cultivate that muse. Blanche Evers was what the French call an article of fantasy, and Gordon had taken a pleasure in finding her deliciously useless. He cultivated utility in other ways, and it pleased and flattered him to feel that he could afford, morally speaking, to have a kittenish wife. He had within himself a fund of common sense to draw upon, so that to espouse a paragon of wisdom would be but to carry water to the fountain. He could easily make up for the deficiencies of a wife who was a little silly, and if she charmed and amused him, he could treat himself to the luxury of these sensations for themselves. He was not in the least afraid of being ruined by it, and if Blanche's birdlike chatter and turns of the head had made a fool of him, he knew it perfectly well, and simply took his stand upon his rights. Every man has a right to a little flower-bed, and life is not all mere kitchen-gardening. Bernard rapidly extemporized this rough explanation of the surprise his friend had offered him, and he found it all-sufficient for his immediate needs. He wrote Blanche a charming note, to which she replied with a great deal of spirit and grace. Her little letter was very prettily turned, and Bernard, reading it over two or three times, said to himself that, to do her justice, she might very well have polished her intellect a trifle during these two or three years. As she was older, she could hardly help being wiser. It even occurred to Bernard that she might have profited by the sort of experience that is known as the discipline of suffering. What had become of Captain Lovelock and that tender passion which was apparently nonetheless genuine for having been expressed in the slang of a humorous period? Had they been permanently separated by judicious guardians, and had she been obliged to obliterate his image from her lightly-beating little heart? Bernard had felt sure at Baden that, beneath her contemptuous airs and that impertinent consciousness of the difficulties of conquest by which a pretty American girl attests her allegiance to a civilization in which young women occupy the highest place — he had felt sure that Blanche had a high appreciation of her handsome Englishman, and that if Lovelock should continue to relish her charms, he might count upon the advantages of reciprocity. But it occurred to Bernard that Captain Lovelock had perhaps been faithless; that, at least, the discourtesy of chance and the inhumanity of an elder brother might have kept him an eternal prisoner at the Hotel de Hollande (where, for all Bernard knew to the contrary, he had been obliged to work out his destiny in the arduous character of a polyglot waiter); so that the poor young girl, casting backward glances along the

path of Mrs. Vivian's retreat, and failing to detect the
onward rush of a rescuing cavalier, had perforce believed herself forsaken, and had been obliged to sum-
mon philosophy to her aid. It was very possible that
her philosophic studies had taught her the art of reflection; and that, as she would have said herself, she
was tremendously toned down. Once, at Baden, when
Gordon Wright happened to take upon himself to
remark that little Miss Evers was bored by her English
gallant, Bernard had ventured to observe, *in petto,* that
Gordon knew nothing about it. But all this was of no
consequence now, and Bernard steered further and
further away from the liability to detect fallacies in his
friend. Gordon had engaged himself to marry, and our
critical hero had not a grain of fault to find with this
resolution. It was a capital thing; it was just what he
wanted; it would do him a world of good. Bernard
rejoiced with him sincerely, and regretted extremely
that a series of solemn engagements to pay visits in
England should prevent his being present at the nuptials.

They were well over, as I have said, when he reached
New York. The honeymoon had waned, and the business of married life had begun. Bernard, at the end,
had sailed from England rather abruptly. A friend who
had a remarkably good cabin on one of the steamers
was obliged by a sudden detention to give it up, and
on his offering it to Longueville, the latter availed
himself gratefully of this opportunity of being a little
less discomposed than usual by the Atlantic billows.
He therefore embarked at two days' notice, a fortnight
earlier than he had intended and than he had written
to Gordon to expect him. Gordon, of course, had
written that he was to seek no hospitality but that
which Blanche was now prepared — they had a charming house — so graciously to dispense; but Bernard,

nevertheless, leaving the ship early in the morning, had betaken himself to an hotel. He wished not to antici- pate his welcome, and he determined to report himself to Gordon first and to come back with his luggage later in the day. After purifying himself of his sea-stains, he left his hotel and walked up the Fifth Avenue with all a newly-landed voyager's enjoyment of terrestrial loco- motion. It was a charming autumn day; there was a golden haze in the air; he supposed it was the Indian summer. The broad sidewalk of the Fifth Avenue was scattered over with dry leaves — crimson and orange and amber. He tossed them with his stick as he passed; they rustled and murmured with the motion, and it reminded him of the way he used to kick them in front of him over these same pavements in his riotous in- fancy. It was a pleasure, after many wanderings, to find himself in his native land again, and Bernard Lon- gueville, as he went, paid his compliments to his mother-city. The brightness and gayety of the place seemed a greeting to a returning son, and he felt a throb of affection for the freshest, the youngest, the easiest and most good-natured of great capitals. On presenting himself at Gordon's door, Bernard was told that the master of the house was not at home; he went in, however, to see the mistress. She was in her drawing room, alone; she had on her bonnet, as if she had been going out. She gave him a joyous, demonstrative little welcome; she was evidently very glad to see him. Ber- nard had thought it possible she had "improved," and she was certainly prettier than ever. He instantly per- ceived that she was still a chatterbox; it remained to be seen whether the quality of her discourse were finer.

"Well, Mr. Longueville," she exclaimed, "where in the world did you drop from, and how long did it take you to cross the Atlantic? Three days, eh? It couldn't have taken you many more, for it was only the other day that Gordon told me you were not to sail till the 20th. You changed your mind, eh? I didn't know you ever changed your mind. Gordon never changes his. That's not a reason, eh, because you are not a bit like Gordon. Well, I never thought you were, except that you are a man. Now what are you laughing at? What should you like me call you? You *are* a man, I suppose; you are not a god. That's what you would like me to call you, I have no doubt. I must keep that for Gordon? I shall certainly keep it a good while. I know a good deal more about gentlemen than I did when I last saw you, and I assure you I don't think they are a bit godlike. I suppose that's why you always drop down from the sky — you think it's more divine. I remember that's the way you arrived at Baden when we were there together; the first thing we knew, you were standing in the midst of us. Do you remember that evening when you presented yourself? You came up and touched Gordon on the shoulder, and he gave a little jump. He will give another little jump when he sees you today. He gives a great many little jumps; I keep him skipping about! I remember perfectly the way we were sitting that evening at Baden, and the way you looked at me when you came up. I saw you before Gordon — I see a good many things before Gordon. What did you look at me that way for? I always meant to ask you. I was dying to know."

"For the simplest reason in the world," said Bernard. "Because you were so pretty."

"Ah no, it wasn't that! I know all about that look. It was something else — as if you knew something about me. I don't know what you can have known. There was very little to know about me, except that I was intensely silly. Really, I was awfully silly that summer at Baden — you wouldn't believe how silly I was. But I don't see how you could have known that — before you had spoken to me. It came out in my conversation — it came out awfully. My mother was a good deal disappointed in Mrs. Vivian's influence; she had expected so much from it. But it was not poor Mrs. Vivian's fault, it was some one's else. Have you ever seen the Vivians again? They are always in Europe; they have gone to live in Paris. That evening when you came up and spoke to Gordon, I never thought that three years afterward I should be married to him, and I don't suppose you did either. Is that what you meant by looking at me? Perhaps you can tell the future. I wish you would tell *my* future!"

"Oh, I can tell that easily," said Bernard.

"What will happen to me?"

"Nothing particular; it will be a little dull — the perfect happiness of a charming woman married to the best fellow in the world."

"Ah, what a horrid future!" cried Blanche, with a little petulant cry. "I want to be happy, but I certainly don't want to be dull. If you say that again you will make me repent of having married the best fellow in the world. I mean to be happy, but I certainly shall not be dull if I can help it."

"I was wrong to say that," said Bernard, "because, after all, my dear young lady, there must be an excitement in having so kind a husband as you have got. Gordon's devotion is quite capable of taking a new form — of inventing a new kindness — every day in the year."

Blanche looked at him an instant, with less than her usual consciousness of her momentary pose.

"My husband *is* very kind," she said gently.

She had hardly spoken the words when Gordon came in. He stopped a moment on seeing Bernard, glanced at his wife, blushed, flushed, and with a loud, frank exclamation of pleasure, grasped his friend by both hands. It was so long since he had seen Bernard that he seemed a good deal moved; he stood there smiling, clasping his hands, looking him in the eyes, unable for some moments to speak. Bernard, on his side, was greatly pleased; it was delightful to him to look into Gordon's honest face again and to return his manly grasp. And he looked well — he looked happy; to see that was more delightful yet. During these few instants, while they exchanged a silent pledge of renewed friendship, Bernard's elastic perception embraced several things besides the consciousness of his own pleasure. He saw that Gordon looked well and happy, but that he looked older, too, and more serious, more marked by life. He looked as if something had happened to him — as, in fact, something had. Bernard saw a latent spark in his friend's eye that seemed to question his own for an impression of Blanche — to question it eagerly, and yet to deprecate judgment. He saw, too — with the fact made more vivid by Gordon's standing there beside her in his manly sincerity and throwing it into contrast — that Blanche was the same little posturing coquette of a Blanche whom, at Baden, he would have treated it as a broad joke that Gordon Wright should dream of marrying. He saw, in a word, that it was what it had first struck him as being — an incongruous union. All this was a good deal for Bernard to see in the course of half a minute, especially through the rather opaque medium of a feeling of irreflective joy; and his impressions at this moment have a value only in so far as they were destined to be confirmed by larger opportunity.

"You have come a little sooner than we expected," said Gordon; "but you are all the more welcome."

"It was rather a risk," Blanche observed. "One should be notified, when one wishes to make a good impression."

"Ah, my dear lady," said Bernard, "you made your impression — as far as I am concerned — a long time ago, and I doubt whether it would have gained anything today by your having prepared an effect."

They were standing before the fireplace, on the great hearthrug, and Blanche, while she listened to this speech, was feeling, with uplifted arm, for a curl that had strayed from her chignon.

"She prepares her effects very quickly," said Gordon, laughing gently. "They follow each other very fast!"

Blanche kept her hand behind her head, which was bent slightly forward; her bare arm emerged from her hanging sleeve, and, with her eyes glancing upward from under her lowered brows, she smiled at her two spectators. Her husband laid his hand on Bernard's arm.

"Isn't she pretty?" he cried; and he spoke with a sort of tender delight in being sure at least of this point.

"Tremendously pretty!" said Bernard. "I told her so half an hour before you came in."

"Ah, it was time I should arrive!" Gordon exclaimed.

Blanche was manifestly not in the least discomposed by this frank discussion of her charms, for the air of distinguished esteem adopted by both of her companions diminished the crudity of their remarks. But she gave a little pout of irritated modesty — it was more becoming than anything she had done yet — and declared that if they wished to talk her over, they were very welcome; but she should prefer their waiting till she got out of the room. So she left them, reminding Bernard that he was to send for his luggage and remain, and promising to give immediate orders for the preparation of his apartment. Bernard opened the door for her to pass out; she gave him a charming nod as he stood there, and he turned back to Gordon with the reflection of her smile in his face. Gordon was watching him; Gordon was dying to know what he thought of her. It was a curious mania of Gordon's, this wanting to know what one thought of the women he loved; but Bernard just now felt abundantly able to humor it. He was so pleased at seeing him tightly married.

"She's a delightful creature," Bernard said, with cordial vagueness, shaking hands with his friend again.

Gordon glanced at him a moment, and then, coloring a little, looked straight out of the window; whereupon Bernard remembered that these were just the terms in which, at Baden, after his companion's absence, he had attempted to qualify Angela Vivian. Gordon was conscious — he was conscious of the oddity of his situation.

"Of course it surprised you," he said, in a moment, still looking out of the window.

"What, my dear fellow?"

"My marriage."

"Well, you know," said Bernard, "everything surprises me. I am of a very conjectural habit of mind. All sorts of ideas come into my head, and yet when the simplest things happen I am always rather startled. I live in a reverie, and I am perpetually waked up by people doing things."

Gordon transferred his eyes from the window to Bernard's face — to his whole person.

"You are waked up? But you fall asleep again!"

"I fall asleep very easily," said Bernard.

Gordon looked at him from head to foot, smiling and shaking his head.

"You are not changed," he said. "You have traveled in unknown lands; you have had, I suppose, all sorts of adventures; but you are the same man I used to know."

"I am sorry for that!"

"You have the same way of representing — of misrepresenting, yourself."

"Well, if I am not changed," said Bernard, "I can ill afford to lose so valuable an art."

"Taking you altogether, I am glad you are the same," Gordon answered, simply; "but you must come into my part of the house."

Chapter XVII

*Y*es, he was conscious — he was very conscious; so Bernard reflected during the two or three first days of his visit to his friend. Gordon knew it must seem strange to so irreverent a critic that a man who had once aspired to the hand of so intelligent a girl — putting other things aside — as Angela Vivian should, as the Ghost in "Hamlet" says, have "declined upon" a young lady who, in force of understanding, was so very much Miss Vivian's inferior; and this knowledge kept him ill at his ease and gave him a certain pitiable awkwardness. Bernard's sense of the anomaly grew rapidly less acute; he made various observations which helped it to seem natural. Blanche was wonderfully pretty; she was very graceful, innocent, amusing. Since Gordon had determined to marry a little goose, he had chosen the animal with extreme discernment. It had quite the plumage of a swan, and it sailed along the stream of life with an extraordinary lightness of motion. He asked himself indeed at times whether Blanche were really so silly as she seemed; he doubted whether any woman could be so silly as Blanche seemed. He had a suspicion at times that, for ends of her own, she was playing a part — the suspicion arising from the fact that, as usually happens in such cases, she overplayed it. Her empty chatter, her futility, her childish coquetry and frivolity — such light wares could hardly be the whole substance of any woman's being; there was something beneath them which Blanche was keeping out of sight. She had a scrap of a mind somewhere, and even a little particle of a heart. If one looked long enough one might catch a glimpse of these possessions. But why should she keep them out of sight, and what were the ends that she proposed to serve by this uncomfortable perversity? Bernard wondered whether she were fond of her husband, and he heard it intimated by several good people in New York who had had some observation of the courtship, that she had married him for his money. He was very sorry to find that this was taken for granted, and he determined, on the whole, not to believe it. He was disgusted with the idea of such a want of gratitude; for, if Gordon Wright had loved Miss Evers for herself, the young lady might certainly have discovered the intrinsic value of so disinterested a suitor. Her mother had the credit of having made the match. Gordon was known to be looking for a wife; Mrs. Evers had put her little featherhead of a daughter very much forward, and Gordon was as easily captivated as a child by the sound of a rattle. Blanche had an affection for him now, however; Bernard saw no reason to doubt that, and certainly she would have been a very flimsy creature indeed if she had not been touched by his inexhaustible kindness. She had every conceivable indulgence, and if she married him for his money, at least she had got what she wanted. She led the most agreeable life conceivable, and she ought to be in high good-humor. It was impossible to have a prettier house, a prettier carriage, more jewels and laces for the adornment of a plump little person. It was impossible to go to more parties, to give better dinners, to have fewer privations or annoyances. Bernard was so much struck with all this that, advancing rapidly in the intimacy of his gracious hostess, he ventured to call her attention to her blessings. She answered that she was perfectly aware of them, and there was no pretty speech she was not prepared to make about Gordon.

"I know what you want to say," she went on; "you want to say that he spoils me, and I don't see why you should hesitate. You generally say everything you want, and you needn't be afraid of me. He doesn't spoil me, simply because I am so bad I can't be spoiled; but that's of no consequence. I was spoiled ages ago; everyone spoiled me — everyone except Mrs. Vivian. I was always fond of having everything I want, and I generally managed to get it. I always had lovely clothes; mamma thought that was a kind of a duty. If it was a duty, I don't suppose it counts as a part of the spoiling. But I was very much indulged, and I know I have everything now. Gordon is a perfect husband; I believe if I were to ask him for a present of his nose, he would cut it off and give it to me. I think I will ask him for a small piece of it some day; it will rather improve him to have an inch or two less. I don't say he's handsome; but he's just as good as he can be. Some people say that if you are very fond of a person you always think them handsome; but I don't agree with that at all. I am very fond of Gordon, and yet I am not blinded by affection, as regards his personal appearance. He's too light for my taste, and too red. And because you think people handsome, it doesn't follow that you are fond of them. I used to have a friend who was awfully handsome — the handsomest man I ever saw — and I was perfectly conscious of his defects. But I'm not conscious of Gordon's, and I don't believe he has got any. He's so intensely kind; it's quite pathetic. One would think he had done me an injury in marrying me, and that he wanted to make up for it. If he has done me an injury I haven't discovered it yet, and I don't believe I ever shall. I certainly shall not as long as he lets me order all the clothes I want. I have ordered five dresses this week, and I mean to order two more. When I told Gordon, what do you think he did? He simply kissed me. Well, if that's not expressive, I don't know what he could have done. He kisses me about seventeen times a day. I suppose it's very improper for a woman to tell anyone how often her husband kisses her; but, as you happen to have seen him do it, I don't suppose you will be scandalized. I know you are not easily scandalized; I am not afraid of you. You are scandalized at my getting so many dresses? Well, I told you I was spoiled — I freely acknowledge it. That's why I was afraid to tell Gordon — because when I was married I had such a lot of things; I was supposed to have dresses enough to last for a year. But Gordon hadn't to pay for them, so there was no harm in my letting him feel that he has a wife. If he thinks I am extravagant, he can easily stop kissing me. You don't think it would be easy to stop? It's very well, then, for those that have never begun!"

Bernard had a good deal of conversation with Blanche, of which, so far as she was concerned, the foregoing remarks may serve as a specimen. Gordon was away from home during much of the day; he had a chemical laboratory in which he was greatly inter-ested, and which he took Bernard to see; it was fitted up with the latest contrivances for the pursuit of ex-perimental science, and was the resort of needy young students, who enjoyed, at Gordon's expense, the op-portunity for pushing their researches. The place did great honor to Gordon's liberality and to his ingenuity; but Blanche, who had also paid it a visit, could never speak of it without a pretty little shudder.

"Nothing would induce me to go there again," she declared, "and I consider myself very fortunate to have escaped from it with my life. It's filled with all sorts of horrible things, that fizzle up and go off, or that make you turn some dreadful color if you look at them. I expect to hear a great clap some day, and half an hour afterward to see Gordon brought home in several hun-dred small pieces, put up in a dozen little bottles. I got a horrid little stain in the middle of my dress that one of the young men — the young *savants* — was so good as to drop there. Did you see the young *savants* who work under Gordon's orders? I thought they were too forlorn; there isn't one of them you would look at. If you can believe it, there wasn't one of them that looked at me; they took no more notice of me than if I had been the charwoman. They might have shown me some attention, at least, as the wife of the proprietor. What is it that Gordon's called — isn't there some other name? If you say 'proprietor,' it sounds as if he kept an hotel. I certainly don't want to pass for the wife of an hotel-keeper. What does he call himself? He must have some name. I hate telling people he's a chemist; it sounds just as if he kept a shop. That's what they call the druggists in England, and I formed the habit while I was there. It makes me feel as if he were some dreadful little man, with big green bottles in the window and 'night-bell' painted outside. He doesn't call himself

anything? Well, that's exactly like Gordon! I wonder
he consents to have a name at all. When I was telling
some one about the young men who work under his
orders — the young *savants* — he said I must not say
that — I must not speak of their working 'under his
orders.' I don't know what he would like me to say!
Under his inspiration!"

During the hours of Gordon's absence, Bernard had
frequent colloquies with his friend's wife, whose irresponsible prattle amused him, and in whom he tried
to discover some faculty, some quality, which might
be a positive guarantee of Gordon's future felicity. But
often, of course, Gordon was an auditor as well; I say
an auditor, because it seemed to Bernard that he had
grown to be less of a talker than of yore. Doubtless,
when a man finds himself united to a garrulous wife,
he naturally learns to hold his tongue; but sometimes,
at the close of one of Blanche's discursive monologues,
on glancing at her husband just to see how he took it,
and seeing him sit perfectly silent, with a fixed, inexpressive smile, Bernard said to himself that Gordon
found the lesson of listening attended with some em-
barrassments. Gordon, as the years went by, was growing a little inscrutable; but this, too, in certain circumstances, was a usual tendency. The operations of the
mind, with deepening experience, became more complex, and people were less apt to emit immature reflections at forty than they had been in their earlier days.
Bernard felt a great kindness in these days for his old
friend; he never yet had seemed to him such a good
fellow, nor appealed so strongly to the benevolence of
his disposition. Sometimes, of old, Gordon used to
irritate him; but this danger appeared completely to
have passed away. Bernard prolonged his visit; it gave
him pleasure to be able to testify in this manner to his
good will. Gordon was the kindest of hosts, and if in

conversation, when his wife was present, he gave precedence to her superior powers, he had at other times a good deal of pleasant bachelor-talk with his guest. He seemed very happy; he had plenty of occupation and plenty of practical intentions. The season went on, and Bernard enjoyed his life. He enjoyed the keen and brilliant American winter, and he found it very pleasant to be treated as a distinguished stranger in his own land — a situation to which his long and repeated absences had relegated him. The hospitality of New York was profuse; the charm of its daughters extreme; the radiance of its skies superb. Bernard was the restless and professionless mortal that we know, wandering in life from one vague experiment to another, constantly gratified and never satisfied, to whom no imperious finality had as yet presented itself; and, nevertheless, for a time he contrived to limit his horizon to the passing hour, and to make a good many hours pass in the drawing room of a demonstrative flirt.

For Mrs. Gordon was a flirt; that had become tolerably obvious. Bernard had known of old that Blanche Evers was one, and two or three months' observation of his friend's wife assured him that she did not judge a certain ethereal coquetry to be inconsistent with the conjugal character. Blanche flirted, in fact, more or less with all men, but her opportunity for playing her harmless batteries upon Bernard were of course exceptionally large. The poor fellow was perpetually under fire, and it was inevitable that he should reply with some precision of aim. It seemed to him all child's play, and it is certain that when his back was turned to his pretty hostess he never found himself thinking of her. He had not the least reason to suppose that she thought of him — excessive concentration of mind was the last vice of which he accused her. But before the winter was over, he discovered that Mrs. Gordon

Wright was being talked about, and that his own name was, as the newspapers say, mentioned in connection with that of his friend's wife. The discovery greatly disgusted him; Bernard Longueville's chronicler must do him the justice to say that it failed to yield him an even transient thrill of pleasure. He thought it very improbable that this vulgar rumor had reached Gordon's ears; but he nevertheless — very naturally — instantly made up his mind to leave the house. He lost no time in saying to Gordon that he had suddenly determined to go to California, and that he was sure he must be glad to get rid of him. Gordon expressed no surprise and no regret. He simply laid his hand on his shoulder and said, very quietly, looking at him in the eyes —

"Very well; the pleasantest things must come to an end."

It was not till an hour afterwards that Bernard said to himself that his friend's manner of receiving the announcement of his departure had been rather odd. He had neither said a word about his staying longer nor urged him to come back again, and there had been (it now seemed to Bernard) an audible undertone of relief in the single sentence with which he assented to his visitor's withdrawal. Could it be possible that poor Gordon was jealous of him, that he had heard this loathsome gossip, or that his own observation had given him an alarm? He had certainly never betrayed the smallest sense of injury; but it was to be remembered that even if he were uneasy, Gordon was quite capable, with his characteristic habit of weighing everything, his own honor included, in scrupulously adjusted scales, of denying himself the luxury of active suspicion. He would never have let a half suspicion make a difference in his conduct, and he would not have dissimulated; he would simply have resisted belief. His hospitality had been without a flaw, and if he had really been wishing Bernard out of his house, he had behaved with admirable self-control. Bernard, however, followed this train of thought a very short distance. It was odious to him to believe that he could have appeared to Gordon, however guiltlessly, to have invaded even in imagination the mystic line of the marital monopoly; not to say that, moreover, if one came to that, he really cared about as much for poor little Blanche as for the weather-cock on the nearest steeple. He simply hurried his preparations for departure, and he told Blanche that he should have to bid her farewell on the following day. He had found her in the drawing room, waiting for dinner. She was expecting company to dine, and Gordon had not yet come down.

She was sitting in the vague glow of the fire-light, in a wonderful blue dress, with two little blue feet crossed on the rug and pointed at the hearth. She received Bernard's announcement with small satisfaction, and expended a great deal of familiar ridicule on his project of a journey to California. Then, suddenly getting up and looking at him a moment —

"I know why you are going," she said.

"I am glad to hear my explanations have not been lost."

"Your explanations are all nonsense. You are going for another reason."

"Well," said Bernard, "if you insist upon it, it's because you are too sharp with me."

"It's because of me. So much as that is true." Bernard wondered what she was going to say — if she were going to be silly enough to allude to the most impudent of fictions; then, as she stood opening and closing her blue fan and smiling at him in the fire-light, he felt that she was silly enough for anything. "It's because of all the talk — it's because of Gordon. You needn't be afraid of Gordon."

"Afraid of him? I don't know what you mean," said Bernard, gravely.

Blanche gave a little laugh.

"You have discovered that people are talking about us — about you and me. I must say I wonder you care. I don't care, and if it's because of Gordon, you might as well know that he doesn't care. If he doesn't care, I don't see why I should; and if I don't, I don't see why you should!"

"You pay too much attention to such insipid drivel in even mentioning it."

"Well, if I have the credit of saying what I shouldn't — to you or to anyone else — I don't see why I shouldn't have the advantage too. Gordon doesn't care — he doesn't care what I do or say. He doesn't care a pin for me!"

She spoke in her usual rattling, rambling voice, and brought out this declaration with a curious absence of resentment.

"You talk about advantage," said Bernard. "I don't see what advantage it is to you to say that."

"I want to — I must — I will! That's the advantage!" This came out with a sudden sharpness of tone; she spoke more excitedly. "He doesn't care a button for me, and he never did! I don't know what he married me for. He cares for something else — he thinks of something else. I don't know what it is — I suppose it's chemistry!"

These words gave Bernard a certain shock, but he had his intelligence sufficiently in hand to contradict them with energy.

"You labor under a monstrous delusion," he exclaimed. "Your husband thinks you fascinating."

This epithet, pronounced with a fine distinctness,

was ringing in the air when the door opened and Gordon came in. He looked for a moment from Bernard to his wife, and then, approaching the latter, he said, softly —

"Do you know that he leaves us tomorrow?"

Chapter XVIII

*B*ernard left then and went to California; but when he arrived there he asked himself why he had come, and was unable to mention any other reason than that he had announced it. He began to feel restless again, and to drift back to that chronic chagrin which had accompanied him through his long journey in the East. He succeeded, however, in keeping these unreasonable feelings at bay for some time, and he strove to occupy himself, to take an interest in Californian problems. Bernard, however, was neither an economist nor a cattle-fancier, and he found that, as the phrase is, there was not a great deal to take hold of. He wandered about, admired the climate and the big peaches, thought a while of going to Japan, and ended by going to Mexico. In this way he passed several months, and justified, in the eyes of other people at

least, his long journey across the Continent. At last he
made it again, in the opposite sense. He went back to
New York, where the summer had already begun, and
here he invented a solution for the difficulty presented
by life to a culpably unoccupied and ill-regulated man.
The solution was not in the least original, and I am
almost ashamed to mention so stale and conventional
a device. Bernard simply hit upon the plan of returning
to Europe. Such as it was, however, he carried it out
with an audacity worthy of a better cause, and was
sensibly happier since he had made up his mind to it.
Gordon Wright and his wife were out of town, but
Bernard went into the country, as boldly as you please,
to inform them of his little project and take a long
leave of them. He had made his arrangements to sail
immediately, and, as at such short notice it was impossible to find good quarters on one of the English
vessels, he had engaged a berth on a French steamer,
which would convey him to Havre. On going down to
Gordon's house in the country, he was conscious of a
good deal of eagerness to know what had become of
that latent irritation of which Blanche had given him
a specimen. Apparently it had quite subsided; Blanche
was wreathed in smiles; she was living in a bower of
roses. Bernard, indeed, had no opportunity for investigating her state of mind, for he found several people
in the house, and Blanche, who had an exalted standard of the duties of a hostess, was occupied in making
life agreeable to her guests, most of whom were gentlemen. She had in this way that great remedy for dissat-
isfaction which Bernard lacked — something interesting to do. Bernard felt a good deal of genuine sadness
in taking leave of Gordon, to whom he contrived to
feel even more kindly than in earlier days. He had quite
forgotten that Gordon was jealous of him — which he
was not, as Bernard said. Certainly, Gordon showed

nothing of it now, and nothing could have been more friendly than their parting. Gordon, also, for a man who was never boisterous, seemed very contented. He was fond of exercising hospitality, and he confessed to Bernard that he was just now in the humor for having his house full of people. Fortune continued to gratify this generous taste; for just as Bernard was coming away another guest made his appearance. The newcomer was none other than the Honorable Augustus Lovelock, who had just arrived in New York, and who, as he added, had long desired to visit the United States. Bernard merely witnessed his arrival, and was struck with the fact that as he presented himself — it seemed quite a surprise — Blanche really stopped chattering.

Chapter XIX

I have called it a stale expedient on Bernard Longueville's part to "go to Europe" again, like the most commonplace American; and it is certain that, as our young man stood and looked out of the window of his inn at Havre, an hour after his arrival at that sea-port, his adventure did not strike him as having any great freshness. He had no plans nor intentions; he had not

even any very definite desires. He had felt the impulse
to come back to Europe, and he had obeyed it; but
now that he had arrived, his impulse seemed to have
little more to say to him. He perceived it, indeed —
mentally — in the attitude of a small street-boy playing
upon his nose with that vulgar gesture which is supposed to represent the elation of successful fraud.
There was a large blank wall before his window, painted
a dirty yellow and much discolored by the weather; a
broad patch of summer sunlight rested upon it and
brought out the full vulgarity of its complexion. Bernard stared a while at this blank wall, which struck him
in some degree as a symbol of his own present moral
prospect. Then suddenly he turned away, with the
declaration that, whatever truth there might be in
symbolism, he, at any rate, had not come to Europe to
spend the precious remnant of his youth in a malodor-
ous Norman sea-port. The weather was very hot, and
neither the hotel nor the town at large appeared to
form an attractive *séjour* for persons of an irritable
nostril. To go to Paris, however, was hardly more attractive than to remain at Havre, for Bernard had a
lively vision of the heated bitumen and the glaring
frontages of the French capital. But if a Norman town
was close and dull, the Norman country was notoriously fresh and entertaining, and the next morning
Bernard got into a calèche, with his luggage, and bade
its proprietor drive him along the coast. Once he had
begun to rumble through this charming landscape, he
was in much better humor with his situation; the air
was freshened by a breeze from the sea; the blooming
country, without walls or fences, lay open to the traveler's eye; the grain-fields and copses were shimmering
in the summer wind; the pink-faced cottages peeped
through the ripening orchard-boughs, and the gray
towers of the old churches were silvered by the morn-

ing-light of France.

At the end of some three hours, Bernard arrived at a little watering-place which lay close upon the shore, in the embrace of a pair of white-armed cliffs. It had a quaint and primitive aspect and a natural picturesqueness which commended it to Bernard's taste. There was evidently a great deal of nature about it, and at this moment, nature, embodied in the clear, gay sunshine, in the blue and quiet sea, in the daisied grass of the high-shouldered downs, had an air of inviting the intelligent observer to postpone his difficulties. Blanquais-les-Galets, as Bernard learned the name of this unfashionable resort to be, was twenty miles from a railway, and the place wore an expression of unaffected rusticity. Bernard stopped at an inn for his noonday breakfast, and then, with his appreciation quickened by the homely felicity of this repast, determined to go no further. He engaged a room at the inn, dismissed his vehicle, and gave himself up to the contemplation of French sea-side manners. These were chiefly to be observed upon a pebbly strand which lay along the front of the village and served as the gathering-point of its idler inhabitants. Bathing in the sea was the chief occupation of these good people, including, as it did, prolonged spectatorship of the process and infinite conversation upon its mysteries. The little world of Blanquais appeared to form a large family party, of highly developed amphibious habits, which sat gossiping all day upon the warm pebbles, occasionally dipping into the sea and drying itself in the sun, without any relaxation of personal intimacy. All this was very amusing to Bernard, who in the course of the day took a bath with the rest. The ocean was, after all, very large, and when one took one's plunge one seemed to have it quite to one's self. When he had dressed himself again, Bernard stretched himself on the beach, feeling happier than he had done in a long time, and pulled his hat over his eyes. The feeling of happiness was an odd one; it had come over him suddenly, without visible cause; but, such as it was, our hero made the most of it. As he lay there it seemed to deepen; his immersion and his exercise in the salt water had given him an agreeable languor. This presently became a drowsiness which was not less agreeable, and Bernard felt himself going to sleep. There were sounds in the air above his head — sounds of the crunching and rattling of the loose, smooth stones as his neighbors moved about on them; of high-pitched French voices exchanging colloquial cries; of the plash of the bathers in the distant water, and the short, soft breaking of the waves. But these things came to his ears more vaguely and remotely, and at last they faded away. Bernard enjoyed half an hour of that light and easy slumber which is apt to overtake idle people in recumbent attitudes in the open air on August afternoons. It brought with it an exquisite sense of rest, and the rest was not spoiled by the fact that it was animated by a charming dream. Dreams are vague things, and this one had the defects of its species; but it was somehow concerned with the image of a young lady whom Bernard had formerly known, and who had beautiful eyes, into which — in the dream — he found himself looking. He waked up to find himself looking into the crown of his hat, which had been resting on the bridge of his nose. He removed it, and half raised himself, resting on his elbow and preparing to taste, in another position, of a little more of that exquisite rest of which mention has just been made. The world about him was still amusing and charming; the chatter of his companions, losing itself in the large sea-presence, the plash of the divers and swimmers, the deep blue of the ocean and the silvery white of the cliff, had that striking air of indifference to the fact that his mind had been absent from them which we are apt to find in mundane things on emerging from a nap. The same people were sitting near him on the beach — the same, and yet not quite the same. He found himself noticing a person whom he had not noticed before — a young lady, who was seated in a low portable chair, some dozen yards off, with her eyes bent upon a book. Her head was in shade; her large parasol made, indeed, an awning for her whole person, which in this way, in the quiet attitude of perusal, seemed to abstract itself from the glare and murmur of the beach. The clear shadow of her umbrella — it was lined with blue — was deep upon her face; but it was not deep enough to prevent Bernard from recognizing a profile that he knew. He suddenly sat upright, with an intensely quickened vision. Was he dreaming still, or had he waked? In a moment he felt that he was acutely awake; he heard her, across the interval, turn the page of her book. For a single instant, as she did so, she looked with level brows at the glittering ocean; then, lowering her eyes, she went on with her reading. In this barely perceptible movement he saw Angela Vivian; it was wonderful how well he remembered her. She was evidently reading very seriously; she was much interested in her book. She was alone; Bernard looked about for her mother, but Mrs. Vivian was not in sight. By this time Bernard had become aware that he was agitated; the exquisite rest of a few moments before had passed away. His agitation struck him as unreasonable; in a few minutes he made up his mind that it was absurd. He had done her an injury — yes; but as she sat there losing herself in a French novel — Bernard could see it was a French novel — he could not make out that she was the worse for it. It had not affected her appearance; Miss Vivian was still a handsome girl. Bernard hoped she would not

look toward him or recognize him; he wished to look
at her at his ease; to think it over; to make up his mind.
The idea of meeting Angela Vivian again had often
come into his thoughts; I may, indeed, say that it was
a tolerably familiar presence there; but the fact, nevertheless, now presented itself with all the violence of an
accident for which he was totally unprepared. He had
often asked himself what he should say to her, how he
should carry himself, and how he should probably find
the young lady; but, with whatever ingenuity he might
at the moment have answered these questions, his
intelligence at present felt decidedly overtaxed. She was
a very pretty girl to whom he had done a wrong; this
was the final attitude into which, with a good deal of
preliminary shifting and wavering, she had settled in
his recollection. The wrong was a right, doubtless, from
certain points of view; but from the girl's own it could
only seem an injury to which its having been inflicted
by a clever young man with whom she had been on
agreeable terms, necessarily added a touch of baseness.

In every disadvantage that a woman suffers at the
hands of a man, there is inevitably, in what concerns
the man, an element of cowardice. When I say "inevitably," I mean that this is what the woman sees in it.
This is what Bernard believed that Angela Vivian saw
in the fact that by giving his friend a bad account of
her he had prevented her making an opulent marriage.
At first he had said to himself that, whether he had
held his tongue or spoken, she had already lost her
chance; but with time, somehow, this reflection had
lost its weight in the scale. It conveyed little re-assur-
ance to his irritated conscience — it had become imponderable and impertinent. At the moment of which
I speak it entirely failed to present itself, even for form's
sake; and as he sat looking at this superior creature who
came back to him out of an episode of his past, he

thought of her simply as an unprotected woman toward whom he had been indelicate. It is not an agreeable thing for a delicate man like Bernard Longueville to have to accommodate himself to such an accident, but this is nevertheless what it seemed needful that he should do. If she bore him a grudge he must think it natural; if she had vowed him a hatred he must allow her the comfort of it. He had done the only thing possible, but that made it no better for her. He had wronged her. The circumstances mattered nothing, and as he could not make it up to her, the only reasonable thing was to keep out of her way. He had stepped into her path now, and the proper thing was to step out of it. If it could give her no pleasure to see him again, it could certainly do him no good to see her. He had seen her by this time pretty well — as far as mere seeing went, and as yet, apparently, he was none the worse for that; but his hope that he should himself escape unperceived had now become acute. It is singular that this hope should not have led him instantly to turn his back and move away; but the explanation of his imprudent delay is simply that he wished to see a little more of Miss Vivian. He was unable to bring himself to the point. Those clever things that he might have said to her quite faded away. The only good taste was to take himself off, and spare her the trouble of inventing civilities that she could not feel. And yet he continued to sit there from moment to moment, arrested, detained, fascinated, by the accident of her not looking round — of her having let him watch her so long. She turned another page, and another, and her reading absorbed her still. He was so near her that he could have touched her dress with the point of his umbrella. At last she raised her eyes and rested them a while on the blue horizon, straight in front of her, but as yet without turning them aside. This, however, augmented the danger of her doing so, and Bernard, with a good deal of an effort, rose to his feet. The effort, doubtless, kept the movement from being either as light or as swift as it might have been, and it vaguely attracted his neighbor's attention. She turned her head and glanced at him, with a glance that evidently expected but to touch him and pass. It touched him, and it was on the point of passing; then it suddenly checked itself; she had recognized him. She looked at him, straight and open-eyed, out of the shadow of her parasol, and Bernard stood there — motionless now — receiving her gaze. How long it lasted need not be narrated. It was probably a matter of a few seconds, but to Bernard it seemed a little eternity. He met her eyes, he looked straight into her face; now that she had seen him he could do nothing else. Bernard's little eternity, however, came to an end; Miss Vivian dropped her eyes upon her book again. She let them rest upon it only a moment; then she closed it and slowly rose from her chair, turning away from Bernard. He still stood looking at her — stupidly, foolishly, helplessly enough, as it seemed to him; no sign of recognition had been exchanged. Angela Vivian hesitated a minute; she now had her back turned to him, and he fancied her light, flexible figure was agitated by her indecision. She looked along the sunny beach which stretched its shallow curve to where the little bay ended and the white wall of the cliffs began. She looked down toward the sea, and up toward the little Casino which was perched on a low embankment, communicating with the beach at two or three points by a short flight of steps. Bernard saw — or supposed he saw — that she was asking herself whither she had best turn to avoid him. He had not blushed when she looked at him — he had rather turned a little pale; but he blushed now, for it really seemed odious to have literally driven the poor girl to bay. Miss Vivian decided to take refuge in the Casino, and she passed along one of the little pathways of planks that were laid here and there across the beach, and directed herself to the nearest flight of steps. Before she had gone two paces a complete change came over Bernard's feeling; his only wish now was to speak to her — to explain — to tell her he would go away. There was another row of steps at a short distance behind him; he rapidly ascended them and reached the little terrace of the Casino. Miss Vivian stood there; she was apparently hesitating again which way to turn. Bernard came straight up to her, with a gallant smile and a greeting. The comparison is a coarse one, but he felt that he was taking the bull by the horns. Angela Vivian stood watching him arrive.

"You didn't recognize me," he said, "and your not recognizing me made me — made me hesitate."

For a moment she said nothing, and then —

"You are more timid than you used to be!" she answered.

He could hardly have said what expression he had expected to find in her face; his apprehension had, perhaps, not painted her obtrusively pale and haughty, aggressively cold and stern; but it had figured something different from the look he encountered. Miss Vivian was simply blushing — that was what Bernard mainly perceived; he saw that her surprise had been extreme — complete. Her blush was re-assuring; it contradicted the idea of impatient resentment, and Bernard took some satisfaction in noting that it was prolonged.

"Yes, I am more timid than I used to be," he said.

In spite of her blush, she continued to look at him very directly; but she had always done that — she always met one's eye; and Bernard now instantly found all the beauty that he had ever found before in her pure, unevasive glance.

"I don't know whether I am more brave," she said; "but I must tell the truth — I instantly recognized you."

"You gave no sign!"

"I supposed I gave a striking one — in getting up and going away."

"Ah!" said Bernard, "as I say, I am more timid than I was, and I didn't venture to interpret that as a sign of recognition."

"It was a sign of surprise."

"Not of pleasure!" said Bernard. He felt this to be a venturesome, and from the point of view of taste perhaps a reprehensible, remark; but he made it because he was now feeling his ground, and it seemed better to make it gravely than with assumed jocosity.

"Great surprises are to me never pleasures," Angela answered; "I am not fond of shocks of any kind. The pleasure is another matter. I have not yet got over my surprise."

"If I had known you were here, I would have written to you beforehand," said Bernard, laughing.

Miss Vivian, beneath her expanded parasol, gave a little shrug of her shoulders.

"Even that would have been a surprise."

"You mean a shock, eh? Did you suppose I was dead?"

Now, at last, she lowered her eyes, and her blush slowly died away.

"I knew nothing about it."

"Of course you couldn't know, and we are all mortal. It was natural that you shouldn't expect — simply on turning your head — to find me lying on the pebbles at Blanquais-les-Galets. You were a great surprise to me, as well; but I differ from you — I like surprises."

"It is rather refreshing to hear that one is a surprise," said the girl.

"Especially when in that capacity one is liked!" Bernard exclaimed.

"I don't say that — because such sensations pass away. I am now beginning to get over mine."

The light mockery of her tone struck him as the echo of an unforgotten air. He looked at her a moment, and then he said —

"You are not changed; I find you quite the same."

"I am sorry for that!" And she turned away.

"What are you doing?" he asked. "Where are you going?"

She looked about her, without answering, up and down the little terrace. The Casino at Blanquais was a much more modest place of reunion than the Conversation-house at Baden-Baden. It was a small, low structure of brightly painted wood, containing but three or four rooms, and furnished all along its front with a narrow covered gallery, which offered a delusive shelter from the rougher moods of the fine, fresh weather. It was somewhat rude and shabby — the subscription for the season was low — but it had a simple picturesqueness. Its little terrace was a very convenient place for a stroll, and the great view of the ocean and of the marble-white crags that formed the broad gate-way of the shallow bay, was a sufficient compensation for the absence of luxuries. There were a few people sitting in the gallery, and a few others scattered upon the terrace; but the pleasure-seekers of Blanquais were, for the most part, immersed in the salt water or disseminated on the grassy downs.

"I am looking for my mother," said Angela Vivian.

"I hope your mother is well."

"Very well, thank you."

"May I help you to look for her?" Bernard asked.

Her eyes paused in their quest, and rested a moment upon her companion.

"She is not here," she said presently. "She has gone home."

"What do you call home?" Bernard demanded.

"The sort of place that we always call home; a bad little house that we have taken for a month."

"Will you let me come and see it?"

"It's nothing to see."

Bernard hesitated a moment.

"Is that a refusal?"

"I should never think of giving it so fine a name."

"There would be nothing fine in forbidding me your door. Don't think that!" said Bernard, with rather a forced laugh.

It was difficult to know what the girl thought; but she said, in a moment —

"We shall be very happy to see you. I am going home."

"May I walk with you so far?" asked Bernard.

"It is not far; it's only three minutes." And Angela moved slowly to the gate of the Casino.

Chapter XX

*B*ernard walked beside her, and for some moments nothing was said between them. As the silence continued, he became aware of it, and it vexed him that she should leave certain things unsaid. She had asked him no question — neither whence he had come, nor how long he would stay, nor what had happened to him since they parted. He wished to see whether this was intention or accident. He was already complaining to himself that she expressed no interest in him, and he was perfectly aware that this was a ridiculous feeling. He had come to speak to her in order to tell her that he was going away, and yet, at the end of five minutes, he had asked leave to come and see her. This sudden gyration of mind was grotesque, and Bernard knew it; but, nevertheless, he had an immense expectation that, if he should give her time, she would manifest some curiosity as to his own situation. He tried to give her time; he held his tongue; but she continued to say nothing. They passed along a sort of winding lane, where two or three fishermen's cottages, with old brown nets suspended on the walls and drying in the sun, stood open to the road, on the other side of which was a patch of salt-looking grass, browsed by a donkey that was not fastidious.

"It's so long since we parted, and we have so much to say to each other!" Bernard exclaimed at last, and he accompanied this declaration with a laugh much more spontaneous than the one he had given a few moments before.

It might have gratified him, however, to observe that his companion appeared to see no ground for joking in the idea that they should have a good deal to say to each other.

"Yes, it's a long time since we spent those pleasant weeks at Baden," she rejoined. "Have you been there again?"

This was a question, and though it was a very simple one, Bernard was charmed with it.

"I wouldn't go back for the world!" he said. "And you?"

"Would I go back? Oh yes; I thought it so agreeable."

With this he was less pleased; he had expected the traces of resentment, and he was actually disappointed at not finding them. But here was the little house of which his companion had spoken, and it seemed, indeed, a rather bad one. That is, it was one of those diminutive structures which are known at French watering-places as "chalets," and, with an exiguity of furniture, are let for the season to families that pride themselves upon their powers of contraction. This one was a very humble specimen of its class, though it was doubtless a not inadequate abode for two quiet and frugal women. It had a few inches of garden, and there were flowers in pots in the open windows, where some extremely fresh white curtains were gently fluttering in the breath of the neighboring ocean. The little door stood wide open.

"This is where we live," said Angela; and she stopped and laid her hand upon the little garden-gate.

"It's very fair," said Bernard. "I think it's better than the pastry-cook's at Baden."

They stood there, and she looked over the gate at the geraniums. She did not ask him to come in; but, on the other hand, keeping the gate closed, she made no movement to leave him. The Casino was now quite out of sight, and the whole place was perfectly still. Suddenly, turning her eyes upon Bernard with a certain strange inconsequence —

"I have not seen you here before," she observed.

He gave a little laugh.

"I suppose it's because I only arrived this morning. I think that if I had been here you would have noticed me."

"You arrived this morning?"

"Three or four hours ago. So, if the remark were not in questionable taste, I should say we had not lost time."

"You may say what you please," said Angela, simply. "Where did you come from?"

Interrogation, now it had come, was most satisfactory, and Bernard was glad to believe that there was an element of the unexpected in his answer.

"From California."

"You came straight from California to this place?"

"I arrived at Havre only yesterday."

"And why did you come here?"

"It would be graceful of me to be able to answer — 'Because I knew you were here.' But unfortunately I did not know it. It was a mere chance; or rather, I feel like saying it was an inspiration."

Angela looked at the geraniums again.

"It was very singular," she said. "We might have been in so many places besides this one. And you might have come to so many places besides this one."

"It is all the more singular, that one of the last persons I saw in America was your charming friend Blanche, who married Gordon Wright. She didn't tell me you were here."

"She had no reason to know it," said the girl. "She is not my friend — as you are her husband's friend."

"Ah no, I don't suppose that. But she might have heard from you."

"She doesn't hear from us. My mother used to write to her for a while after she left Europe, but she has given it up." She paused a moment, and then she added — "Blanche is too silly!"

Bernard noted this, wondering how it bore upon his theory of a spiteful element in his companion. Of course Blanche was silly; but, equally of course, this young lady's perception of it was quickened by Blanche's having married a rich man whom she herself might have married.

"Gordon doesn't think so," Bernard said.

Angela looked at him a moment.

"I am very glad to hear it," she rejoined, gently.

"Yes, it is very fortunate."

"Is he well?" the girl asked. "Is he happy?"

"He has all the air of it."

"I am very glad to hear it," she repeated. And then she moved the latch of the gate and passed in. At the same moment her mother appeared in the open doorway. Mrs. Vivian had apparently been summoned by the sound of her daughter's colloquy with an unrecognized voice, and when she saw Bernard she gave a sharp little cry of surprise. Then she stood gazing at him.

Since the dispersion of the little party at Baden-Baden he had not devoted much meditation to this conscientious gentlewoman who had been so tenderly anxious to establish her daughter properly in life; but

there had been in his mind a tacit assumption that if
Angela deemed that he had played her a trick Mrs.
Vivian's view of his conduct was not more charitable.
He felt that he must have seemed to her very unkind,
and that in so far as a well-regulated conscience per-
mitted the exercise of unpractical passions, she honored him with a superior detestation. The instant he
beheld her on her threshold this conviction rose to the
surface of his consciousness and made him feel that
now, at least, his hour had come.

"It is Mr. Longueville, whom we met at Baden," said
Angela to her mother, gravely.

Mrs. Vivian began to smile, and stepped down
quickly toward the gate.

"Ah, Mr. Longueville," she murmured, "it's so long
— it's so pleasant — it's so strange —"

And suddenly she stopped, still smiling. Her smile
had an odd intensity; she was trembling a little, and
Bernard, who was prepared for hissing scorn, perceived
with a deep, an almost violent, surprise, a touching
agitation, an eager friendliness.

"Yes, it's very long," he said; "it's very pleasant. I have
only just arrived; I met Miss Vivian."

"And you are not coming in?" asked Angela's
mother, very graciously.

"Your daughter has not asked me!" said Bernard.

"Ah, my dearest," murmured Mrs. Vivian, looking
at the girl.

Her daughter returned her glance, and then the elder
lady paused again, and simply began to smile at Bernard, who recognized in her glance that queer little
intimation — shy and cautious, yet perfectly discernible
— of a desire to have a private understanding with what
he felt that she mentally termed his better nature,
which he had more than once perceived at Baden-
Baden.

"Ah no, she has not asked me," Bernard repeated, laughing gently.

Then Angela turned her eyes upon him, and the expression of those fine organs was strikingly agreeable. It had, moreover, the merit of being easily interpreted; it said very plainly, "Please don't insist, but leave me alone." And it said it not at all sharply — very gently and pleadingly. Bernard found himself understanding it so well that he literally blushed with intelligence.

"Don't you come to the Casino in the evening, as you used to come to the Kursaal?" he asked.

Mrs. Vivian looked again at her daughter, who had passed into the door-way of the cottage; then she said —

"We will go this evening."

"I shall look for you eagerly," Bernard rejoined. *"Auf wiedersehen,* as we used to say at Baden!"

Mrs. Vivian waved him a response over the gate, her daughter gave him a glance from the threshold, and he took his way back to his inn.

He awaited the evening with great impatience; he fancied he had made a discovery, and he wished to confirm it. The discovery was that his idea that she bore him a grudge, that she was conscious of an injury, that he was associated in her mind with a wrong, had all been a morbid illusion. She had forgiven, she had forgotten, she didn't care, she had possibly never cared! This, at least, was his theory now, and he longed for a little more light upon it. His old sense of her being a complex and intricate girl had, in that quarter of an hour of talk with her, again become lively, so that he was not absolutely sure his apprehensions had been vain. But, with his quick vision of things, he had got the impression, at any rate, that she had no vulgar resentment of any slight he might have put upon her, or any disadvantage he might have caused her. Her feeling about such a matter would be large and original. Bernard desired to see more of that, and in the evening, in fact, it seemed to him that he did so.

The terrace of the Casino was far from offering the brilliant spectacle of the promenade in front of the gaming-rooms at Baden. It had neither the liberal illumination, the distinguished frequenters, nor the superior music which formed the attraction of that celebrated spot; but it had a modest animation of its own, in which the starlight on the open sea took the place of clustered lamps, and the mighty resonance of the waves performed the function of an orchestra. Mrs. Vivian made her appearance with her daughter, and Bernard, as he used to do at Baden, chose a corner to place some chairs for them. The crowd was small, for most of the visitors had compressed themselves into one of the rooms, where a shrill operetta was being performed by a strolling troupe. Mrs. Vivian's visit was a short one; she remained at the Casino less than half an hour. But Bernard had some talk with Angela. He sat beside her — her mother was on the other side, talking with an old French lady whose acquaintance she had made on the beach. Between Bernard and Angela several things were said. When his friends went away Bernard walked home with them. He bade them good-night at the door of their chalet, and then slowly strolled back to the Casino. The terrace was nearly empty; everyone had gone to listen to the operetta, the sound of whose contemporary gayety came through the open, hot-looking windows in little thin quavers and catches. The ocean was rumbling just beneath; it made a ruder but richer music. Bernard stood looking at it a moment; then he went down the steps to the beach. The tide was rather low; he walked slowly down to the line of the breaking waves. The sea looked huge and black and simple; everything was vague in the unassisted darkness. Bernard stood there some time; there was nothing but the sound and the sharp, fresh smell. Suddenly he put his hand to his heart; it was beating very fast. An immense conviction had come over him — abruptly, then and there — and for a moment he held his breath. It was like a word spoken in the darkness — he held his breath to listen. He was in love with Angela Vivian, and his love was a throbbing passion! He sat down on the stones where he stood — it filled him with a kind of awe.

Chapter XXI

*I*t filled him with a kind of awe, and the feeling was by no means agreeable. It was not a feeling to which even a man of Bernard Longueville's easy power of extracting the savor from a sensation could rapidly habituate himself, and for the rest of that night it was far from making of our hero the happy man that a lover just coming to self-consciousness is supposed to be. It was wrong — it was dishonorable — it was impossible — and yet it *was;* it was, as nothing in his own personal experience had ever been. He seemed hitherto to have been living by proxy, in a vision, in reflection

— to have been an echo, a shadow, a futile attempt; but this at last was life itself, this was a fact, this was reality. For these things one lived; these were the things that people had died for. Love had been a fable before this — doubtless a very pretty one; and passion had been a literary phrase — employed obviously with considerable effect. But now he stood in a personal relation to these familiar ideas, which gave them a very much keener import; they had laid their hand upon him in the darkness, he felt it upon his shoulder, and he knew by its pressure that it was the hand of destiny. What made this sensation a shock was the element that was mixed with it; the fact that it came not simply and singly, but with an attendant shadow in which it immediately merged and lost itself. It was forbidden fruit — he knew it the instant he had touched it. He felt that he had pledged himself *not* to do just this thing which was gleaming before him so divinely — not to widen the crevice, not to open the door that would flood him with light. Friendship and honor were at stake; they stood at his left hand, as his newborn passion stood already at his right; they claimed him as well, and their grasp had a pressure which might become acutely painful. The soul is a still more tender organism than the body, and it shrinks from the prospect of being subjected to violence. Violence — spiritual violence — was what our luxurious hero feared; and it is not too much to say that as he lingered there by the sea, late into the night, while the gurgitation of the waves grew deeper to his ear, the prospect came to have an element of positive terror. The two faces of his situation stood confronting each other; it was a rigid, brutal opposition, and Bernard held his breath for a while with the wonder of what would come of it. He sat a long time upon the beach; the night grew very cold, but he had no sense of it. Then he went away and passed before

the Casino again, and wandered through the village.
The Casino was shrouded in darkness and silence, and
there was nothing in the streets of the little town but
the salt smell of the sea, a vague aroma of fish and the
distant sound of the breakers. Little by little, Bernard
lost the feeling of having been startled, and began to
perceive that he could reason about his trouble.
Trouble it was, though this seems an odd name for the
consciousness of a bright enchantment; and the first
thing that reason, definitely consulted, told him about
the matter was that he had been in love with Angela
Vivian anytime these three years. This sapient faculty
supplied him with further information; only two or
three of the items of which, however, it is necessary to
reproduce. He had been a great fool — an incredible
fool — not to have discovered before this what was the
matter with him! Bernard's sense of his own shrewdness — always tolerably acute — had never received such
a bruise as this present perception that a great many
things had been taking place in his clever mind without his clever mind suspecting them. But it little mattered, his reason went on to declare, what he had
suspected or what he might now feel about it; his
present business was to leave Blanquais-les-Galets at
sunrise the next morning and never rest his eyes upon
Angela Vivian again. This was his duty; it had the merit
of being perfectly plain and definite, easily apprehended, and unattended, as far as he could discover,
with the smallest material difficulties. Not only this,
reason continued to remark; but the moral difficulties
were equally inconsiderable. He had never breathed a
word of his passion to Miss Vivian — quite the contrary;
he had never committed himself nor given her the
smallest reason to suspect his hidden flame; and he was
therefore perfectly free to turn his back upon her — he
could never incur the reproach of trifling with her

affections. Bernard was in that state of mind when it is the greatest of blessings to be saved the distress of choice — to see a straight path before you and to feel that you have only to follow it. Upon the straight path I have indicated, he fixed his eyes very hard; of course he would take his departure at the earliest possible hour on the morrow. There was a streak of morning in the eastern sky by the time he knocked for re-admittance at the door of the inn, which was opened to him by a mysterious old woman in a nightcap and meager accessories, whose identity he failed to ascertain; and he laid himself down to rest — he was very tired — with his attention fastened, as I say, on the idea — on the very image — of departure.

On waking up the next morning, rather late, he found, however, that it had attached itself to a very different object. His vision was filled with the brightness of the delightful fact itself, which seemed to impregnate the sweet morning air and to flutter in the light, fresh breeze that came through his open window from the sea. He saw a great patch of the sea between a couple of red-tiled roofs; it was bluer than any sea had ever been before. He had not slept long — only three or four hours; but he had quite slept off his dread. The shadow had dropped away and nothing was left but the beauty of his love, which seemed to shine in the freshness of the early day. He felt absurdly happy — as if he had discovered El Dorado; quite apart from consequences — he was not thinking of consequences, which of course were another affair — the feeling was intrinsically the finest one he had ever had, and — as a mere feeling — he had not done with it yet. The consideration of consequences could easily be deferred, and there would, meanwhile, be no injury to anyone in his extracting, very quietly, a little subjective joy from the state of his heart. He would let the flower bloom for a day before plucking it up by the roots. Upon this latter course he was perfectly resolved, and in view of such an heroic resolution the subjective interlude appeared no more than his just privilege. The project of leaving Blanquais-les-Galets at nine o'clock in the morning dropped lightly from his mind, making no noise as it fell; but another took its place, which had an air of being still more excellent and which consisted of starting off on a long walk and absenting himself for the day. Bernard grasped his stick and wandered away; he climbed the great shoulder of the further cliff and found himself on the level downs. Here there was apparently no obstacle whatever to his walking as far as his fancy should carry him. The summer was still in a splendid mood, and the hot and quiet day — it was a Sunday — seemed to constitute a deep, silent smile on the face of nature. The sea glistened on one side, and the crops ripened on the other; the larks, losing themselves in the dense sunshine, made it ring here and there in undiscoverable spots; this was the only sound save when Bernard, pausing now and then in his walk, found himself hearing far below him, at the base of the cliff, the drawling murmur of a wave. He walked a great many miles and passed through half a dozen of those rude fishing-hamlets, lodged in some sloping hollow of the cliffs, so many of which, of late years, all along the Norman coast, have adorned themselves with a couple of hotels and a row of bathing-machines. He walked so far that the shadows had begun to lengthen before he bethought himself of stopping; the afternoon had come on and had already begun to wane. The grassy downs still stretched before him, shaded here and there with shallow but windless dells. He looked for the softest place and then flung himself down on the grass; he lay there for a long time, thinking of many things. He had determined to give himself up to a day's happiness; it was happiness of a very harmless kind — the satisfaction of thought, the bliss of mere consciousness; but such as it was it did not elude him nor turn bitter in his heart, and the long summer day closed upon him before his spirit, hovering in perpetual circles round the idea of what *might* be, had begun to rest its wing. When he rose to his feet again it was too late to return to Blanquais in the same way that he had come; the evening was at hand, the light was already fading, and the walk he had taken was one which even if he had not felt very tired, he would have thought it imprudent to attempt to repeat in the darkness. He made his way to the nearest village, where he was able to hire a rustic *carriole*, in which primitive conveyance, gaining the high-road, he jogged and jostled through the hours of the evening slowly back to his starting-point. It wanted an hour of midnight by the time he reached his inn, and there was nothing left for him but to go to bed.

He went in the unshaken faith that he should leave Blanquais early on the morrow. But early on the morrow it occurred to him that it would be simply grotesque to go off without taking leave of Mrs. Vivian and her daughter, and offering them some explanation of his intention. He had given them to understand that, so delighted was he to find them there, he would remain at Blanquais at least as long as they. He must have seemed to them wanting in civility, to spend a whole bright Sunday without apparently troubling his head about them, and if the unlucky fact of his being in love with the girl were a reason for doing his duty, it was at least not a reason for being rude. He had not yet come to that — to accepting rudeness as an incident of virtue; it had always been his theory that virtue had the best manners in the world, and he flattered himself at any rate that he could guard his integrity without making himself ridiculous. So, at what he thought a proper hour, in the course of the morning, he retraced his steps along the little lane through which, two days ago, Angela Vivian had shown him the way to her mother's door. At this humble portal he knocked; the windows of the little chalet were open, and the white curtains, behind the flower-pots, were fluttering as he had seen them before. The door was opened by a neat young woman, who informed him very promptly that Madame and Mademoiselle had left Blanquais a couple of hours earlier. They had gone to Paris — yes, very suddenly, taking with them but little luggage, and they had left her — she had the honor of being the *femme de chambre of ces dames* — to put up their remaining possessions and follow as soon as possible. On Bernard's expressing surprise and saying that he had supposed them to be fixed at the sea-side for the rest of the season, the femme de chambre, who seemed a very intelligent person, begged to remind him that the season was drawing to a close, that Madame had taken the chalet but for five weeks, only ten days of which period were yet to expire, that *ces dames*, as Monsieur perhaps knew, were great travelers, who had been half over the world and thought nothing of breaking camp at an hour's notice, and that, in fine, Madame might very well have received a telegram summoning her to another part of the country.

"And where have the ladies gone?" asked Bernard.

"For the moment, to Paris."

"And in Paris where have they gone?"

"*Dame, chez elles* — to their house," said the femme de chambre, who appeared to think that Bernard asked too many questions.

But Bernard persisted.

"Where is their house?"

The waiting-maid looked at him from head to foot.

"If Monsieur wishes to write, many of Madame's letters come to her banker," she said, inscrutably.

"And who is her banker?"

"He lives in the Rue de Provençe."

"Very good – I will find him out," said our hero, turning away.

The discriminating reader who has been so good as to interest himself in this little narrative will perhaps at this point exclaim with a pardonable consciousness of shrewdness: "Of course he went the next day to the Rue de Provençe!" Of course, yes; only as it happens Bernard did nothing of the kind. He did one of the most singular things he ever did in his life – a thing that puzzled him even at the time, and with regard to which he often afterward wondered whence he had drawn the ability for so remarkable a feat – he simply spent a fortnight at Blanquais-les-Galets. It was a very quiet fortnight; he spoke to no one, he formed no relations, he was company to himself. It may be added that he had never found his own company half so good. He struck himself as a reasonable, delicate fellow, who looked at things in such a way as to make him refrain – refrain successfully, that was the point – from concerning himself practically about Angela Vivian. His saying that he would find out the banker in the Rue de Provençe had been for the benefit of the femme de chambre, whom he thought rather impertinent; he had really no intention whatever of entering that classic thoroughfare. He took long walks, rambled on the beach, along the base of the cliffs and among the brown sea-caves, and he thought a good deal of certain incidents which have figured at an earlier stage of this narrative. He had forbidden himself the future, as an object of contemplation, and it was therefore a matter of necessity that his imagination should take refuge among the warm and familiar episodes of the past. He

wondered why Mrs. Vivian should have left the place
so suddenly, and was of course struck with the analogy
between this incident and her abrupt departure from
Baden. It annoyed him, it troubled him, but it by no
means rekindled the alarm he had felt on first perceiving the injured Angela on the beach. That alarm had
been quenched by Angela's manner during the hour
that followed and during their short talk in the evening. This evening was to be forever memorable, for it
had brought with it the revelation which still, at moments, suddenly made Bernard tremble; but it had also
brought him the assurance that Angela cared as little
as possible for anything that a chance acquaintance
might have said about her. It is all the more singular,
therefore, that one evening, after he had been at Blanquais a fortnight, a train of thought should suddenly
have been set in motion in his mind. It was kindled
by no outward occurrence, but by some wandering
spark of fancy or of memory, and the immediate effect
of it was to startle our hero very much as he had been
startled on the evening I have described. The circumstances were the same; he had wandered down to the
beach alone, very late, and he stood looking at the
duskily-tumbling sea. Suddenly the same voice that
had spoken before murmured another phrase in the
darkness, and it rang upon his ear for the rest of the
night. It startled him, as I have said, at first; then, the
next morning, it led him to take his departure for Paris.
During the journey it lingered in his ear; he sat in the
corner of the railway-carriage with his eyes closed,
abstracted, on purpose to prolong the reverberation. If
it were not true it was at least, as the Italians have it,
ben trovato, and it was wonderful how well it bore
thinking of. It bears telling less well; but I can at least
give a hint of it. The theory that Angela hated him had
evaporated in her presence, and another of a very

different sort had sprung into being. It fitted a great many of the facts, it explained a great many contradictions, anomalies, mysteries, and it accounted for Miss Vivian's insisting upon her mother's leaving Blanquais at a few hours' notice, even better than the theory of her resentment could have done. At any rate, it obliterated Bernard's scruples very effectually, and led him on his arrival in Paris to repair instantly to the Rue de Provençe. This street contains more than one banker, but there is one with whom Bernard deemed Mrs. Vivian most likely to have dealings. He found he had reckoned rightly, and he had no difficulty in procuring her address. Having done so, however, he by no means went immediately to see her; he waited a couple of days – perhaps to give those obliterated scruples I have spoken of a chance to revive. They kept very quiet, and it must be confessed that Bernard took no great pains to recall them to life. After he had been in Paris three days, he knocked at Mrs. Vivian's door.

Chapter XXII

It was opened by the little waiting-maid whom he had

seen at Blanquais, and who looked at him very hard before she answered his inquiry.

"You see I have found Mrs. Vivian's dwelling, though you wouldn't give me the address," Bernard said to her, smiling.

"Monsieur has put some time to it!" the young woman answered dryly. And she informed him that Madame was at home, though Mademoiselle, for whom he had not asked, was not.

Mrs. Vivian occupied a diminutive apartment at the summit of one of the tall white houses which ornament the neighborhood of the Arc de Triomphe. The early days of September had arrived, but Paris was still a city of absentees. The weather was warm and charming, and a certain savor of early autumn in the air was in accord with the somewhat melancholy aspect of the empty streets and closed shutters of this honorable quarter, where the end of the monumental vistas seemed to be curtained with a hazy emanation from the Seine. It was late in the afternoon when Bernard was ushered into Mrs. Vivian's little high-nestling drawing room, and a patch of sunset tints, faintly red, rested softly upon the gilded wall. Bernard had seen these ladies only in borrowed and provisional abodes; but here was a place where they were really living and which was stamped with their tastes, their habits, their charm. The little *salon* was very elegant; it contained a multitude of pretty things, and it appeared to Bernard to be arranged in perfection. The long windows – the ceiling being low, they were really very short – opened upon one of those solid balconies, occupying the width of the apartment, which are often in Paris a compensation for living up five flights of stairs, and this balcony was filled with flowers and cushions. Bernard stepped out upon it to await the coming of Mrs. Vivian, and, as she was not quick to appear, he had time to see that his friends enjoyed a magnificent view. They looked up at the triumphal Arch, which presented itself at a picturesque angle, and near the green tree-tops of the Champs Elysées, beyond which they caught a broad gleam of the Seine and a glimpse, blue in the distance, of the great towers of Notre Dame. The whole vast city lay before them and beneath them, with its ordered brilliancy and its mingled aspect of compression and expansion; and yet the huge Parisian murmur died away before it reached Mrs. Vivian's sky-parlor, which seemed to Bernard the brightest and quietest little habitation he had ever known.

His hostess came rustling in at last; she seemed agitated; she knocked over with the skirt of her dress a little gilded chair which was reflected in the polished *parquet* as in a sheet of looking-glass. Mrs. Vivian had a fixed smile — she hardly knew what to say.

"I found your address at the banker's," said Bernard. "Your maid, at Blanquais, refused to give it to me."

Mrs. Vivian gave him a little look — there was always more or less of it in her face — which seemed equivalent to an entreaty that her interlocutor should spare her.

"Maids are so strange," she murmured; "especially the French!"

It pleased Bernard for the moment not to spare her, though he felt a sort of delight of kindness for her.

"Your going off from Blanquais so suddenly, without leaving me any explanation, any clue, any message of any sort — made me feel at first as if you didn't wish that I should look you up. It reminded me of the way you left Baden — do you remember? — three years ago."

"Baden was so charming — but one couldn't stay forever," said Mrs. Vivian.

"I had a sort of theory one could. Our life was so pleasant that it seemed a shame to break the spell, and if no one had moved I am sure we might be sitting there now."

Mrs. Vivian stared, still with her little fixed smile. "I think we should have had bad weather."

"Very likely," said Bernard, laughing. "Nature would have grown jealous of our good-humor — of our tranquil happiness. And after all, here we are together again — that is, some of us. But I have only my own audacity to thank for it. I was quite free to believe that you were not at all pleased to see me re-appear — and it is only because I am not easy to discourage — am indeed probably a rather impudent fellow — that I have ventured to come here today."

"I am very glad to see you re-appear, Mr. Longueville," Mrs. Vivian declared with the accent of veracity.

"It was your daughter's idea, then, running away from Blanquais?"

Mrs. Vivian lowered her eyes.

"We were obliged to go to Fontainebleau. We have but just come back. I thought of writing to you," she softly added.

"Ah, what pleasure that would have given me!"

"I mean, to tell you where we were, and that we should have been so happy to see you."

"I thank you for the intention. I suppose your daughter wouldn't let you carry it out."

"Angela is so peculiar," Mrs. Vivian said, simply.

"You told me that the first time I saw you."

"Yes, at Siena," said Mrs. Vivian.

"I am glad to hear you speak frankly of that place!"

"Perhaps it's better," Mrs. Vivian murmured. She got up and went to the window; then stepping upon the balcony, she looked down a moment into the street. "She will come back in a moment," she said, coming into the room again. "She has gone to see a friend who lives just beside us. We don't mind about Siena now," she added, softly.

Bernard understood her – understood this to be a retraction of the request she had made of him at Baden.

"Dear little woman," he said to himself, "she wants to marry her daughter still – only now she wants to marry her to me!"

He wished to show her that he understood her, and he was on the point of seizing her hand, to do he didn't know what – to hold it, to press it, to kiss it – when he heard the sharp twang of the bell at the door of the little apartment.

Mrs. Vivian fluttered away.

"It's Angela," she cried, and she stood there waiting and listening, smiling at Bernard, with her handkerchief pressed to her lips.

In a moment the girl came into the drawing room, but on seeing Bernard she stopped, with her hand on the door-knob. Her mother went to her and kissed her.

"It's Mr. Longueville, dearest – he has found us out."

"Found us out?" repeated Angela, with a little laugh. "What a singular expression!"

She was blushing as she had blushed when she first saw him at Blanquais. She seemed to Bernard now to have a great and peculiar brightness – something she had never had before.

"I certainly have been looking for you," he said. "I was greatly disappointed when I found you had taken flight from Blanquais."

"Taken flight?" She repeated his words as she had repeated her mother's. "That is also a strange way of speaking!"

"I don't care what I say," said Bernard, "so long as I make you understand that I have wanted very much to see you again, and that I have wondered every day whether I might venture –"

"I don't know why you shouldn't venture!" she interrupted, giving her little laugh again. "We are not so terrible, are we, mamma? — that is, when once you have climbed our five flights of stairs."

"I came up very fast," said Bernard, "and I find your apartment magnificent."

"Mr. Longueville must come again, must he not, dear?" asked mamma.

"I shall come very often, with your leave," Bernard declared.

"It will be immensely kind," said Angela, looking away.

"I am not sure that you will think it that."

"I don't know what you are trying to prove," said Angela; "first that we ran away from you, and then that we are not nice to our visitors."

"Oh no, not that!" Bernard exclaimed; "for I assure you I shall not care how cold you are with me."

She walked away toward another door, which was masked with a curtain that she lifted.

"I am glad to hear that, for it gives me courage to say that I am very tired, and that I beg you will excuse me."

She glanced at him a moment over her shoulder; then she passed out, dropping the curtain.

Bernard stood there face to face with Mrs. Vivian, whose eyes seemed to plead with him more than ever. In his own there was an excited smile.

"Please don't mind that," she murmured. "I know it's true that she is tired."

"Mind it, dear lady?" cried the young man. "I delight in it. It's just what I like."

"Ah, she's very peculiar!" sighed Mrs. Vivian.

"She is strange — yes. But I think I understand her a little."

"You must come back tomorrow, then."

"I hope to have many tomorrows!" cried Bernard as

he took his departure.

Chapter XXIII

*A*nd he had them in fact. He called the next day at
the same hour, and he found the mother and the
daughter together in their pretty *salon.* Angela was very
gentle and gracious; he suspected Mrs. Vivian had
given her a tender little lecture upon the manner in
which she had received him the day before. After he
had been there five minutes, Mrs. Vivian took a de-
canter of water that was standing upon a table and went
out on the balcony to irrigate her flowers. Bernard
watched her a while from his place in the room; then
she moved along the balcony and out of sight. Some
ten minutes elapsed without her re-appearing, and then
Bernard stepped to the threshold of the window and
looked for her. She was not there, and as he came and
took his seat near Angela again, he announced, rather
formally, that Mrs. Vivian had passed back into one
of the other windows.

Angela was silent a moment — then she said —
"Should you like me to call her?"

She *was* very peculiar — that was very true; yet Bernard held to his declaration of the day before that he now understood her a little.

"No, I don't desire it," he said. "I wish to see you alone; I have something particular to say to you."

She turned her face toward him, and there was something in its expression that showed him that he looked to her more serious than he had ever looked. He sat down again; for some moments he hesitated to go on.

"You frighten me," she said laughing; and in spite of her laugh this was obviously true.

"I assure you my state of mind is anything but formidable. I am afraid of *you*, on the contrary; I am humble and apologetic."

"I am sorry for that," said Angela. "I particularly dislike receiving apologies, even when I know what they are for. What yours are for, I can't imagine."

"You don't dislike me — you don't hate me?" Bernard suddenly broke out.

"You don't ask me that humbly. Excuse me therefore if I say I have other, and more practical, things to do."

"You despise me," said Bernard.

"That is not humble either, for you seem to insist upon it."

"It would be after all a way of thinking of me, and I have a reason for wishing you to do that."

"I remember very well that you used to have a reason for everything. It was not always a good one."

"This one is excellent," said Bernard, gravely. "I have been in love with you for three years."

She got up slowly, turning away.

"Is that what you wished to say to me?"

She went toward the open window, and he followed her.

"I hope it doesn't offend you. I don't say it lightly — it's not a piece of gallantry. It's the very truth of my being. I didn't know it till lately — strange as that may seem. I loved you long before I knew it — before I ventured or presumed to know it. I was thinking of you when I seemed to myself to be thinking of other things. It is very strange — there are things in it I don't understand. I traveled over the world, I tried to interest, to divert myself; but at bottom it was a perfect failure. To see you again — that was what I wanted. When I saw you last month at Blanquais I knew it; then everything became clear. It was the answer to the riddle. I wished to read it very clearly — I wished to be sure; therefore I didn't follow you immediately. I questioned my heart — I cross-questioned it. It has borne the examination, and now I am sure. I am very sure. I love you as my life — I beg you to listen to me!"

She had listened — she had listened intently, looking straight out of the window and without moving.

"You have seen very little of me," she said, presently, turning her illuminated eye on him.

"I have seen enough," Bernard added, smiling. "You must remember that at Baden I saw a good deal of you."

"Yes, but that didn't make you like me. I don't understand."

Bernard stood there a moment, frowning, with his eyes lowered.

"I can imagine that. But I think I can explain."

"Don't explain now," said Angela. "You have said enough; explain some other time." And she went out on the balcony.

Bernard, of course, in a moment was beside her, and, disregarding her injunction, he began to explain.

"I thought I disliked you — but I have come to the conclusion it was just the contrary. In reality I was in love with you. I had been so from the first time I saw you — when I made that sketch of you at Siena."

"That in itself needs an explanation. I was not at all

nice then — I was very rude, very perverse. I was horrid!"

"Ah, you admit it!" cried Bernard, with a sort of quick elation.

She had been pale, but she suddenly blushed.

"Your own conduct was singular, as I remember it. It was not exactly agreeable."

"Perhaps not; but at least it was meant to be. I didn't know how to please you then, and I am far from supposing that I have learned now. But I entreat you to give me a chance."

She was silent a while; her eyes wandered over the great prospect of Paris.

"Do you know how you can please me now?" she said, at last. "By leaving me alone."

Bernard looked at her a moment, then came straight back into the drawing room and took his hat.

"You see I avail myself of the first chance. But I shall come back tomorrow."

"I am greatly obliged to you for what you have said. Such a speech as that deserves to be listened to with consideration. You may come back tomorrow," Angela added.

On the morrow, when he came back, she received him alone.

"How did you know, at Baden, that I didn't like you?" he asked, as soon as she would allow him.

She smiled, very gently.

"You assured me yesterday that you did like me."

"I mean that I supposed I didn't. How did you know that?"

"I can only say that I observed."

"You must have observed very closely, for, superficially, I rather had the air of admiring you," said Bernard.

"It was very superficial."

"You don't mean that; for, after all, that is just what

my admiration, my interest in you, were not. They were deep, they were latent. They were not superficial — they were subterranean."

"You are contradicting yourself, and I am perfectly consistent," said Angela. "Your sentiments were so well hidden that I supposed I displeased you."

"I remember that at Baden, you used to contradict yourself," Bernard answered.

"You have a terrible memory!"

"Don't call it terrible, for it sees everything now in a charming light — in the light of this understanding that we have at last arrived at, which seems to shine backward — to shine full on those Baden days."

"Have we at last arrived at an understanding?" she asked, with a grave directness which Bernard thought the most beautiful thing he had ever seen.

"It only depends upon you," he declared; and then he broke out again into a protestation of passionate tenderness. "Don't put me off this time," he cried. "You have had time to think about it; you have had time to get over the surprise, the shock. I love you, and I offer you everything that belongs to me in this world." As she looked at him with her dark, clear eyes, weighing this precious vow and yet not committing herself — "Ah, you don't forgive me!" he murmured.

She gazed at him with the same solemn brightness. "What have I to forgive you?"

This question seemed to him enchanting. He reached forward and took her hands, and if Mrs. Vivian had come in she would have seen him kneeling at her daughter's feet.

But Mrs. Vivian remained in seclusion, and Bernard saw her only the next time he came.

"I am very happy, because I think my daughter is happy," she said.

"And what do you think of me?"

"I think you are very clever. You must promise me
to be very good to her."

"I am clever enough to promise that."

"I think you are good enough to keep it," said Mrs.
Vivian. She looked as happy as she said, and her happiness gave her a communicative, confidential tendency. "It is very strange how things come about —
how the wheel turns round," she went on. "I suppose
there is no harm in my telling you that I believe she
always cared for you."

"Why didn't you tell me before?" said Bernard, with
almost filial reproachfulness.

"How could I? I don't go about the world offering
my daughter to people — especially to indifferent people."

"At Baden you didn't think I was indifferent. You
were afraid of my not being indifferent enough."

Mrs. Vivian colored.

"Ah, at Baden I was a little too anxious!"

"Too anxious I shouldn't speak to your daughter!"
said Bernard, laughing.

"At Baden," Mrs. Vivian went on, "I had views. But
I haven't any now — I have given them up."

"That makes your acceptance of me very flattering!"
Bernard exclaimed, laughing still more gaily.

"I have something better," said Mrs. Vivian, laying
her fingertips on his arm. "I have confidence."

Bernard did his best to encourage this gracious sentiment, and it seemed to him that there was something
yet to be done to implant it more firmly in Angela's
breast.

"I have a confession to make to you," he said to her
one day. "I wish you would listen to it."

"Is it something very horrible?" Angela asked.

"Something very horrible indeed. I once did you an
injury."

"An injury?" she repeated, in a tone which seemed to reduce the offence to contemptible proportions by simple vagueness of mind about it.

"I don't know what to call it," said Bernard. "A poor service — an ill-turn."

Angela gave a shrug, or rather an imitation of a shrug; for she was not a shrugging person.

"I never knew it."

"I misrepresented you to Gordon Wright," Bernard went on.

"Why do you speak to me of him?" she asked rather sadly.

"Does it displease you?"

She hesitated a little.

"Yes, it displeases me. If your confession has anything to do with him, I would rather not hear it."

Bernard returned to the subject another time — he had plenty of opportunities. He spent a portion of every day in the company of these dear women; and these days were the happiest of his life. The autumn weather was warm and soothing, the *quartier* was still deserted, and the uproar of the great city, which seemed a hundred miles away, reached them through the dense October air with a softened and muffled sound. The evenings, however, were growing cool, and before long they lighted the first fire of the season in Mrs. Vivian's heavily draped little chimneypiece. On this occasion Bernard sat there with Angela, watching the bright crackle of the wood and feeling that the charm of winter nights had begun. These two young persons were alone together in the gathering dusk; it was the hour before dinner, before the lamp had been lighted.

"I insist upon making you my confession," said Bernard. "I shall be very unhappy until you let me do it."

"Unhappy? You are the happiest of men."

"I lie upon roses, if you will; but this memory, this remorse, is a folded rose-leaf. I was completely mistaken about you at Baden; I thought all manner of evil of you — or at least I said it."

"Men are dull creatures," said Angela.

"I think they are. So much so that, as I look back upon that time, there are some things I don't understand even now."

"I don't see why you should look back. People in our position are supposed to look forward."

"You don't like those Baden days yourself," said Bernard. "You don't like to think of them."

"What a wonderful discovery!"

Bernard looked at her a moment in the brightening fire-light.

"What part was it you tried to play there?"

Angela shook her head.

"Men are dull creatures."

"I have already granted that, and I am eating humble pie in asking for an explanation."

"What did you say of me?" Angela asked, after a silence.

"I said you were a coquette. Remember that I am simply historical."

She got up and stood in front of the fire, having her hand on the chimneypiece and looking down at the blaze. For some moments she remained there. Bernard could not see her face.

"I said you were a dangerous woman to marry," he went on deliberately. "I said it because I thought it. I gave Gordon an opinion about you — it was a very unfavorable one. I couldn't make you out — I thought you were playing a double part. I believed that you were ready to marry him, and yet I saw — I thought I saw —" and Bernard paused again.

"What did you see?" and Angela turned toward him.

"That you were encouraging me – playing with me."

"And you didn't like that?"

"I liked it immensely – for myself! But didn't like it for Gordon; and I must do myself the justice to say that I thought more of him than of myself."

"You were an excellent friend," said Angela, simply.

"I believe I was. And I am so still," Bernard added.

She shook her head sadly.

"Poor Mr. Wright!"

"He is a dear good fellow," said Bernard.

"Thoroughly good, and dear, doubtless to his wife, the affectionate Blanche."

"You don't like him – you don't like her," said Bernard.

"Those are two very different matters. I am very sorry for Mr. Wright."

"You needn't be that. He is doing very well."

"So you have already informed me. But I am sorry for him, all the same."

"That doesn't answer my question," Bernard exclaimed, with a certain irritation. "What part were you playing?"

"What part do you think?"

"Haven't I told you I gave it up, long ago?"

Angela stood with her back to the fire, looking at him; her hands were locked behind her.

"Did it ever strike you that my position at Baden was a charming one? – knowing that I had been handed over to you to be put under the microscope – like an insect with a pin stuck through it!"

"How in the world did you know it? I thought we were particularly careful."

"How can a woman help knowing such a thing? She guesses it – she discovers it by instinct; especially if she be a proud woman."

"Ah," said Bernard, "if pride is a source of information, you must be a prodigy of knowledge!"

"I don't know that you are particularly humble!" the girl retorted. "The meekest and most submissive of her sex would not have consented to have such a bargain as that made about her — such a trick played upon her!"

"My dearest Angela, it was no bargain — no trick!" Bernard interposed.

"It was a clumsy trick — it was a bad bargain!" she declared. "At any rate I hated it — I hated the idea of your pretending to pass judgment upon me; of your having come to Baden for the purpose. It was as if Mr. Wright had been buying a horse and you had undertaken to put me through my paces!"

"I undertook nothing — I declined to undertake."

"You certainly made a study of me — and I was determined you should get your lesson wrong. I determined to embarrass, to mislead, to defeat you. Or rather, I didn't determine; I simply obeyed a natural impulse of self-defense — the impulse to evade the fierce light of criticism. I wished to put you in the wrong."

"You did it all very well. You put me admirably in the wrong."

"The only justification for my doing it at all was my doing it well," said Angela.

"You were justified then! You must have hated me fiercely."

She turned her back to him and stood looking at the fire again.

"Yes, there are some things that I did that can be accounted for only by an intense aversion."

She said this so naturally that in spite of a certain theory that was touched upon a few pages back, Bernard was a good deal bewildered. He rose from the sofa where he had been lounging and went and stood beside her a moment. Then he passed his arm round her waist and murmured an almost timorous —

"Really?"

"I don't know what you are trying to make me say!" she answered.

He looked down at her for a moment as he held her close to him.

"I don't see, after all, why I should wish to make you say it. It would only make my remorse more acute."

She was musing, with her eyes on the fire, and for a moment she made no answer; then, as if her attention were returning —

"Are you still talking about your remorse?" she asked.

"You see I put it very strongly."

"That I was a horrid creature?"

"That you were not a woman to marry."

"Ah, my poor Bernard," said Angela, "I can't attempt to prove to you that you are not inconsistent!"

The month of September drew to a close, and she consented to fix a day for their wedding. The last of October was the moment selected, and the selection was almost all that was wanting to Bernard's happiness. I say "almost," for there was a solitary spot in his consciousness which felt numb and dead — unpervaded by the joy with which the rest of his spirit seemed to thrill and tingle. The removal of this hard grain in the sweet savor of life was needed to complete his felicity. Bernard felt that he had made the necessary excision when, at the end of the month, he wrote to Gordon Wright of his engagement. He had been putting off the performance of this duty from day to day — it seemed so hard to accomplish it gracefully. He did it at the end very briefly; it struck him that this was the best way. Three days after he had sent his letter there arrived one from Gordon himself, informing

Bernard that he had suddenly determined to bring
Blanche to Europe. She was not well, and they would
lose no time. They were to sail within a week after his
writing. The letter contained a postscript — "Captain
Lovelock comes with us."

Chapter XXIV

*B*ernard prepared for Gordon's arrival in Paris,
which, according to his letter, would take place in a
few days. He was not intending to stop in England;
Blanche desired to proceed immediately to the French
capital, to confer with her man-milliner, after which it
was probable that they would go to Italy or to the East
for the winter. "I have given her a choice of Rome or
the Nile," said Gordon, "but she tells me she doesn't
care a fig where we go."

I say that Bernard prepared to receive his friends,
and I mean that he prepared morally — or even intel-
lectually. Materially speaking, he could simply hold
himself in readiness to engage an apartment at a hotel
and to go to meet them at the station. He expected to
hear from Gordon as soon as this interesting trio
should reach England, but the first notification he

received came from a Parisian hotel. It came to him in the shape of a very short note, in the morning, shortly before lunch, and was to the effect that his friends had alighted in the Rue de la Paix the night before.

"We were tired, and I have slept late," said Gordon; "otherwise you should have heard from me earlier. Come to lunch, if possible. I want extremely to see you."

Bernard, of course, made a point of going to lunch. In as short a time as possible he found himself in Gordon's sitting room at the Hotel Middlesex. The table was laid for the midday repast, and a gentleman stood with his back to the door, looking out of the window. As Bernard came in, this gentleman turned and exhibited the ambrosial beard, the symmetrical shape, the monocular appendage, of Captain Lovelock.

The Captain screwed his glass into his eye, and greeted Bernard in his usual fashion — that is, as if he had parted with him overnight.

"Oh, good morning! Beastly morning, isn't it? I suppose you are come to luncheon — I have come to luncheon. It ought to be on table, you know — it's nearly two o'clock. But I dare say you have noticed foreigners are never punctual — it's only English servants that are punctual. And they don't understand luncheon, you know — they can't make out our eating at this sort of hour. You know they always dine so beastly early. Do you remember the sort of time they used to dine at Baden? — half-past five, half-past six; some unearthly hour of that kind. That's the sort of time you dine in America. I found they'd invite a man at half-past six. That's what I call being in a hurry for your food. You know they always accuse the Americans of making a rush for their victuals. I am bound to say that in New York, and that sort of place, the victuals were very good when you got them. I hope you don't mind my saying anything about America? You know the Americans are so deucedly thin-skinned — they always bristle up if you say anything against their institutions. The English don't care a rap what you say — they've got a different sort of temper, you know. With the Americans I'm deuced careful — I never breathe a word about anything. While I was over there I went in for being complimentary. I laid it on thick, and I found they would take all I could give them. I didn't see much of their institutions, after all; I went in for seeing the people. Some of the people were charming — upon my soul, I was surprised at some of the people. I dare say you know some of the people I saw; they were as nice people as you would see anywhere. There were always a lot of people about Mrs. Wright, you know; they told me they were all the best people. You know she is always late for everything. She always comes in after everyone is there — looking so devilish pretty, pulling on her gloves. She wears the longest gloves I ever saw in my life. Upon my word, if they don't come, I think I will ring the bell and ask the waiter what's the matter. Wouldn't you ring the bell? It's a great mistake, their trying to carry out their ideas of lunching. That's Wright's character, you know; he's always trying to carry out some idea. When I am abroad, I go in for the foreign breakfast myself. You may depend upon it they had better give up trying to do this sort of thing at this hour."

Captain Lovelock was more disposed to conversation than Bernard had known him before. His discourse of old had been languid and fragmentary, and our hero had never heard him pursue a train of ideas through so many involutions. To Bernard's observant eye, indeed, the Captain was an altered man. His manner betrayed a certain restless desire to be agreeable, to anticipate judgment – a disposition to smile, and be civil, and entertain his auditor, a tendency to move about and look out of the window and at the clock. He struck Bernard as a trifle nervous – as less solidly planted on his feet than when he lounged along the Baden gravel-walks by the side of his usual companion – a lady for whom, apparently, his admiration was still considerable. Bernard was curious to see whether he would ring the bell to inquire into the delay attending the service of lunch; but before this sentiment, rather idle under the circumstances, was gratified, Blanche passed into the room from a neighboring apartment. To Bernard's perception Blanche, at least, was always Blanche; she was a person in whom it would not have occurred to him to expect any puzzling variation, and the tone of her little, soft, thin voice instantly rang in his ear like an echo of yesterday's talk. He had already remarked to himself that after however long an interval one might see Blanche, she re-appeared with an air of familiarity. This was in some sense, indeed, a proof of the agreeable impression she made, and she looked exceedingly pretty as she now suddenly stopped on seeing our two gentlemen, and gave a little cry of surprise.

"Ah! I didn't know you were here. They never told me. Have you been waiting a long time? How d' ye do? You must think we are polite." She held out her hand to Bernard, smiling very graciously. At Captain Lovelock she barely glanced. "I hope you are very well," she went on to Longueville; "but I needn't ask that. You're as blooming as a rose. What in the world has happened to you? You look so brilliant – so fresh. Can you say that to a man – that he looks fresh? Or can you only say that about butter and eggs?"

"It depends upon the man," said Captain Lovelock. "You can't say that a man's fresh who spends his time in running about after *you!*"

"Ah, are you here?" cried Blanche with another little cry of surprise. "I didn't notice you — I thought you were the waiter. This is what he calls running about after me," she added, to Bernard; "coming to breakfast without being asked. How queerly they have arranged the table!" she went on, gazing with her little elevated eyebrows at this piece of furniture. "I always thought that in Paris, if they couldn't do anything else, they could arrange a table. I don't like that at all — those horrid little dishes on each side! Don't you think those things ought to be off the table, Mr. Longueville? I don't like to see a lot of things I'm not eating. And I told them to have some flowers — pray, where are the flowers? Do they call those things flowers? They look as if they had come out of the landlady's bonnet! Mr. Longueville, do look at those objects."

"They are not like me — they are not very fresh," laughed Bernard.

"It's no great matter — we have not got to eat them," growled Captain Lovelock.

"I should think you would expect to — with the luncheon you usually make!" rejoined Blanche. "Since you are here, though I didn't ask you, you might as well make yourself useful. Will you be so good as to ring the bell? If Gordon expects that we are going to wait another quarter of an hour for him he exaggerates the patience of a long-suffering wife. If you are very curious to know what he is about, he is writing letters, by way of a change. He writes about eighty a day; his correspondents must be strong people! It's a lucky thing for me that I am married to Gordon; if I were not he might write to me — to me, to whom it's a misery to have to answer even an invitation to dinner! To begin with, I don't know how to spell. If Captain Lovelock ever boasts that he has had letters from me, you may know it's an invention. He has never had anything but telegrams — three telegrams — that I sent him in America about a pair of slippers that he had left at our house and that I didn't know what to do with. Captain Lovelock's slippers are no trifle to have on one's hands — on one's feet, I suppose I ought to say. For telegrams the spelling doesn't matter; the people at the office correct it — or if they don't you can put it off on them. I never see anything nowadays but Gordon's back," she went on, as they took their places at table — "his noble broad back, as he sits writing his letters. That's my principal view of my husband. I think that now we are in Paris I ought to have a portrait of it by one of the great artists. It would be such a characteristic pose. I have quite forgotten his face and I don't think I should know it."

Gordon's face, however, presented itself just at this moment; he came in quickly, with his countenance flushed with the pleasure of meeting his old friend again. He had the sun-scorched look of a traveler who has just crossed the Atlantic, and he smiled at Bernard with his honest eyes.

"Don't think me a great brute for not being here to receive you," he said, as he clasped his hand. "I was writing an important letter and I put it to myself in this way: 'If I interrupt my letter I shall have to come back and finish it; whereas if I finish it now, I can have all the rest of the day to spend with him.' So I stuck to it to the end, and now we can be inseparable."

"You may be sure Gordon reasoned it out," said Blanche, while her husband offered his hand in silence to Captain Lovelock.

"Gordon's reasoning is as fine as other people's feeling!" declared Bernard, who was conscious of a desire to say something very pleasant to Gordon, and who did not at all approve of Blanche's little ironical tone about her husband.

"And Bernard's compliments are better than either," said Gordon, laughing and taking his seat at table.

"I have been paying him compliments," Blanche went on. "I have been telling him he looks so brilliant, so blooming — as if something had happened to him, as if he had inherited a fortune. He must have been doing something very wicked, and he ought to tell us all about it, to amuse us. I am sure you are a dreadful Parisian, Mr. Longueville. Remember that we are three dull, virtuous people, exceedingly bored with each other's society, and wanting to hear something strange and exciting. If it's a little improper, that won't spoil it."

"You certainly are looking uncommonly well," said Gordon, still smiling, across the table, at his friend. "I see what Blanche means —"

"My dear Gordon, that's a great event," his wife interposed.

"It's a good deal to pretend, certainly," he went on, smiling always, with his red face and his blue eyes. "But this is no great credit to me, because Bernard's superb condition would strike anyone. You look as if you were going to marry the Lord Mayor's daughter!"

If Bernard was blooming, his bloom at this juncture must have deepened, and in so doing indeed have contributed an even brighter tint to his expression of salubrious happiness. It was one of the rare occasions of his life when he was at a loss for a verbal expedient.

"It's a great match," he nevertheless murmured, jestingly. "You must excuse my inflated appearance."

"It has absorbed you so much that you have had no time to write to me," said Gordon. "I expected to hear from you after you arrived."

"I wrote to you a fortnight ago — just before receiving your own letter. You left New York before my letter reached it."

"Ah, it will have crossed us," said Gordon. "But now that we have your society I don't care. Your letters, of course, are delightful, but that is still better."

In spite of this sympathetic statement Bernard cannot be said to have enjoyed his lunch; he was thinking of something else that lay before him and that was not agreeable. He was like a man who has an acrobatic feat to perform — a wide ditch to leap, a high pole to climb — and who has a presentiment of fractures and bruises. Fortunately he was not obliged to talk much, as Mrs. Gordon displayed even more than her usual vivacity, rendering her companions the graceful service of lifting the burden of conversation from their shoulders.

"I suppose you were surprised to see us rushing out here so suddenly," she observed in the course of the repast. "We had said nothing about it when you last saw us, and I believe we are supposed to tell you everything, ain't we? I certainly have told you a great many things, and there are some of them I hope you haven't repeated. I have no doubt you have told them all over Paris, but I don't care what you tell in Paris — Paris isn't so easily shocked. Captain Lovelock doesn't repeat what I tell him; I set him up as a model of discretion. I have told him some pretty bad things, and he has liked them so much he has kept them all to himself. I say my bad things to Captain Lovelock, and my good things to other people; he doesn't know the difference and he is perfectly content."

"Other people as well often don't know the difference," said Gordon, gravely. "You ought always to tell us which are which."

Blanche gave her husband a little impertinent stare.

"When I am not appreciated," she said, with an attempt at superior dryness, "I am too proud to point it out. I don't know whether you know that I'm

proud," she went on, turning to Gordon and glancing
at Captain Lovelock; "it's a good thing to know. I
suppose Gordon will say that I ought to be too proud
to point *that* out; but what are you to do when no one
has any imagination? You have a grain or two, Mr.
Longueville; but Captain Lovelock hasn't a speck. As
for Gordon, *je n'en parle pas!* But even you, Mr. Longueville, would never imagine that I am an interesting
invalid — that we are traveling for my delicate health.
The doctors haven't given me up, but I have given them
up. I know I don't look as if I were out of health; but
that's because I always try to look my best. My appearance proves nothing — absolutely nothing. Do you
think my appearance proves anything, Captain
Lovelock?"

Captain Lovelock scrutinized Blanche's appearance
with a fixed and solemn eye; and then he replied —

"It proves you are very lovely."

Blanche kissed her fingertips to him in return for
this compliment.

"You only need to give Captain Lovelock a chance,"
she rattled on, "and he is as clever as anyone. That's
what I like to do to my friends — I like to make chances
for them. Captain Lovelock is like my dear little blue
terrier that I left at home. If I hold out a stick he will
jump over it. He won't jump without the stick; but as
soon as I produce it he knows what he has to do. He
looks at it a moment and then he gives his little hop.
He knows he will have a lump of sugar, and Captain
Lovelock expects one as well. Dear Captain Lovelock,
shall I ring for a lump? Wouldn't it be touching?
Garçon, un morceau de sucre pour Monsieur le Capitaine!
But what I give Monsieur le Capitaine is *moral* sugar!
I usually administer it in private, and he shall have a
good big morsel when you go away."

Gordon got up, turning to Bernard and looking at

his watch.

"Let us go away, in that case," he said, smiling, "and leave Captain Lovelock to receive his reward. We will go and take a walk; we will go up the Champs Elysées. Good morning, Monsieur le Capitaine."

Neither Blanche nor the Captain offered any opposition to this proposal, and Bernard took leave of his hostess and joined Gordon, who had already passed into the antechamber.

Chapter XXV

Gordon took his arm and they gained the street; they strolled in the direction of the Champs Elysées.

"For a little exercise and a good deal of talk, it's the pleasantest place," said Gordon. "I have a good deal to say; I have a good deal to ask you."

Bernard felt the familiar pressure of his friend's hand, as it rested on his arm, and it seemed to him never to have lain there with so heavy a weight. It held him fast — it held him to account; it seemed a physical symbol of responsibility. Bernard was not reassured by hearing that Gordon had a great deal to say, and he expected a sudden explosion of bitterness on the subject of Blanche's irremediable triviality. The afternoon was a lovely one — the day was a perfect example of the mellowest mood of autumn. The air was warm and filled with a golden haze, which seemed to hang about the bare Parisian trees, as if with a tender impulse to drape their nakedness. A fine day in Paris brings out a wonderfully bright and appreciative multitude of strollers and loungers, and the liberal spaces of the Champs Elysées were on this occasion filled with those placid votaries of inexpensive entertainment who abound in the French capital. The benches and chairs on the edge of the great avenue exhibited a dense fraternity of gazers, and up and down the broad walk passed the slow-moving and easily pleased pedestrians. Gordon, in spite of his announcement that he had a good deal to say, confined himself at first to superficial allusions, and Bernard after a while had the satisfaction of perceiving that he was not likely, for the moment, to strike the note of conjugal discord. He appeared, indeed, to feel no desire to speak of Blanche in any manner whatever. He fell into the humor of the hour and the scene, looked at the crowd, talked about trifles. He remarked that Paris was a wonderful place after all, and that a little glimpse of the Parisian picture was a capital thing as a change; said he was very glad they had come, and that for his part he was willing to stay three months.

"And what have you been doing with yourself?" he asked. "How have you been occupied, and what are you meaning to do?"

Bernard said nothing for a moment, and Gordon presently glanced at his face to see why he was silent. Bernard, looking askance, met his companion's eyes, and then, resting his own upon them, he stopped short. His heart was beating; it was a question of saying to

Gordon outright, "I have been occupied in becoming engaged to Angela Vivian." But he couldn't say it, and yet he must say something. He tried to invent something; but he could think of nothing, and still Gordon was looking at him.

"I am so glad to see you!" he exclaimed, for want of something better; and he blushed — he felt foolish, he felt false — as he said it.

"My dear Bernard!" Gordon murmured gratefully, as they walked on. "It's very good of you to say that; I am very glad we are together again. I want to say something," he added, in a moment; "I hope you won't mind it —" Bernard gave a little laugh at his companion's scruples, and Gordon continued. "To tell the truth, it has sometimes seemed to me that we were not so good friends as we used to be — that something had come between us — I don't know what, I don't know why. I don't know what to call it but a sort of lowering of the temperature. I don't know whether you have felt it, or whether it has been simply a fancy of mine. Whatever it may have been, it's all over, isn't it? We are too old friends — too good friends — not to stick together. Of course, the rubs of life may occasionally loosen the cohesion; but it is very good to feel that, with a little direct contact, it may easily be re-established. Isn't that so? But we shouldn't reason about these things; one feels them, and that's enough."

Gordon spoke in his clear, cheerful voice, and Bernard listened intently. It seemed to him there was an undertone of pain and effort in his companion's speech; it was that of an unhappy man trying to be wise and make the best of things.

"Ah, the rubs of life — the rubs of life!" Bernard repeated vaguely.

"We mustn't mind them," said Gordon, with a conscientious laugh. "We must toughen our hides; or, at the worst, we must plaster up our bruises. But why should we choose this particular place and hour for talking of the pains of life?" he went on. "Are we not in the midst of its pleasures? I mean, henceforth, to cultivate its pleasures. What are yours, just now, Bernard? Isn't it supposed that in Paris one must amuse one's self? How have you been amusing yourself?"

"I have been leading a very quiet life," said Bernard.

"I notice that's what people always say when they have been particularly dissipated. What have you done? Whom have you seen that one knows?"

Bernard was silent a moment.

"I have seen some old friends of yours," he said at last. "I have seen Mrs. Vivian and her daughter."

"Ah!" Gordon made this exclamation, and then stopped short. Bernard looked at him, but Gordon was looking away; his eyes had caught some one in the crowd. Bernard followed the direction they had taken, and then Gordon went on: "Talk of the devil — excuse the adage! Are not those the ladies in question?"

Mrs. Vivian and her daughter were, in fact, seated among a great many other quiet people, in a couple of hired chairs, at the edge of the great avenue. They were turned toward our two friends, and when Bernard distinguished them, in the well-dressed multitude, they were looking straight at Gordon Wright.

"They see you!" said Bernard.

"You say that as if I wished to run away," Gordon answered. "I don't want to run away; on the contrary, I want to speak to them."

"That's easily done," said Bernard, and they advanced to the two ladies.

Mrs. Vivian and her daughter rose from their chairs as they came; they had evidently rapidly exchanged observations, and had decided that it would facilitate their interview with Gordon Wright to receive him standing. He made his way to them through the crowd, blushing deeply, as he always did when excited; then he stood there bare-headed, shaking hands with each of them, with a fixed smile, and with nothing, apparently, to say. Bernard watched Angela's face; she was giving his companion a beautiful smile. Mrs. Vivian was delicately cordial.

"I was sure it was you," said Gordon at last. "We were just talking of you."

"Did Mr. Longueville deny it was we?" asked Mrs. Vivian, archly; "after we had supposed that we had made an impression on him!"

"I knew you were in Paris — we were in the act of talking of you," Gordon went on. "I am very glad to see you."

Bernard had shaken hands with Angela, looking at her intently; and in her eyes, as his own met them, it seemed to him that there was a gleam of mockery. At whom was she mocking — at Gordon, or at himself? Bernard was uncomfortable enough not to care to be mocked; but he felt even more sorry that Gordon should be.

"We also knew you were coming — Mr. Longueville had told us," said Mrs. Vivian; "and we have been expecting the pleasure of seeing Blanche. Dear little Blanche!"

"Dear little Blanche will immediately come and see you," Gordon replied.

"Immediately, we hope," said Mrs. Vivian. "We shall be so very glad." Bernard perceived that she wished to say something soothing and sympathetic to poor Gordon; having it, as he supposed, on her conscience that, after having once encouraged him to regard himself as indispensable (in the capacity of son-in-law) to her happiness, she should now present to him the spectacle of a felicity which had established itself without his aid. "We were so very much interested in your marriage," she went on. "We thought it so — so delightful."

Gordon fixed his eyes on the ground for a moment. "I owe it partly to you," he answered. "You had done so much for Blanche. You had so cultivated her mind and polished her manners that her attractions were doubled, and I fell an easy victim to them."

He uttered these words with an exaggerated solemnity, the result of which was to produce, for a moment, an almost embarrassing silence. Bernard was rapidly becoming more and more impatient of his own embarrassment, and now he exclaimed, in a loud and jovial voice —

"Blanche makes victims by the dozen! I was a victim last winter; we are all victims!"

"Dear little Blanche!" Mrs. Vivian murmured again.

Angela had said nothing; she had simply stood there, making no attempt to address herself to Gordon, and yet with no affectation of reserve or of indifference. Now she seemed to feel the impulse to speak to him.

"When Blanche comes to see us, you must be sure to come with her," she said, with a friendly smile.

Gordon looked at her, but he said nothing.

"We were so sorry to hear she is out of health," Angela went on.

Still Gordon was silent, with his eyes fixed on her expressive and charming face.

"It is not serious," he murmured at last.

"She used to be so well — so bright," said Angela, who also appeared to have the desire to say something kind and comfortable.

Gordon made no response to this; he only looked at her.

"I hope you are well, Miss Vivian," he broke out at last.

"Very well, thank you."

"Do you live in Paris?"

"We have pitched our tent here for the present."

"Do you like it?"

"I find it no worse than other places."

Gordon appeared to desire to talk with her; but he could think of nothing to say. Talking with her was a pretext for looking at her; and Bernard, who thought she had never been so handsome as at that particular moment, smiling at her troubled ex-lover, could easily conceive that his friend should desire to prolong this privilege.

"Have you been sitting here long?" Gordon asked, thinking of something at last.

"Half an hour. We came out to walk, and my mother felt tired. It is time we should turn homeward," Angela added.

"Yes, I am tired, my daughter. We must take a *voiture*, if Mr. Longueville will be so good as to find us one," said Mrs. Vivian.

Bernard, professing great alacrity, looked about him; but he still lingered near his companions. Gordon had thought of something else. "Have you been to Baden again?" Bernard heard him ask. But at this moment Bernard espied at a distance an empty hackney-carriage crawling up the avenue, and he was obliged to go and signal to it. When he came back, followed by the vehicle, the two ladies, accompanied by Gordon, had come to the edge of the pavement. They shook hands with Gordon before getting into the cab, and Mrs. Vivian exclaimed —

"Be sure you give our love to your dear wife!"

Then the two ladies settled themselves and smiled their adieux, and the little victoria rumbled away at an easy pace, while Bernard stood with Gordon, looking after it. They watched it a moment, and then Gordon turned to his companion. He looked at Bernard for some moments intently, with a singular expression.

"It is strange for me to see her!" he said, presently.

"I hope it is not altogether disagreeable," Bernard answered smiling.

"She is delightfully handsome," Gordon went on.

"She is a beautiful woman."

"And the strange thing is that she strikes me now so differently," Gordon continued. "I used to think her so mysterious — so ambiguous. She seems to be now so simple."

"Ah," said Bernard, laughing, "that's an improvement!"

"So simple and so good!" Gordon exclaimed.

Bernard laid his hand on his companion's shoulder, shaking his head slowly.

"You must not think too much about that," he said.

"So simple — so good — so charming!" Gordon repeated.

"Ah, my dear Gordon!" Bernard murmured.

But still Gordon continued.

"So intelligent, so reasonable, so sensible."

"Have you discovered all that in two minutes' talk?"

"Yes, in two minutes' talk. I shouldn't hesitate about her now!"

"It's better you shouldn't say that," said Bernard.

"Why shouldn't I say it? It seems to me it's my duty to say it."

"No — your duty lies elsewhere," said Bernard. "There are two reasons. One is that you have married another woman."

"What difference does that make?" cried Gordon.

Bernard made no attempt to answer this inquiry; he simply went on —

"The other is — the other is —"

But here he paused.

"What is the other?" Gordon asked.

"That I am engaged to marry Miss Vivian."

And with this Bernard took his hand off Gordon's shoulder.

Gordon stood staring.

"To marry Miss Vivian?"

Now that Bernard had heard himself say it, audibly, distinctly, loudly, the spell of his apprehension seemed broken, and he went on bravely.

"We are to be married very shortly. It has all come about within a few weeks. It will seem to you very strange — perhaps you won't like it. That's why I have hesitated to tell you."

Gordon turned pale; it was the first time Bernard had ever seen him do so; evidently he did not like it. He stood staring and frowning.

"Why, I thought — I thought," he began at last — "I thought that you disliked her!"

"I supposed so, too," said Bernard. "But I have got over that."

Gordon turned away, looking up the great avenue into the crowd. Then turning back, he said —

"I am very much surprised."

"And you are not pleased!"

Gordon fixed his eyes on the ground a moment.

"I congratulate you on your engagement," he said at last, looking up with a face that seemed to Bernard hard and unnatural.

"It is very good of you to say that, but of course you can't like it! I was sure you wouldn't like it. But what could I do? I fell in love with her, and I couldn't run away simply to spare you a surprise. My dear Gordon," Bernard added, "you will get used to it."

"Very likely," said Gordon, dryly. "But you must give me time."

"As long as you like!"

Gordon stood for a moment again staring down at

the ground.

"Very well, then, I will take my time," he said. "Goodbye!"

And he turned away, as if to walk off alone.

"Where are you going?" asked Bernard, stopping him.

"I don't know — to the hotel, anywhere. To try to get used to what you have told me."

"Don't try too hard; it will come of itself," said Bernard.

"We shall see!"

And Gordon turned away again.

"Do you prefer to go alone?"

"Very much — if you will excuse me!"

"I have asked you to excuse a greater want of ceremony!" said Bernard, smiling.

"I have not done so yet!" Gordon rejoined; and marching off, he mingled with the crowd.

Bernard watched him till he lost sight of him, and then, dropping into the first empty chair that he saw, he sat and reflected that his friend liked it quite as little as he had feared.

Chapter XXVI

*B*ernard sat thinking for a long time; at first with a good deal of mortification — at last with a good deal of bitterness. He felt angry at last; but he was not angry with himself. He was displeased with poor Gordon, and with Gordon's displeasure. He was uncomfortable, and he was vexed at his discomfort. It formed, it seemed to him, no natural part of his situation; he had had no glimpse of it in the book of fate where he registered on a fair blank page his betrothal to a charming girl. That Gordon should be surprised, and even a little shocked and annoyed — this was his right and his privilege; Bernard had been prepared for that, and had determined to make the best of it. But it must not go too far; there were limits to the morsel of humble pie that he was disposed to swallow. Something in Gordon's air and figure, as he went off in a huff, looking vicious and dangerous — yes, that was positively his look — left a sinister impression on Bernard's mind, and, after a while, made him glad to take refuge in being angry. One would like to know what Gordon expected, *par exemple!* Did he expect Bernard to give up

Angela simply to save him a shock; or to back out of his engagement by way of an ideal reparation? No, it was too absurd, and, if Gordon had a wife of his own, why in the name of justice should not Bernard have one?

Being angry was a relief, but it was not exactly a solution, and Bernard, at last, leaving his place, where for an hour or two he had been absolutely unconscious of everything that went on around him, wandered about for some time in deep restlessness and irritation. At one moment he thought of going back to Gordon's hotel, to see him, to explain. But then he became aware that he was too angry for that – to say nothing of Gordon's being too angry also; and, moreover, that there was nothing to explain. He was to marry Angela Vivian; that was a very simple fact – it needed no explanation. Was it so wonderful, so inconceivable, an incident so unlikely to happen? He went, as he always did on Sunday, to dine with Mrs. Vivian, and it seemed to him that he perceived in the two ladies some symptoms of a discomposure which had the same origin as his own. Bernard, on this occasion, at dinner, failed to make himself particularly agreeable; he ate fast – as if he had no idea what he was eating, and talked little; every now and then his eyes rested for some time upon Angela, with a strange, eagerly excited expression, as if he were looking her over and trying to make up his mind about her afresh. This young lady bore his inscrutable scrutiny with a deal of superficial composure; but she was also silent, and she returned his gaze, from time to time, with an air of unusual anxiety. She was thinking, of course, of Gordon, Bernard said to himself; and a woman's first meeting, in after years, with an ex-lover must always make a certain impression upon her. Gordon, however, had never been a lover, and if Bernard noted Angela's gravity it was not because he felt jealous. "She is simply sorry for him," he said to himself; and by the time he had finished his dinner it began to come back to him that he was sorry, too. Mrs. Vivian was probably sorry as well, for she had a slightly confused and preoccupied look — a look from which, even in the midst of his chagrin, Bernard extracted some entertainment. It was Mrs. Vivian's intermittent conscience that had been reminded of one of its lapses; her meeting with Gordon Wright had recalled the least exemplary episode of her life — the time when she whispered mercenary counsel in the ear of a daughter who sat, grave and pale, looking at her with eyes that wondered. Mrs. Vivian blushed a little now, when she met Bernard's eyes; and to remind herself that she was after all a virtuous woman, talked as much as possible about superior and harmless things — the beauty of the autumn weather, the pleasure of seeing French papas walking about on Sunday with their progeny in their hands, the peculiarities of the pulpit-oratory of the country as exemplified in the discourse of a Protestant *pasteur* whom she had been to hear in the morning.

When they rose from table and went back into her little drawing room, she left her daughter alone for awhile with Bernard. The two were standing together before the fire; Bernard watched Mrs. Vivian close the door softly behind her. Then, looking for a moment at his companion —

"He is furious!" he announced at last.

"Furious?" said Angela. "Do you mean Mr. Wright?"

"The amiable, reasonable Gordon. He takes it very hard."

"Do you mean about me?" asked Angela.

"It's not with you he's furious, of course; it is with me. He won't let me off easily."

Angela looked for a moment at the fire.

"I am very sorry for him," she said, at last.

"It seems to me I am the one to be pitied," said Bernard; "and I don't see what compassion you, of all people in the world, owe him."

Angela again rested her eyes on the fire; then presently, looking up —

"He liked me very much," she remarked.

"All the more shame to him!" cried Bernard.

"What do you mean?" asked the girl, with her beautiful stare.

"If he liked you, why did he give you up?"

"He didn't give me up."

"What do *you* mean, please?" asked Bernard, staring back at her.

"I sent him away — I refused him," said Angela.

"Yes; but you thought better of it, and your mother had persuaded you that if he should ask you again, you had better accept him. Then it was that he backed out — in consequence of what I said to him on his return from England."

She shook her head slowly, with a strange smile.

"My poor Bernard, you are talking very wildly. He *did* ask me again."

"That night?" cried Bernard.

"The night he came back from England — the last time I saw him, until today."

"After I had denounced you?" our puzzled hero exclaimed, frowning portentously.

"I am sorry to let you know the small effect of your words!"

Bernard folded his hands together — almost devoutly — and stood gazing at her with a long, inarticulate murmur of satisfaction.

"Ah! then, I didn't injure you — I didn't deprive you of a chance?"

"Oh, sir, the intention on your part was the same!"

Angela exclaimed.

"Then all my uneasiness, all my remorse, were wasted?" he went on.

But she kept the same tone, and its tender archness only gave a greater sweetness to his sense of relief.

"It was a very small penance for you to pay."

"You dismissed him definitely, and that was why he vanished?" asked Bernard, wondering still.

"He gave me another 'chance,' as you elegantly express it, and I declined to take advantage of it."

"Ah, well, now," cried Bernard, "I *am* sorry for him!"

"I was very kind — very respectful," said Angela. "I thanked him from the bottom of my heart; I begged his pardon very humbly for the wrong — if wrong it was — that I was doing him. I didn't in the least require of him that he should leave Baden at seven o'clock the next morning. I had no idea that he would do so, and that was the reason that I insisted to my mother that we ourselves should go away. When we went I knew nothing about his having gone, and I supposed he was still there. I didn't wish to meet him again."

Angela gave this information slowly, softly, with pauses between the sentences, as if she were recalling the circumstances with a certain effort; and meanwhile Bernard, with his transfigured face and his eyes fixed upon her lips, was moving excitedly about the room.

"Well, he can't accuse me, then!" he broke out again. "If what I said had no more effect upon him than that, I certainly did him no wrong."

"I think you are rather vexed he didn't believe you," said Angela.

"I confess I don't understand it. He had all the air of it. He certainly had not the air of a man who was going to rush off and give you the last proof of his confidence."

"It was not a proof of confidence," said Angela. "It

had nothing to do with me. It was as between himself and you; it was a proof of independence. He did believe you, more or less, and what you said fell in with his own impressions — strange impressions that they were, poor man! At the same time, as I say, he liked me, too; it was out of his liking me that all his trouble came! He caught himself in the act of listening to you too credulously — and that seemed to him unmanly and dishonorable. The sensation brought with it a reaction, and to prove to himself that in such a matter he could be influenced by nobody, he marched away, an hour after he had talked with you, and, in the teeth of his perfect mistrust, confirmed by your account of my irregularities — heaven forgive you both! — again asked me to be his wife. But he hoped I would refuse!"

"Ah," cried Bernard, "the recreant! He deserved — he deserved —"

"That I should accept him?" Angela asked, smiling still.

Bernard was so much affected by this revelation, it seemed to him to make such a difference in his own responsibility and to lift such a weight off his conscience, that he broke out again into the liveliest ejaculations of relief.

"Oh, I don't care for anything, now, and I can do what I please! Gordon may hate me, and I shall be sorry for him; but it's not my fault, and I owe him no reparation. No, no; I am free!"

"It's only I who am not, I suppose," said Angela, "and the reparation must come from me! If he is unhappy, I must take the responsibility."

"Ah yes, of course," said Bernard, kissing her.

"But why should he be unhappy?" asked Angela. "If I refused him, it was what he wanted."

"He is hard to please," Bernard rejoined. "He has got a wife of his own."

"If Blanche doesn't please him, he is certainly difficult;" and Angela mused a little. "But you told me the other day that they were getting on so well."

"Yes, I believe I told you," Bernard answered, musing a little too.

"You are not attending to what I say."

"No, I am thinking of something else — I am thinking of what it was that made you refuse him that way, at the last, after you had let your mother hope." And Bernard stood there, smiling at her.

"Don't think anymore; you will not find out," the girl declared, turning away.

"Ah, it was cruel of you to let me think I was wrong all these years," he went on; "and, at the time, since you meant to refuse him, you might have been more frank with me."

"I thought my fault had been that I was too frank."

"I was densely stupid, and you might have made me understand better."

"Ah," said Angela, "you ask a great deal of a girl!"

"Why have you let me go on so long thinking that my deluded words had had an effect upon Gordon — feeling that I had done you a brutal wrong? It was real to me, the wrong — and I have told you of the pangs and the shame which, for so many months, it has cost me! Why have you never undeceived me until today, and then only by accident?"

At this question Angela blushed a little; then she answered, smiling —

"It was my vengeance."

Bernard shook his head.

"That won't do — you don't mean it. You never cared — you were too proud to care; and when I spoke to you about my fault, you didn't even know what I meant. You might have told me, therefore, that my remorse was idle, that what I said to Gordon had not been of the smallest consequence, and that the rupture had come from yourself."

For some time Angela said nothing, then at last she gave him one of the deeply serious looks with which her face was occasionally ornamented.

"If you want really to know, then — can't you see that your remorse seemed to me connected in a certain way with your affection; a sort of guarantee of it? You thought you had injured some one or other, and that seemed to be mixed up with your loving me, and therefore I let it alone."

"Ah," said Bernard, "my remorse is all gone, and yet I think I love you about as much as ever! So you see how wrong you were not to tell me."

"The wrong to you I don't care about. It is very true I might have told you for Mr. Wright's sake. It would perhaps have made him look better. But as you never attacked him for deserting me, it seemed needless for me to defend him."

"I confess," said Bernard, "I am quite at sea about Gordon's look in the matter. Is he looking better now — or is he looking worse? You put it very well just now; I was attending to you, though you said I was not. If he hoped you would refuse him, with whom is his quarrel at present? And why was he so cool to me for months after we parted at Baden? If that was his state of mind, why should he accuse me of inconsistency?"

"There is something in it, after all, that a woman can understand. I don't know whether a man can. He hoped I would refuse him, and yet when I had done so he was vexed. After a while his vexation subsided, and he married poor Blanche; but, on learning today that I had accepted you, it flickered up again. I suppose that was natural enough; but it won't be serious."

"What will not be serious, my dear?" asked Mrs.

Vivian, who had come back to the drawing room, and who, apparently, could not hear that the attribute in question was wanting in any direction, without some alarm.

"Shall I tell mamma, Bernard?" said Angela.

"Ah, my dear child, I hope it's nothing that threatens your mutual happiness," mamma murmured, with gentle earnestness.

"Does it threaten our mutual happiness, Bernard?" the girl went on, smiling.

"Let Mrs. Vivian decide whether we ought to let it make us miserable," said Bernard. "Dear Mrs. Vivian, you are a casuist, and this is a nice case."

"Is it anything about poor Mr. Wright?" the elder lady inquired.

"Why do you say 'poor' Mr. Wright?" asked Bernard.

"Because I am sadly afraid he is not happy with Blanche."

"How did you discover that — without seeing them together?"

"Well, perhaps you will think me very fanciful," said Mrs. Vivian; "but it was by the way he looked at Angela. He has such an expressive face."

"He looked at me very kindly, mamma," Angela observed.

"He regularly stared, my daughter. In anyone else I should have said it was rude. But his situation is so peculiar; and one could see that he admired you still." And Mrs. Vivian gave a little soft sigh.

"Ah! she is thinking of the thirty thousand a year," Bernard said to himself.

"I am sure I hope he admires me still," the girl cried, laughing. "There is no great harm in that."

"He was comparing you with Blanche — and he was struck with the contrast."

"It couldn't have been in my favor. If it's a question

of being looked at, Blanche bears it better than I."

"Poor little Blanche!" murmured Mrs. Vivian, sweetly.

"Why did you tell me he was so happy with her?" Angela asked, turning to Bernard, abruptly.

Bernard gazed at her a moment, with his eyebrows raised.

"I never saw anyone ask such sudden questions!" he exclaimed.

"You can answer me at your leisure," she rejoined, turning away.

"It was because I adored you."

"You wouldn't say that at your leisure," said the girl.

Mrs. Vivian stood watching them.

"You, who are so happy together, you ought to think kindly of others who are less fortunate."

"That is very true, Mrs. Vivian; and I have never thought of anyone so kindly as I have of Gordon for the last year."

Angela turned round again.

"Is Blanche so very bad, then?"

"You will see for yourself!"

"Ah, no," said Mrs. Vivian, "she is not bad; she is only very light. I am so glad she is to be near us again. I think a great deal can be done by association. We must help her, Angela. I think we helped her before."

"It is also very true that she is light, Mrs. Vivian," Bernard observed, "and if you could make her a little heavier, I should be tremendously grateful."

Bernard's prospective mother-in-law looked at him a little.

"I don't know whether you are laughing at me — I always think you are. But I shall not give up Blanche for that. I never give up anyone that I have once tried to help. Blanche will come back to me."

Mrs. Vivian had hardly spoken when the sharp little

vibration of her door-bell was heard in the hall. Bernard stood for a moment looking at the door of the drawing room.

"It is poor Gordon come to make a scene!" he announced.

"Is that what you mean — that he opposed your marriage?" asked Mrs. Vivian, with a frightened air.

"I don't know what he proposes to do with Blanche," said Bernard, laughing.

There were voices in the hall. Angela had been listening.

"You say she will come back to you, mamma," she exclaimed. "Here she is arrived!"

Chapter XXVII

*A*t the same moment the door was thrown open, and Mrs. Gordon appeared on the threshold with a gentleman behind her. Blanche stood an instant looking into the lighted room and hesitating — flushed a little, smiling, extremely pretty.

"May I come in?" she said, "and may I bring in Captain Lovelock?"

The two ladies, of course, fluttering toward her with every demonstration of hospitality, drew her into the room, while Bernard proceeded to greet the Captain, who advanced with a certain awkward and bashful majesty, almost sweeping with his great stature Mrs. Vivian's humble ceiling. There was a tender exchange of embraces between Blanche and her friends, and the charming visitor, losing no time, began to chatter with her usual volubility. Mrs. Vivian and Angela made her companion graciously welcome; but Blanche begged they wouldn't mind him — she had only brought him as a watchdog.

"His place is on the rug," she said. "Captain Lovelock, go and lie down on the rug."

"Upon my soul, there is nothing else but rugs in these French places!" the Captain rejoined, looking round Mrs. Vivian's *salon.* "Which rug do you mean?"

Mrs. Vivian had remarked to Blanche that it was very kind of her to come first, and Blanche declared that she could not have laid her head on her pillow before she had seen her dear Mrs. Vivian.

"Do you suppose I would wait because I am married?" she inquired, with a keen little smile in her charming eyes. "I am not so much married as that, I can tell you! Do you think I look much as if I were married, with no one to bring me here tonight but Captain Lovelock?"

"I am sure Captain Lovelock is a very gallant escort," said Mrs. Vivian.

"Oh, he was not afraid — that is, he was not afraid of the journey, though it lay all through those dreadful wild Champs Elysées. But when we arrived, he was afraid to come in — to come up here. Captain Lovelock is so modest, you know — in spite of all the success he had in America. He will tell you about the success he had in America; it quite makes up for the defeat of the

British army in the Revolution. They *were* defeated in
the Revolution, the British, weren't they? I always told
him so, but he insists they were not. 'How do we come
to be free, then?' I always ask him; 'I suppose you admit
that we are free.' Then he becomes personal and says
that I am free enough, certainly. But it's the general
fact I mean; I wish you would tell him about the
general fact. I think he would believe you, because he
knows you know a great deal about history and all that.
I don't mean this evening, but some time when it is
convenient. He didn't want to come in — he wanted
to stay in the carriage and smoke a cigar; he thought
you wouldn't like it, his coming with me the first time.
But I told him he needn't mind that, for I would
certainly explain. I would be very careful to let you
know that I brought him only as a substitute. A substitute for whom? A substitute for my husband, of
course. My dear Mrs. Vivian, of course I ought to bring
you some pretty message from Gordon — that he is
dying to come and see you, only that he had nineteen
letters to write and that he couldn't possibly stir from
his fireside. I suppose a good wife ought to invent
excuses for her husband — ought to throw herself into
the breach; isn't that what they call it? But I am afraid
I am not a good wife. Do you think I am a good wife,
Mr. Longueville? You once stayed three months with
us, and you had a chance to see. I don't ask you that
seriously, because you never tell the truth. I always do;
so I will say I am not a good wife. And then the breach
is too big, and I am too little. Oh, I am too little, Mrs.
Vivian; I know I am too little. I am the smallest woman
living; Gordon can scarcely see me with a microscope,
and I believe he has the most powerful one in America.
He is going to get another here; that is one of the things
he came abroad for; perhaps it will do better. I *do* tell
the truth, don't I, Mrs. Vivian? I have that merit, if I

haven't any other. You once told me so at Baden; you said you could say one thing for me, at any rate — that I didn't tell fibs. You were very nice to me at Baden," Blanche went on, with her little intent smile, laying her hand in that of her hostess. "You see, I have never forgotten it. So, to keep up my reputation, I must tell the truth about Gordon. He simply said he wouldn't come — voilà! He gave no reason and he didn't send you any pretty message. He simply declined, and he went out somewhere else. So you see he isn't writing letters. I don't know where he can have gone; perhaps he has gone to the theater. I know it isn't proper to go to the theater on Sunday evening; but they say charity begins at home, and as Gordon's doesn't begin at home, perhaps it doesn't begin anywhere. I told him that if he wouldn't come with me I would come alone, and he said I might do as I chose — that he was not in a humor for making visits. I wanted to come to you very much; I had been thinking about it all day; and I am so fond of a visit like this in the evening, without being invited. Then I thought perhaps you had a salon — doesn't everyone in Paris have a salon? I tried to have a salon in New York, only Gordon said it wouldn't do. He said it wasn't in our manners. Is this a salon tonight, Mrs. Vivian? Oh, do say it is; I should like so much to see Captain Lovelock in a salon! By good fortune he happened to have been dining with us; so I told him he must bring me here. I told you I would explain, Captain Lovelock," she added, "and I hope you think I have made it clear."

The Captain had turned very red during this wandering discourse. He sat pulling his beard and shifting the position which, with his stalwart person, he had taken up on a little gilded chair — a piece of furniture which every now and then gave a delicate creak.

"I always understand you well enough till you begin

to explain," he rejoined, with a candid, even if embar-
rassed, laugh. "Then, by Jove, I'm quite in the woods.
You see such a lot more in things than most people.
Doesn't she, Miss Vivian?"

"Blanche has a fine imagination," said Angela, smiling frankly at the charming visitor.

When Blanche was fairly adrift upon the current of
her articulate reflections, it was the habit of her companions — indeed, it was a sort of tacit agreement
among them — simply to make a circle and admire.
They sat about and looked at her — yawning, perhaps,
a little at times, but on the whole very well entertained,
and often exchanging a smiling commentary with each
other. She looked at them, smiled at them each, in
succession. Everyone had his turn, and this always
helped to give Blanche an audience. Incoherent and
aimless as much of her talk was, she never looked
prettier than in the attitude of improvisation — or
rather, I should say, than in the hundred attitudes
which she assumed at such a time. Perpetually moving,
she was yet constantly graceful, and while she twisted
her body and turned her head, with charming hands
that never ceased to gesticulate, and little, conscious,
brilliant eyes that looked everywhere at once — eyes
that seemed to chatter even faster than her lips — she
made you forget the nonsense she poured forth, or
think of it only as a part of her personal picturesqueness. The thing was a regular performance; the practice
of unlimited chatter had made her perfect. She rested
upon her audience and held it together, and the sight
of half a dozen pairs of amused and fascinated faces
led her from one piece of folly to another. On this
occasion, her audience was far from failing her, for
they were all greatly interested. Captain Lovelock's
interest, as we know, was chronic, and our three other
friends were much occupied with a matter with which

Blanche was intimately connected. Bernard, as he listened to her, smiling mechanically, was not encouraged. He remembered what Mrs. Vivian had said shortly before she came in, and it was not pleasant to him to think that Gordon had been occupied half the day in contrasting the finest girl in the world with this magnified butterfly. The contrast was sufficiently striking as Angela sat there near her, very still, bending her handsome head a little, with her hands crossed in her lap, and on her lips a kind but inscrutable smile. Mrs. Vivian was on the sofa next to Blanche, one of whose hands, when it was not otherwise occupied, she occasionally took into her own.

"Dear little Blanche!" she softly murmured, at intervals.

These few remarks represent a longer pause than Mrs. Gordon often suffered to occur. She continued to deliver herself upon a hundred topics, and it hardly matters where we take her up.

"I haven't the least idea what we are going to do. I have nothing to say about it whatever. Gordon tells me every day I must decide, and then I ask Captain Lovelock what he thinks; because, you see, he always thinks a great deal. Captain Lovelock says he doesn't care a fig — that he will go wherever I go. So you see that doesn't carry us very far. I want to settle on some place where Captain Lovelock won't go, but he won't help me at all. I think it will look better for him not to follow us; don't you think it will look better, Mrs. Vivian? Not that I care in the least where we go — or whether Captain Lovelock follows us, either. I don't take any interest in anything, Mrs. Vivian; don't you think that is very sad? Gordon may go anywhere he likes — to St. Petersburg, or to Bombay."

"You might go to a worse place than Bombay," said Captain Lovelock, speaking with the authority of an

Anglo-Indian rich in reminiscences.

Blanche gave him a little stare.

"Ah well, that's knocked on the head! From the way you speak of it, I think you would come after us; and the more I think of that, the more I see it wouldn't do. But we have got to go to some southern place, because I am very unwell. I haven't the least idea what's the matter with me, and neither has anyone else; but that doesn't make any difference. It's settled that I am out of health. One might as well be out of it as in it, for all the advantage it is. If you are out of health, at any rate you can come abroad. It was Gordon's discovery — he's always making discoveries. You see it's because I'm so silly; he can always put it down to my being an invalid. What I should like to do, Mrs. Vivian, would be to spend the winter with you — just sitting on the sofa beside you and holding your hand. It would be rather tiresome for you; but I really think it would be better for me than anything else. I have never forgotten how kind you were to me before my marriage — that summer at Baden. You were everything to me — you and Captain Lovelock. I am sure I should be happy if I never went out of this lovely room. You have got it so beautifully arranged — I mean to do my own room just like it when I go home. And you have got such lovely clothes. You never used to say anything about it, but you and Angela always had better clothes than I. Are you always so quiet and serious — never talking about *chiffons* — always reading some wonderful book? I wish you would let me come and stay with you. If you only ask me, Gordon would be too delighted. He wouldn't have to trouble about me anymore. He could go and live over in the Latin Quarter — that's the desire of his heart — and think of nothing but old bottles. I know it isn't very good manners to beg for an invitation," Blanche went on, smiling with a gentler radi-

ance; "but when it's a question of one's health. One
wants to keep one's self alive — doesn't one? One wants
to keep one's self going. It would be so good for me,
Mrs. Vivian; it would really be very good for me!"

She had turned round more and more to her hostess
as she talked; and at last she had given both her hands
to Mrs. Vivian, and sat looking at her with a singular
mixture of earnestness and jocosity. It was hard to
know whether Blanche were expressing a real desire or
a momentary caprice, and whether this abrupt little
petition were to be taken seriously, or treated merely
as a dramatic *pose* in a series of more or less effective
attitudes. Her smile had become almost a grimace, she
was flushed, she showed her pretty teeth; but there was
a little passionate quiver in her voice.

"My dear child," said Mrs. Vivian, "we should be
delighted to have you pay us a visit, and we should be
so happy if we could do you any good. But I am afraid
you would very soon get tired of us, and I ought to tell
you, frankly, that our little home is to be — a broken
up. You know there is to be a — a change," the good
lady continued, with a hesitation which apparently
came from a sense of walking on uncertain ground,
while she glanced with a smile at Bernard and Angela.

Blanche sat there with her little excited, yet innocent
— too innocent — stare; her eyes followed Mrs. Vivian's.
They met Bernard's for an instant, and for some reason, at this moment, Bernard flushed.

He rose quickly and walked away to the window
where he stood looking out into the darkness. "The
devil — the devil!" he murmured to himself; "she
doesn't even know we are to be married — Gordon
hasn't been able to trust himself to tell her!" And this
fact seemed pregnant with evidence as to Gordon's
state of mind; it did not appear to simplify the situation. After a moment, while Bernard stood there with

his back turned — he felt rather awkward and foolish — he heard Blanche begin with her little surprised voice.

"Ah, you are going away? You are going to travel? But that's charming; we can travel together. You are not going to travel? What then are you going to do? You are going back to America? Ah, but you mustn't do that, as soon as I come abroad; that's not nice or friendly, Mrs. Vivian, to your poor little old Blanche. You are not going back to America? Ah, then, I give it up! What's the great mystery? Is it something about Angela? There was always a mystery about Angela. I hope you won't mind my saying it, my dear; but I was always afraid of you. My husband — he admires you so much, you know — has often tried to explain you to me; but I have never understood. What are you going to do now? Are you going into a convent? Are you going to be — A-a-h!"

And, suddenly, quickly, interrupting herself, Mrs. Gordon gave a long, wondering cry. Bernard heard her spring to her feet, and the two other ladies rise from their seats. Captain Lovelock got up as well; Bernard heard him knock over his little gilded chair. There was a pause, during which Blanche went through a little mute exhibition of amazement and pleasure. Bernard turned round, to receive half a dozen quick questions.

"What are you hiding away for? What are you blushing for? I never saw you do anything like that before! Why do you look so strange, and what are you making me say? Angela, is it true — is there something like that?" Without waiting for the answer to this last question, Blanche threw herself upon Mrs. Vivian. "My own Mrs. Vivian," she cried, "*is* she married?"

"My dear Blanche," said Bernard, coming forward, "has not Gordon told you? Angela and I are not married, but we hope to be before long. Gordon only knew it this morning; we ourselves have only known it a short time. There is no mystery about it, and we only want your congratulations."

"Well, I must say you have been very quiet about it!" cried Blanche. "When I was engaged, I wrote you all a letter."

"By Jove, she wrote to me!" observed Captain Lovelock.

Angela went to her and kissed her.

"Your husband doesn't seem to have explained me very successfully!"

Mrs. Gordon held Bernard's intended for a moment at arm's length, with both her hands, looking at her with eyes of real excitement and wonder. Then she folded her in a prolonged, an exaggerated, embrace.

"Why didn't he tell me – why didn't he tell me?" she presently began. "He has had all day to tell me, and it was very cruel of him to let me come here without knowing it. Could anything be more absurd – more awkward? You don't think it's awkward – you don't mind it? Ah well, you are very good! But I like it, Angela – I like it extremely, immensely. I think it's delightful, and I wonder it never occurred to me. Has it been going on long? Ah, of course, it has been going on! Didn't it begin at Baden, and didn't I see it there? Do you mind my alluding to that? At Baden we were all so mixed up that one couldn't tell who was attentive to whom! But Bernard has been very faithful, my dear; I can assure you of that. When he was in America he wouldn't look at another woman. I know something about that! He stayed three months in my house and he never spoke to me. Now I know why, Mr. Bernard; but you might have told me at the time. The reason was certainly good enough. I always want to know why, you know. Why Gordon never told me, for instance; that's what I want to know!"

Blanche refused to sit down again; she declared that she was so agitated by this charming news that she could not be quiet, and that she must presently take her departure. Meanwhile she congratulated each of her friends half a dozen times; she kissed Mrs. Vivian again, she almost kissed Bernard; she inquired about details; she longed to hear all about Angela's "things." Of course they would stop for the wedding; but meantime she must be very discreet; she must not intrude too much. Captain Lovelock addressed to Angela a few fragmentary, but well-intentioned sentences, pulling his beard and fixing his eyes on the door-knob — an implement which presently turned in his manly fist, as he opened the door for his companion to withdraw. Blanche went away in a flutter of ejaculations and protestations which left our three friends in Mrs. Vivian's little drawing room standing looking at each other as the door closed behind her.

"It certainly would have been better taste in him to tell her," said Bernard, frowning, "and not let other people see how little communication there is between them. It has mortified her."

"Poor Mr. Wright had his reasons," Mrs. Vivian suggested, and then she ventured to explain: "He still cares for Angela, and it was painful to him to talk about her marrying some one else."

This had been Bernard's own reflection, and it was no more agreeable as Mrs. Vivian presented it; though Angela herself seemed indifferent to it — seemed, indeed, not to hear it, as if she were thinking of something else.

"We must simply marry as soon as possible; tomorrow, if necessary," said Bernard, with some causticity. "That's the best thing we can do for everyone. When once Angela is married, Gordon will stop thinking of her. He will never permit his imagination to hover

about a married woman; I am very sure of that. He
doesn't approve of that sort of thing, and he has the
same law for himself as for other people."

"It doesn't matter," said Angela, simply.

"How do you mean, my daughter, it doesn't matter?"

"I don't feel obliged to feel so sorry for him now."

"Now? Pray, what has happened? I am more sorry
than ever, since I have heard poor Blanche's dreadful
tone about him."

The girl was silent a moment; then she shook her
head, lightly.

"Her tone — her tone? Dearest mother, don't you
see? She is intensely in love with him!"

Chapter XXVIII

This observation struck Bernard as extremely ingenious and worthy of his mistress's fine intelligence; he
greeted it with enthusiasm, and thought of it for the
next twelve hours. The more he thought of it the more
felicitous it seemed to him, and he went to Mrs.
Vivian's the next day almost for the express purpose
of saying to Angela that, decidedly, she was right. He
was admitted by his old friend, the little *femme de*

chambre, who had long since bestowed upon him, definitively, her confidence; and as in the antechamber he heard the voice of a gentleman raised and talking with some emphasis, come to him from the *salon,* he paused a moment, looking at her with an interrogative eye.

"Yes," said Mrs. Vivian's attendant, "I must tell Monsieur frankly that another gentleman is there. Moreover, what does it matter? Monsieur would perceive it for himself!"

"Has he been here long?" asked Bernard.

"A quarter of an hour. It probably doesn't seem long to the gentleman!"

"Is he alone with Mademoiselle?"

"He asked for Mademoiselle only. I introduced him into the *salon,* and Mademoiselle, after conversing a little while with Madame, consented to receive him. They have been alone together, as I have told Monsieur, since about three o'clock. Madame is in her own apartment. The position of Monsieur," added this discriminating woman, "certainly justifies him in entering the *salon.*"

Bernard was quite of this opinion, and in a moment more he had crossed the threshold of the little drawing room and closed the door behind him.

Angela sat there on a sofa, leaning back with her hands clasped in her lap and her eyes fixed upon Gordon Wright, who stood squarely before her, as if he had been making her a resolute speech. Her face wore a look of distress, almost of alarm; she kept her place, but her eyes gave Bernard a mute welcome. Gordon turned and looked at him slowly from head to foot. Bernard remembered, with a good deal of vividness, the last look his friend had given him in the Champs Elysées the day before; and he saw with some satisfaction that this was not exactly a repetition of that expression of cold horror. It was a question, however, whether the horror were changed for the better. Poor Gordon looked intensely sad and grievously wronged. The keen resentment had faded from his face, but an immense reproach was there — a heavy, helpless, appealing reproach. Bernard saw that he had not a scene of violence to dread — and yet, when he perceived what was coming, he would almost have preferred violence. Gordon did not offer him his hand, and before Bernard had had time to say anything, began to speak again, as if he were going on with what he had been saying to Angela.

"You have done me a great wrong — you have done me a cruel wrong! I have been telling it to Miss Vivian; I came on purpose to tell her. I can't really tell her; I can't tell her the details; it's too painful! But you know what I mean! I couldn't stand it any longer. I thought of going away — but I couldn't do that. I must come and say what I feel. I can't bear it now."

This outbreak of a passionate sense of injury in a man habitually so undemonstrative, so little disposed to call attention to himself, had in it something at once of the touching and the terrible. Bernard, for an instant, felt almost bewildered; he asked himself whether he had not, after all, been a monster of duplicity. He was guilty of the weakness of taking refuge in what is called, I believe, in legal phrase, a side-issue.

"Don't say all this before Angela!" he exclaimed, with a kind of artificial energy. "You know she is not in the least at fault, and that it can only give her pain. The thing is between ourselves."

Angela was sitting there, looking up at both the men. "I like to hear it," she said.

"You have a singular taste!" Bernard declared.

"I know it's between ourselves," cried Gordon, "and that Miss Vivian is not at fault. She is only too lovely, too wise, too good! It is you and I that are at fault — horribly at fault! You see I admit it, and you don't. I never dreamed that I should live to say such things as this to you; but I never dreamed you would do what you have done! It's horrible, most horrible, that such a difference as this should come between two men who believed themselves — or whom I believed, at least — the best friends in the world. For it is a difference — it's a great gulf, and nothing will ever fill it up. I must say so; I can't help it. You know I don't express myself easily; so, if I break out this way, you may know what I feel. I know it is a pain to Miss Vivian, and I beg her to forgive me. She has so much to forgive that she can forgive that, too. I can't pretend to accept it; I can't sit down and let it pass. And then, it isn't only my feelings; it's the right; it's the justice. I must say to her that you have no right to marry her; and beg of her to listen to me and let you go."

"My dear Gordon, are you crazy?" Bernard demanded, with an energy which, this time at least, was sufficiently real.

"Very likely I am crazy. I am crazy with disappointment and the bitterness of what I have lost. Add to that the wretchedness of what I have found!"

"Ah, don't say that, Mr. Wright," Angela begged.

He stood for an instant looking at her, but not heeding her words. "Will you listen to me again? Will you forget the wrong I did you? — my stupidity and folly and unworthiness? Will you blot out the past and let me begin again. I see you as clearly now as the light of that window. Will you give me another chance?"

Angela turned away her eyes and covered her face with her hands. "You *do* pain me!" she murmured.

"You go too far," said Bernard. "To what position does your extraordinary proposal relegate your wife?"

Gordon turned his pleading eyes on his old friend

without a ray of concession; but for a moment he
hesitated. "Don't speak to me of my wife. I have no
wife."

"Ah, poor girl!" said Angela, springing up from the
sofa.

"I am perfectly serious," Gordon went on, addressing
himself again to her. "No, after all, I am not crazy; I
see only too clearly — I see what *should* be; when people
see that, you call them crazy. Bernard has no right —
he must give you up. If you really care for him, you
should help him. He is in a very false position; you
shouldn't wish to see him in such a position. I can't
explain to you — if it were even for my own sake. But
Bernard must have told you; it is not possible that he
has not told you?"

"I have told Angela everything, Gordon," said Bernard.

"I don't know what you mean by your having done
me a wrong!" the girl exclaimed.

"If he has told you, then — I may say it! In listening
to him, in believing him."

"But you didn't believe me," Bernard exclaimed,
"since you immediately went and offered yourself to
Miss Vivian!"

"I believed you all the same! When did I ever not
believe you?"

"The last words I ever heard from Mr. Wright were
words of the deepest kindness," said Angela.

She spoke with such a serious, tender grace, that
Gordon seemed stirred to his depths again.

"Ah, give me another chance!" he moaned.

The poor girl could not help her tone, and it was in
the same tone that she continued —

"If you think so well of me, try and be reasonable."

Gordon looked at her, slowly shaking his head.

"Reasonable — reasonable? Yes, you have a right to

say that, for you are full of reason. But so am I. What I ask is within reasonable limits."

"Granting your happiness were lost," said Bernard – "I say that only for the argument – is that a ground for your wishing to deprive me of mine?"

"It is not yours – it is mine, that you have taken! You put me off my guard, and then you took it! Yours is elsewhere, and you are welcome to it!"

"Ah," murmured Bernard, giving him a long look and turning away, "it is well for you that I am willing still to regard you as my best friend!"

Gordon went on, more passionately, to Angela.

"He put me off my guard – I can't call it anything else. I know I gave him a great chance – I encouraged him, urged him, tempted him. But when once he had spoken, he should have stood to it. He shouldn't have had two opinions – one for me, and one for himself! He put me off my guard. It was because I still resisted him that I went to you again, that last time. But I was still afraid of you, and in my heart I believed him. As I say, I always believed him; it was his great influence upon me. He is the cleverest, the most intelligent, the most brilliant of men. I don't think that a grain less than I ever thought it," he continued, turning again to Bernard. "I think it only the more, and I don't wonder that you find a woman to believe it. But what have you done but deceive me? It was just my belief in your intelligence that reassured me. When Miss Vivian refused me a second time, and I left Baden, it was at first with a sort of relief. But there came back a better feeling – a feeling faint compared to this feeling of today, but strong enough to make me uneasy and to fill me with regret. To quench my regret, I kept thinking of what you had said, and it kept me quiet. Your word had such weight with me!"

"How many times more would you have wished to

be refused, and how many refusals would have been required to give me my liberty?" asked Bernard.

"That question means nothing, because you never knew that I had again offered myself to Miss Vivian."

"No; you told me very little, considering all that you made me tell you."

"I told you beforehand that I should do exactly as I chose."

"You should have allowed me the same liberty!"

"Liberty!" cried Gordon. "Hadn't you liberty to range the whole world over? Couldn't he have found a thousand other women?"

"It is not for me to think so," said Angela, smiling a little.

Gordon looked at her a moment.

"Ah, you cared for him from the first!" he cried.

"I had seen him before I ever saw you," said the girl.

Bernard suppressed an exclamation. There seemed to flash through these words a sort of retrospective confession which told him something that she had never directly told him. She blushed as soon as she had spoken, and Bernard found a beauty in this of which the brightness blinded him to the awkward aspect of the fact she had just presented to Gordon. At this fact Gordon stood staring; then at last he apprehended it – largely.

"Ah, then, it had been a plot between you!" he cried out.

Bernard and Angela exchanged a glance of pity.

"We had met for five minutes, and had exchanged a few words before I came to Baden. It was in Italy – at Siena. It was a simple accident that I never told you," Bernard explained.

"I wished that nothing should be said about it," said Angela.

"Ah, you loved him!" Gordon exclaimed.

Angela turned away — she went to the window. Bernard followed her for three seconds with his eyes; then he went on —

"If it were so, I had no reason to suppose it. You have accused me of deceiving you, but I deceived only myself. You say I put you off your guard, but you should rather say you put me on mine. It was, thanks to that, that I fell into the most senseless, the most brutal of delusions. The delusion passed away — it had contained the germ of better things. I saw my error, and I bitterly repented of it; and on the day you were married I felt free."

"Ah, yes, I have no doubt you waited for that!" cried Gordon. "It may interest you to know that my marriage is a miserable failure."

"I am sorry to hear it — but I can't help it."

"You have seen it with your own eyes. You know all about it, and I needn't tell you."

"My dear Mr. Wright," said Angela, pleadingly, turning round, "in Heaven's name, don't say that!"

"Why shouldn't I say it? I came here on purpose to say it. I came here with an intention — with a plan. You know what Blanche is — you needn't pretend, for kindness to me, that you don't. You know what a precious, what an inestimable wife she must make me — how devoted, how sympathetic she must be, and what a household blessing at every hour of the day. Bernard can tell you all about us — he has seen us in the sanctity of our home." Gordon gave a bitter laugh and went on, with the same strange, serious air of explaining his plan. "She despises me, she hates me, she cares no more for me than for the button on her glove — by which I mean that she doesn't care a hundredth part as much. You may say that it serves me right, and that I have got what I deserve. I married her *because* she was silly. I wanted a silly wife; I had an idea you were too wise. Oh, yes, that's what I thought of you! Blanche knew why I picked her out, and undertook to supply the article required. Heaven forgive her! She has certainly kept her engagement. But you can imagine how it must have made her like me — knowing why I picked her out! She has disappointed me all the same. I thought she had a heart; but that was a mistake. It doesn't matter, though, because everything is over between us."

"What do you mean, everything is over?" Bernard demanded.

"Everything will be over in a few weeks. Then I can speak to Miss Vivian seriously."

"Ah! I am glad to hear this is not serious," said Bernard.

"Miss Vivian, wait a few weeks," Gordon went on. "Give me another chance then. Then it will be perfectly right; I shall be free."

"You speak as if you were going to put an end to your wife!"

"She is rapidly putting an end to herself. She means to leave me."

"Poor, unhappy man, do you know what you are saying?" Angela murmured.

"Perfectly. I came here to say it. She means to leave me, and I mean to offer her every facility. She is dying to take a lover, and she has got an excellent one waiting for her. Bernard knows whom I mean; I don't know whether you do. She was ready to take one three months after our marriage. It is really very good of her to have waited all this time; but I don't think she can go more than a week or two longer. She is recommended a southern climate, and I am pretty sure that in the course of another ten days I may count upon their starting together for the shores of the Mediterranean. The shores of the Mediterranean, you know, are lovely, and I hope they will do her a world of good. As soon as they have left Paris I will let you know; and then you will of course admit that, virtually, I am free."

"I don't understand you."

"I suppose you are aware," said Gordon, "that we have the advantage of being natives of a country in which marriages may be legally dissolved."

Angela stared; then, softly —

"Are you speaking of a divorce?"

"I believe that is what they call it," Gordon answered, gazing back at her with his densely clouded blue eyes. "The lawyers do it for you; and if she goes away with Lovelock, nothing will be more simple than for me to have it arranged."

Angela stared, I say; and Bernard was staring, too. Then the latter, turning away, broke out into a tremendous, irrepressible laugh.

Gordon looked at him a moment; then he said to Angela, with a deeper tremor in his voice —

"He was my dearest friend."

"I never felt more devoted to you than at this moment!" Bernard declared, smiling still.

Gordon had fixed his somber eyes upon the girl again.

"Do you understand me now?"

Angela looked back at him for some instants.

"Yes," she murmured at last.

"And will you wait, and give me another chance?"

"Yes," she said, in the same tone.

Bernard uttered a quick exclamation, but Angela checked him with a glance, and Gordon looked from one of them to the other.

"Can I trust you?" Gordon asked.

"I will make you happy," said Angela.

Bernard wondered what under the sun she meant; but he thought he might safely add —

"I will abide by her choice."

Gordon actually began to smile.

"It won't be long, I think; two or three weeks."

Angela made no answer to this; she fixed her eyes on the floor.

"I shall see Blanche as often as possible," she presently said.

"By all means! The more you see her the better you will understand me."

"I understand you very well now. But you have shaken me very much, and you must leave me. I shall see you also — often."

Gordon took up his hat and stick; he saw that Bernard did not do the same.

"And Bernard?" he exclaimed.

"I shall ask him to leave Paris," said Angela.

"Will you go?"

"I will do what Angela requests," said Bernard.

"You have heard what she requests; it's for you to come now."

"Ah, you must at least allow me to take leave!" cried Bernard.

Gordon went to the door, and when he had opened it he stood for a while, holding it and looking at his companions. Then —

"I assure you she won't be long!" he said to Angela, and rapidly passed out.

The others stood silent till they heard the outer door of the apartment close behind him.

"And now please to elucidate!" said Bernard, folding his arms.

Angela gave no answer for some moments; then she turned upon him a smile which appeared incongruous, but which her words presently helped to explain.

"He is intensely in love with his wife!"

Chapter XXIX

*T*his statement was very effective, but it might well have seemed at first to do more credit to her satiric powers than to her faculty of observation. This was the light in which it presented itself to Bernard; but, little by little, as she amplified the text, he grew to think well of it, and at last he was quite ready to place it, as a triumph of sagacity, on a level with that other discovery which she had made the evening before and with regard to which his especial errand today had been to congratulate her afresh. It brought him, however, less satisfaction than it appeared to bring to his clever companion; for, as he observed plausibly enough, Gordon was quite out of his head, and, this being the case, of what importance was the secret of his heart?

"The secret of his heart and the condition of his head are one and the same thing," said Angela. "He is turned upside down by the wretchedly false position that he has got into with his wife. She has treated him badly, but he has treated her wrongly. They are in love with each other, and yet they both do nothing but hide it. He is not in the least in love with poor me — not today anymore than he was three years ago. He thinks he is, because he is full of sorrow and bitterness, and because the news of our engagement has given him a shock. But that's only a pretext — a chance to pour out the grief and pain which have been accumulating in his heart under a sense of his estrangement from Blanche. He is too proud to attribute his feelings to that cause, even to himself; but he wanted to cry out and say he was hurt, to demand justice for a wrong; and the revelation of the state of things between you and me — which of course strikes him as incongruous; we must allow largely for that — came to him as a sudden opportunity. No, no," the girl went on, with a generous ardor in her face, following further the train of her argument, which she appeared to find extremely attractive, "I know what you are going to say and I deny it. I am not fanciful, or sophistical, or irrational, and I know perfectly what I am about. Men are so stupid; it's only women that have real discernment. Leave me alone, and I shall do something. Blanche is silly, yes, very silly; but she is not so bad as her husband accused her of being, in those dreadful words which he will live to repent of. She is wise enough to care for him, greatly, at bottom, and to feel her little heart filled with rage and shame that he doesn't appear to care for her. If he would take her a little more seriously — it's an immense pity he married her because she was silly! — she would be flattered by it, and she would try and deserve it. No, no, no! she doesn't, in reality, care a straw for Captain Lovelock, I assure you, I promise you she doesn't. A woman can tell. She is in danger, possibly, and if her present situation, as regards her husband, lasts, she might do something as horrid as he said. But she would do it out of spite — not out of affection for the Captain, who must be got immediately out of the way. She only keeps him to torment her husband and make Gordon come back to her. She would drop him forever tomorrow." Angela paused a moment, reflecting, with a kindled eye. "And she shall!"

Bernard looked incredulous.

"How will that be, Miss Solomon?"

"You shall see when you come back."

"When I come back? Pray, where am I going?"

"You will leave Paris for a fortnight – as I promised our poor friend."

Bernard gave an irate laugh.

"My dear girl, you are ridiculous! Your promising it was almost as childish as his asking it."

"To play with a child you must be childish. Just see the effect of this abominable passion of love, which you have been crying up to me so! By its operation Gordon Wright, the most sensible man of our acquaintance, is reduced to the level of infancy! If you will only go away, I will manage him."

"You certainly manage me! Pray, where shall I go?"

"Wherever you choose. I will write to you every day."

"That will be an inducement," said Bernard. "You know I have never received a letter from you."

"I write the most delightful ones!" Angela exclaimed; and she succeeded in making him promise to start that night for London.

She had just done so when Mrs. Vivian presented herself, and the good lady was not a little astonished at being informed of his intention.

"You surely are not going to give up my daughter to oblige Mr. Wright?" she observed.

"Upon my word, I feel as if I were!" said Bernard.

"I will explain it, dear mamma," said Angela. "It is very interesting. Mr. Wright has made a most fearful scene; the state of things between him and Blanche is dreadful."

Mrs. Vivian opened her clear eyes.

"You really speak as if you liked it!"

"She does like it — she told Gordon so," said Bernard. "I don't know what she is up to! Gordon has taken leave of his wits; he wishes to put away his wife."

"To put her away?"

"To repudiate her, as the historians say!"

"To repudiate little Blanche!" murmured Mrs. Vivian, as if she were struck with the incongruity of the operation.

"I mean to keep them together," said Angela, with a firm decision.

Her mother looked at her with admiration.

"My dear daughter, I will assist you."

The two ladies had such an air of mysterious competence to the task they had undertaken that it seemed to Bernard that nothing was left to him but to retire into temporary exile. He accordingly betook himself to London, where he had social resources which would, perhaps, make exile endurable. He found himself, however, little disposed to avail himself of these resources, and he treated himself to no pleasures but those of memory and expectation. He ached with a sense of his absence from Mrs. Vivian's deeply familiar sky-parlor, which seemed to him for the time the most sacred spot on earth — if on earth it could be called — and he consigned to those generous postal receptacles which ornament with their brilliant hue the London street-corners, an inordinate number of the most voluminous epistles that had ever been dropped into them. He took long walks, alone, and thought all the way of Angela, to whom, it seemed to him, that the character of ministering angel was extremely becoming. She was faithful to her promise of writing to him every day, and she was an angel who wielded — so at least Bernard thought, and he was particular about letters — a very ingenious pen. Of course she had only one topic — the success of her operations with regard to Gordon. "Mamma has undertaken Blanche," she wrote, "and I am devoting myself to Mr. W. It is really very interesting." She told Bernard all about it in detail, and he also found it interesting; doubly so, indeed, for it must be confessed that the charming figure of the mistress of his affections attempting to heal a great social breach with her light and delicate hands, divided his attention pretty equally with the distracted, the distorted, the almost ludicrous, image of his old friend.

Angela wrote that Gordon had come back to see her the day after his first visit, and had seemed greatly troubled on learning that Bernard had taken himself off. "It was because you insisted on it, of course," he said; "it was not from feeling the justice of it himself." "I told him," said Angela, in her letter, "that I had made a point of it, but that we certainly ought to give you a little credit for it. But I couldn't insist upon this, for fear of sounding a wrong note and exciting afresh what I suppose he would be pleased to term his jealousy. He asked me where you had gone, and when I told him — 'Ah, how he must hate me!' he exclaimed. 'There you are quite wrong,' I answered. 'He feels as kindly to you as — as I do.' He looked as if he by no means believed this; but, indeed, he looks as if he believed nothing at all. He is quite upset and demoralized. He stayed half an hour and paid me his visit — trying hard to 'please' me again! Poor man, he is in a charming state to please the fair sex! But if he doesn't please me, he interests me more and more; I make bold to say that to you. You would have said it would be very awkward; but, strangely enough, I found it very easy. I suppose it is because I am so interested. Very likely it was awkward for him, poor fellow, for I can certify that he was not a whit happier at the end of his half-hour, in spite of the privilege he had enjoyed. He said nothing more about you, and we talked of Paris and New York, of Baden and Rome. Imagine the situation! I shall make no resistance whatever to it; I shall simply let him perceive that conversing with me on these topics does not make him feel a bit more comfortable, and that he must look elsewhere for a remedy. I said not a word about Blanche."

She spoke of Blanche, however, the next time. "He came again this afternoon," she said in her second letter, "and he wore exactly the same face as yesterday — namely, a very unhappy one. If I were not entirely too wise to believe his account of himself, I might suppose that he was unhappy because Blanche shows symptoms of not taking flight. She has been with us a great deal — she has no idea what is going on — and I can't honestly say that she chatters any less than usual. But she is greatly interested in certain shops that she is buying out, and especially in her visits to her tailor. Mamma has proposed to her — in view of your absence — to come and stay with us, and she doesn't seem afraid of the idea. I told her husband today that we had asked her, and that we hoped he had no objection. 'None whatever; but she won't come.' 'On the contrary, she says she will.' 'She will pretend to, up to the last minute; and then she will find a pretext for backing out.' 'Decidedly, you think very ill of her,' I said. 'She hates me,' he answered, looking at me strangely. 'You say that of everyone,' I said. 'Yesterday you said it of Bernard.' 'Ah, for him there would be more reason!' he exclaimed. 'I won't attempt to answer for Bernard,' I went on, 'but I will answer for Blanche. Your idea of her hating you is a miserable delusion. She cares for you more than for anyone in the world. You only misunderstand each other, and with a little good will on both sides you can easily get out of your tangle.' But he wouldn't listen to me; he stopped me short. I saw I should excite him if I insisted; so I dropped the subject. But it is not for long; he *shall* listen to me."

Later she wrote that Blanche had in fact "backed out," and would not come to stay with them, having given as an excuse that she was perpetually trying on dresses, and that at Mrs. Vivian's she should be at an inconvenient distance from the temple of these sacred rites, and the high priest who conducted the worship. "But we see her every day," said Angela, "and mamma is constantly with her. She likes mamma better than me. Mamma listens to her a great deal and talks to her a little — I can't do either when we are alone. I don't know what she says — I mean what mamma says; what Blanche says I know as well as if I heard it. We see nothing of Captain Lovelock, and mamma tells me she has not spoken of him for two days. She thinks this is a better symptom, but I am not so sure. Poor Mr. Wright treats it as a great triumph that Blanche should behave as he foretold. He is welcome to the comfort he can get out of this, for he certainly gets none from anything else. The society of your correspondent is not that balm to his spirit which he appeared to expect, and this in spite of the fact that I have been as gentle and kind with him as I know how to be. He is very silent — he sometimes sits for ten minutes without speaking; I assure you it isn't amusing. Sometimes he looks at me as if he were going to break out with that crazy idea to which he treated me the other day. But he says nothing, and then I see that he is not thinking of me — he is simply thinking of Blanche. The more he thinks of her the better."

"My dear Bernard," she began on another occasion, "I hope you are not dying of *ennui*, etc. Over here things are going so-so. He asked me yesterday to go with him to the Louvre, and we walked about among the pictures for half an hour. Mamma thinks it a very

strange sort of thing for me to be doing, and though
she delights, of all things, in a good cause, she is not
sure that this cause is good enough to justify the means.
I admit that the means are very singular, and, as far as
the Louvre is concerned, they were not successful. We
sat and looked for a quarter of an hour at the great
Venus who has lost her arms, and he said never a word.
I think he doesn't know what to say. Before we separated he asked me if I heard from you. 'Oh, yes,' I said,
'every day.' 'And does he speak of me?' 'Never!' I
answered; and I think he looked disappointed." Bernard had, in fact, in writing to Angela, scarcely mentioned his name. "He had not been here for two days,"
she continued, at the end of a week; "but last evening,
very late — too late for a visitor — he came in. Mamma
had left the drawing room, and I was sitting alone; I
immediately saw that we had reached a crisis. I thought
at first he was going to tell me that Blanche had carried
out his prediction; but I presently saw that this was not
where the shoe pinched; and, besides, I knew that
mamma was watching her too closely. 'How can I have
ever been such a dull-souled idiot?' he broke out, as
soon as he had got into the room. 'I like to hear you
say that,' I said, 'because it doesn't seem to me that you
have been at all wise.' 'You are cleverness, kindness, tact,
in the most perfect form!' he went on. As a veracious
historian I am bound to tell you that he paid me a
bushel of compliments, and thanked me in the most
flattering terms for my having let him bore me so for
a week. 'You have not bored me,' I said; 'you have
interested me.' 'Yes,' he cried, 'as a curious case of
monomania. It's a part of your kindness to say that;
but I know I have bored you to death; and the end of
it all is that you despise me. You can't help despising
me; I despise myself. I used to think that I was a man,
but I have given that up; I am a poor creature! I used

Confidence

to think I could take things quietly and bear them bravely. But I can't! If it were not for very shame I could sit here and cry to you.' 'Don't mind me,' I said; 'you know it is a part of our agreement that I was not to be critical.' 'Our agreement?' he repeated, vaguely. 'I see you have forgotten it,' I answered; 'but it doesn't in the least matter; it is not of that I wish to talk to you. All the more that it hasn't done you a particle of good. I have been extremely nice with you for a week; but you are just as unhappy now as you were at the beginning. Indeed, I think you are rather worse.' 'Heaven forgive me, Miss Vivian, I believe I am!' he cried. 'Heaven will easily forgive you; you are on the wrong road. To catch up with your happiness, which has been running away from you, you must take another; you must travel in the same direction as Blanche; you must not separate yourself from your wife.' At the sound of Blanche's name he jumped up and took his usual tone; he knew all about his wife, and needed no information. But I made him sit down again, and I made him listen to me. I made him listen for half an hour, and at the end of the time he was interested. He had all the appearance of it; he sat gazing at me, and at last the tears came into his eyes. I believe I had a moment of eloquence. I don't know what I said, nor how I said it, to what point it would bear examination, nor how, if you had been there, it would seem to you, as a disinterested critic, to hang together; but I know that after a while there were tears in my own eyes. I begged him not to give up Blanche; I assured him that she is not so foolish as she seems; that she is a very delicate little creature to handle, and that, in reality, whatever she does, she is thinking only of him. He had been all goodness and kindness to her, I knew that; but he had not, from the first, been able to conceal from her that he regarded her chiefly as a pretty kitten. She wished to be more than that, and she took refuge in flirting, simply to excite his jealousy and make him feel strongly about her. He has felt strongly, and he was feeling strongly now; he was feeling passionately — that was my whole contention. But he had perhaps never made it plain to those rather near-sighted little mental eyes of hers, and he had let her suppose something that couldn't fail to rankle in her mind and torment it. 'You have let her suppose,' I said, 'that you were thinking of me, and the poor girl has been jealous of me. I know it, but from nothing she herself has said. She has said nothing; she has been too proud and too considerate. If you don't think that's to her honor, I do. She has had a chance every day for a week, but she has treated me without a grain of spite. I have appreciated it, I have understood it, and it has touched me very much. It ought to touch you, Mr. Wright. When she heard I was engaged to Mr. Longueville, it gave her an immense relief. And yet, at the same moment you were protesting, and denouncing, and saying those horrible things about her! I know how she appears — she likes admiration. But the admiration in the world which she would most delight in just now would be yours. She plays with Captain Lovelock as a child does with a wooden harlequin, she pulls a string and he throws up his arms and legs. She has about as much intention of eloping with him as a little girl might have of eloping with a pasteboard Jim Crow. If you were to have a frank explanation with her, Blanche would very soon throw Jim Crow out of the window. I very humbly entreat you to cease thinking of me. I don't know what wrong you have ever done me, or what kindness I have ever done you, that you should feel obliged to trouble your head about me. You see all I am — I tell you now. I am nothing in the least remarkable. As for your thinking ill of me at Baden, I never knew it nor cared about it.

If it had been so, you see how I should have got over it. Dear Mr. Wright, we might be such good friends, if you would only believe me. She's so pretty, so charming, so universally admired. You said just now you had bored me, but it's nothing — in spite of all the compliments you have paid me — to the way I have bored you. If *she* could only know it — that I have bored you! Let her see for half an hour that I am out of your mind — the rest will take care of itself. She might so easily have made a quarrel with me. The way she has behaved to me is one of the prettiest things I have ever seen, and you shall see the way I shall always behave to her! Don't think it necessary to say out of politeness that I have not bored you; it is not in the least necessary. You know perfectly well that you are disappointed in the charm of my society. And I have done my best, too. I can honestly affirm that!' For some time he said nothing, and then he remarked that I was very clever, but he didn't see a word of sense in what I said. 'It only proves,' I said, 'that the merit of my conversation is smaller than you had taken it into your head to fancy. But I have done you good, all the same. Don't contradict me; you don't know yet; and it's too late for us to argue about it. You will tell me tomorrow.'"

Chapter XXX

Some three evenings after he received this last report of the progress of affairs in Paris, Bernard, upon whom the burden of exile sat none the more lightly as the days went on, turned out of the Strand into one of the theaters. He had been gloomily pushing his way through the various London densities — the November fog, the nocturnal darkness, the jostling crowd. He was too restless to do anything but walk, and he had been saying to himself, for the thousandth time, that if he had been guilty of a misdemeanor in succumbing to the attractions of the admirable girl who showed to such advantage in letters of twelve pages, his fault was richly expiated by these days of impatience and be-reavement. He gave little heed to the play; his thoughts were elsewhere, and, while they rambled, his eyes wan-dered round the house. Suddenly, on the other side of it, he beheld Captain Lovelock, seated squarely in his orchestra-stall, but, if Bernard was not mistaken, pay-ing as little attention to the stage as he himself had done. The Captain's eyes, it is true, were fixed upon the scene; his head was bent a little, his magnificent beard rippled over the expanse of his shirt-front. But Bernard was not slow to see that his gaze was heavy and opaque, and that, though he was staring at the actresses, their charms were lost upon him. He saw that, like himself, poor Lovelock had matter for reflection in his manly breast, and he concluded that Blanche's ponderous swain was also suffering from a sense of disjunction. Lovelock sat in the same posture all the evening, and that his imagination had not projected itself into the play was proved by the fact that during the *entractes* he gazed with the same dull fixedness at the curtain. Bernard forbore to interrupt him; we know that he was not at this moment socially inclined, and he judged that the Captain was as little so, inasmuch as causes even more imperious than those which had operated in his own case must have been at the bottom of his sudden appearance in London. On leaving the theater, however, Bernard found himself detained with the crowd in the vestibule near the door, which, wide open to the street, was a scene of agitation and confusion. It had come on to rain, and the raw dampness mingled itself with the dusky uproar of the Strand. At last, among the press of people, as he was passing out, our hero became aware that he had been brought into contact with Lovelock, who was walking just beside him. At the same moment Lovelock noticed him – looked at him for an instant, and then looked away. But he looked back again the next instant, and the two men then uttered that inarticulate and inexpressive exclamation which passes for a sign of greeting among gentlemen of the Anglo-Saxon race, in their moments of more acute self-consciousness.

"Oh, are you here?" said Bernard. "I thought you were in Paris."

"No; I ain't in Paris," Lovelock answered with some dryness. "Tired of the beastly hole!"

"Oh, I see," said Bernard. "Excuse me while I put up my umbrella."

He put up his umbrella, and from under it, the next moment, he saw the Captain waving two fingers at him out of the front of a hansom. When he returned to his hotel he found on his table a letter superscribed in Gordon Wright's hand. This communication ran as follows:

"I believe you are making a fool of me. In Heaven's name, come back to Paris! G. W."

Bernard hardly knew whether to regard these few words as a further declaration of war, or as an overture to peace; but he lost no time in complying with the summons they conveyed. He started for Paris the next morning, and in the evening, after he had removed the dust of his journey and swallowed a hasty dinner, he rang at Mrs. Vivian's door. This lady and her daughter gave him a welcome which — I will not say satisfied him, but which, at least, did something toward soothing the still unhealed wounds of separation.

"And what is the news of Gordon?" he presently asked.

"We have not seen him in three days," said Angela.

"He is cured, dear Bernard; he must be. Angela has been wonderful," Mrs. Vivian declared.

"You should have seen mamma with Blanche," her daughter said, smiling. "It was most remarkable."

Mrs. Vivian smiled, too, very gently.

"Dear little Blanche! Captain Lovelock has gone to London."

"Yes, he thinks it a beastly hole. Ah, no," Bernard added, "I have got it wrong."

But it little mattered. Late that night, on his return to his own rooms, Bernard sat gazing at his fire. He had not begun to undress; he was thinking of a good many things. He was in the midst of his reflections when there came a rap at his door, which the next moment was flung open. Gordon Wright stood there, looking at him — with a gaze which Bernard returned for a moment before bidding him to come in. Gordon came in and came up to him; then he held out his hand. Bernard took it with great satisfaction; his last feeling had been that he was very weary of this ridiculous quarrel, and it was an extreme relief to find it was over.

"It was very good of you to go to London," said Gordon, looking at him with all the old serious honesty of his eyes.

"I have always tried to do what I could to oblige you," Bernard answered, smiling.

"You must have cursed me over there," Gordon went on.

"I did, a little. As you were cursing me here, it was permissible."

"That's over now," said Gordon. "I came to welcome you back. It seemed to me I couldn't lay my head on my pillow without speaking to you."

"I am glad to get back," Bernard admitted, smiling still. "I can't deny that. And I find you as I believed I should." Then he added, seriously — "I knew Angela would keep us good friends."

For a moment Gordon said nothing. Then, at last —

"Yes, for that purpose it didn't matter which of us should marry her. If it had been I," he added, "she would have made you accept it."

"Ah, I don't know!" Bernard exclaimed.

"I am sure of it," said Gordon earnestly — almost argumentatively. "She's an extraordinary woman."

"Keeping you good friends with me — that's a great thing. But it's nothing to her keeping you good friends with your wife."

Gordon looked at Bernard for an instant; then he

fixed his eyes for some time on the fire.

"Yes, that is the greatest of all things. A man should value his wife. He should believe in her. He has taken her, and he should keep her — especially when there is a great deal of good in her. I was a great fool the other day," he went on. "I don't remember what I said. It was very weak."

"It seemed to me feeble," said Bernard. "But it is quite within a man's rights to be a fool once in a while, and you had never abused of the license."

"Well, I have done it for a lifetime — for a lifetime." And Gordon took up his hat. He looked into the crown of it for a moment, and then he fixed his eyes on Bernard's again. "But there is one thing I hope you won't mind my saying. I have come back to my old impression of Miss Vivian."

"Your old impression?"

And Miss Vivian's accepted lover frowned a little.

"I mean that she's not simple. She's very strange."

Bernard's frown cleared away in a sudden, almost eager smile.

"Say at once that you dislike her! That will do capitally."

Gordon shook his head, and he, too, almost smiled a little.

"It's not true. She's very wonderful. And if I did dislike her, I should struggle with it. It would never do for me to dislike your wife!"

After he had gone, when the night was half over, Bernard, lying awake a while, gave a laugh in the still darkness, as this last sentence came back to him.

On the morrow he saw Blanche, for he went to see Gordon. The latter, at first, was not at home; but he had a quarter of an hour's talk with his wife, whose powers of conversation were apparently not in the smallest degree affected by anything that had occurred.

"I hope you enjoyed your visit to London," she said. "Did you go to buy Angela a set of diamonds in Bond Street? You didn't buy anything — you didn't go into a shop? Then pray what did you go for? Excuse my curiosity — it seems to me it's rather flattering. I never know anything unless I am told. I haven't any powers of observation. I noticed you went — oh, yes, I observed that very much; and I thought it very strange, under the circumstances. Your most intimate friend arrived in Paris, and you choose the next day to make a little tour! I don't like to see you treat my husband so; he would never have done it to you. And if you didn't stay for Gordon, you might have staid for Angela. I never heard of anything so monstrous as a gentleman rushing away from the object of his affection, for no particular purpose that anyone could discover, the day after she has accepted him. It was not the day after? Well, it was too soon, at any rate. Angela couldn't in the least tell me what you had gone for; she said it was for a 'change.' That was a charming reason! But she was very much ashamed of you — and so was I; and at last we all sent Captain Lovelock after you to bring you back. You came back without him? Ah, so much the better; I suppose he is still looking for you, and, as he isn't very clever, that will occupy him for some time. We want to occupy him; we don't approve of his being so idle. However, for my own part, I am very glad you were away. I was a great deal at Mrs. Vivian's, and I shouldn't have felt nearly so much at liberty to go if I had known I should always find you there making love to Mademoiselle. It wouldn't have seemed to me discreet, — I know what you are going to say — that it's the first time you ever heard of my wishing to avoid an indiscretion. It's a taste I have taken up lately, — for the same reason you went to London, for a 'change.'" Here Blanche paused for an appreciable moment; and then she added — "Well, I must say, I have never seen anything so lovely as Mrs. Vivian's influence. I hope mamma won't be disappointed in it this time."

When Bernard next saw the other two ladies, he said to them that he was surprised at the way in which clever women incurred moral responsibilities.

"We like them," said Mrs. Vivian. "We delight in them!"

"Well," said Bernard, "I wouldn't for the world have it on my conscience to have reconciled poor Gordon to Mrs. Blanche."

"You are not to say a word against Blanche," Angela declared. "She's a little miracle."

"It will be all right, dear Bernard," Mrs. Vivian added, with soft authority.

"I have taken a great fancy to her," the younger lady went on.

Bernard gave a little laugh.

"Gordon is right in his ultimate opinion. You are very strange!"

"You may abuse me as much as you please; but I will never hear a word against Mrs. Gordon."

And she never would in future; though it is not recorded that Bernard availed himself in any special degree of the license offered him in conjunction with this warning.

Blanche's health within a few days had, according to her own account, taken a marvelous turn for the better; but her husband appeared still to think it proper that they should spend the winter beneath a brilliant sun, and he presently informed his friends that they had at last settled it between them that a voyage up the Nile must be, for a thoroughly united couple, a very agreeable pastime. To perform this expedition advantageously they must repair to Cairo without delay, and for this reason he was sure that Bernard and Angela would easily understand their not making a point of waiting for the wedding. These happy people quite understood it. Their nuptials were to be celebrated with extreme simplicity. If, however, Gordon was not able to be present, he, in conjunction with his wife, bought for Angela, as a bridal gift, a necklace of the most beautiful pearls the Rue de la Paix could furnish; and on his arrival at Cairo, while he waited for his dragoman to give the signal for starting, he found time, in spite of the exactions of that large correspondence which has been more than once mentioned in the course of our narrative, to write Bernard the longest letter he had ever addressed to him. The letter reached Bernard in the middle of his honeymoon.

CPSIA information can be obtained at www.ICGtesting.com
Printed in the USA
LVOW12s1539170414

382145LV00003B/781/P